MIGHTY
the fallen

DIANNA ROMAN

For information address diannaromanbooks@hotmail.com

Published by Wild One Press LLC
Editing by Jennifer Green
Proofing by Margaret Neal

ISBN: 978-1-959553-40-3 (ebook)
ISBN: 978-1-959553-41-0 (Trade Paperback)

CONTENT ADVISORY

This is a work of fiction with some topics based on real life experiences. Several establishments mentioned are fictional and not based on actual places.

Please be advised this work contains the following topics, should be read at your own discretion, and should not be relied upon as factual medical, mental health, or recovery advice:

- Discussions of driving while intoxicated
- Descriptions of physical injuries sustained in a car accident
- Consensual casual sex between two college students
- Explicit sexual content
- Casual intimacy between an MC and a stranger at a nightclub, no cheating
- Insinuations of depression and feelings of low self-worth
- Self-deprecating terminology about physical disabilities
- Discussions of opioid addiction and recovery
- The use of alcohol for pain and sleep management
- Self body shaming
- Use of CBD for pain management and recreational use
- Discussions about erectile dysfunction caused by nerve damage
- Paternal conflict
- Sarcasm about children by a side character
- Explicit adult language

If you or someone you know is struggling with addiction, depression, or thoughts of suicide, please seek out assistance.

I dreamt about this.

Deserving you.
You looking at me
like I earned you.

DEDICATION

to Brian—
I know I'll find you in Heaven
because you've already
been through Hell

WHEN YOU ARE OLD

How many loved your moments of sad grace
And loved your beauty with love false or true
But one man loved the pilgrim Soul in you
And loved the sorrows of your changing face
-W.B. Yeats

REMY

prologue

15 years ago

"You're seriously not coming out with us?"

Head down, I tediously wrap a sheet of newspaper around a coffee mug at the kitchen counter like it's requiring all my attention. I don't even know why this mug is in our kitchen. It looks like one from the Sunshine Diner over by the college arena. Five bucks says Jamie stole it on some early morning hangover breakfast run.

"No, I want to finish packing so I don't have anything left to do tomorrow besides load up my car."

"It's our last night here. How can you miss this?"

"We went out last night! Did you forget all the groaning you did this morning? Because I haven't."

Glancing at the clock, I can see it's already ten p.m. Is he ever going to leave?

"I'm recovered!" He laughs, snagging his jacket off the hook by the door to our rental duplex. "And that's what our twenties are for. You only live once."

I'm well aware that this is our last night here. It already took me most of the evening to break away from my parents after the graduation ceremony. Now, if my beloved roommate would just get the heck out, what's left of the night may not be ruined.

"You call ending up with your face in a gutter *living*?" I challenge, pulling open a kitchen drawer to see if there's anything left that I can grab to keep up the ruse of packing.

I seriously do not need the box of crap that I gathered while he was dragging his heels for the last hour. All my things are ready to go, and half of my boxes are already in the U-Haul trailer I rented.

"Hold up. Why do you smell so good?"

When did he move this close? Inching back, I flash him what I hope is a bemused expression.

"What?"

Sniffing the air, he pursues me like the pain in the ass that he is. How have I endured four years of college living with him?

Brow furrowing, he points at me. "You're wearing cologne!"

"Yeah. So?" I laugh nervously, giving him a playful shove to push him away. "I wanted to feel like I'd washed all of last night off me."

Turning away, I yank open another drawer, but it's empty, so I move on to the next. If Chris flakes on me because he sees Jamie is still here, I'm never speaking to my roommate again. It's my last chance to see Chris before we both leave tomorrow. Apparently, I'm willing to throw away four years of friendship to do so. My stomach twists into knots over how disloyal that makes me sound, but... Well, I've been fully aware of how stupid I am for the Panthers' star tight end for quite some time.

"You showered before the ceremony and then you showered when you got home," he says suspiciously, drumming his fingertips against the counter. "One would think that would be enough to wash off a few hours at the bar from the night before."

God, he's annoying. And perceptive, which is...also annoying.

"Not expecting company, are you?" he ventures coyly, accusingly.

Super annoying!

"What? No."

Me and my stupid nervous laughter. He's going to see right through me. My cheeks are probably as red as my T-shirt. I hate lying to him, but what am I supposed to say?

Jamie, could you please leave so Chris can fuck me one last time?

God, I'd never hear the end of it. He's not a fan of my…fandom, but I don't want to hear it. Not tonight.

I can practically feel his suspicious gaze. Sighing, I swipe up another sheet of newspaper and flash him a withering look.

"I'm tired, *Jay*. I don't feel like getting drunk again when I have to drive all day tomorrow. And we're probably not going to go more than a day without talking to each other. We'll be texting all the time, *and* I'll see you again this summer before my doctorate program starts."

He nudges his glasses up the bridge of his nose and then raises his hands in surrender. "I know. Jeez, you make me sound needy. I was just making sure you weren't going to engage in any *bad* decisions on your last night in town."

I snort at that, although I know exactly what he's implying. "That's rich, coming from the guy who's about to head out for a night of debauchery."

"A night of *art*," he corrects, which has me snorting as he heads to the door again. "Go-go dancing is an art. Besides, I only look, never touch. If one of them happens to fall into my lap or writes his phone number on my chest…" He shrugs. "What's a guy supposed to do?"

My stomach flips watching him swipe his keys off the hook on the wall. Finally!

I *am* being a terrible friend. He's the one who pointed out that we're young, though. Why shouldn't I engage in a few bad decisions?

Or…the same one. Over and over.

I get a wave and a farewell from him that feels three hours overdue. As soon as the door closes behind him, my legs act like someone just fired a starting gun at a track meet. Racing across the living room, my bare feet make a squeaking sound against the hardwood flooring when I jerk to a stop at my bedroom doorway. Reaching around the doorframe, I flip the switch on the wall inside, turning out the light—my sign that the coast is clear.

It's been three weeks since I've seen Chris. Seen him *here*. Sneaking glances at him during the final for the one class we had together this semester doesn't count. He got approval to complete his classwork remotely these last few weeks after he got invited to the NFL draft. It left me in limbo, both silently hoping for his dreams to come true and wishing that they wouldn't, so he could finally have an excuse to stay in my orbit. The orbit of people who aren't perfect superhumans. To be honest, though, my brain can't fathom him as anything other than a star athlete.

Shaking my head, I walk to the sofa, the only piece of furniture left in the living room. He got selected in the first round of the draft. Of course, he did. I never doubted he would. That has nothing to do with my foolish crush. Granted, I've learned more about football these past two years than I ever imagined I would, but I'm far from an expert on the game. Still, it would be obvious to anyone with half an inkling about football that he's a phenomenon.

Rubbing my stomach, the thought drops the bottom out of it. Now that he's made it, why would he show up tonight? He left again after finals last week for mini-camp, where draftees go to get acclimated to the NFL playbook. He's really in. It's begun.

A thirty-two-million-dollar contract. He can have whatever—and who-ever—he wants. But…he *did say* he'd be here.

Flopping down on the couch, I throw my forearm over my eyes. Maybe if I close them, it'll blot out the incessant thoughts that have been spinning me up over the past month.

It's over. It's really over.

No more Chris. No more *me and Chris*.

I know we made no promises. The only hints he ever dropped were that he couldn't wait to leave here and never look back. I understood that for what it included—*me*. I'd be part of the past he wants to leave behind, not the future he's been so eager for. He never said it any plainer because he didn't have to, not that we spent much of our time together talking.

A punch of lust warms my cheeks. Shifting, I adjust myself through my shorts. To be fair, when he's within reach, I don't exactly have talking on the brain either. That's the thing about me and Chris—there's a pow-erful force that draws us together like nothing could disrupt it. I'm gaso-line, and he's a flamethrower.

Whenever he talks about the future, though, ours are separate. It's almost like he's reinforcing that I'll be far away from him, like he thinks I'll forget. I know I've heard this from Jamie dozens of times, too—harsh reminders that a Panthers tight end and a wallflower, future physi-cal therapist like me, can only be fuck buddies, but I resent it. Chris chose *me*.

I still shiver each time I think of the way he held my gaze. I was wait-ing for Jamie outside of one of his classes that they share. I ran into him at a bar shortly after that. We chatted about nothing worth any merit; all I remember is the way we couldn't take our eyes off each other. He ran his hand down my arm before he left, and I cataloged the move in my brain like it was the equivalent of receiving someone's letterman jacket. A week later, I saw him in the back of the library and it was nothing short of a lightning bolt striking between us. Any doubt I had over his interest in guys, or rather *me*, was resolved when I nervously admitted that I didn't have a girlfriend because I preferred *boyfriends*.

"And do you have one at the moment?" he asked, voice dropping as he stepped closer.

"No." I gulped, backing into a shelf until the book spines dug into my lower back.

He rested his hands on a shelf above my head, his meaty biceps framing my face. His gaze slid down my body, and for the first time in my life, I knew what it was like to feel truly desirable.

"Would you be up for having a *special friend*?"

I knew immediately what he meant, but I got stuck on the words. I've never been good at innuendo.

"I… Sure. I can always use another friend."

His breath gusted out of his nostrils, amused. He glanced down at where my hands were holding a book to my chest like it was a shield. It was both a test and an invitation. He waited patiently as I figured that out, and then finally worked up the nerve. Reaching out, I stroked the back of my knuckles over his abs, my hand trembling. His slow inhale was a sexual validation I hadn't known I'd been looking for my entire adult life. He leaned his hips against mine, showing me how hard he was, meeting how hard *I* was.

"This can't go anywhere, though," he warned in front of my lips. "I've worked too hard to be distracted. And no one can find out. I want to be known for football, not my personal life."

I was so lost in the silent storm that had been brewing between us, I'd have agreed to anything. I got it. He didn't want any attention drawn to himself. Neither did I. All I wanted was *his* attention. And somehow, I'd gotten it. *Me*—boring Jeremy Tanner, who shouldn't even have existed on Chris Mightener's radar. Who's ever had the chance to have their fantasy man choose them?

He did choose me, though. He chose me for a reason and kept coming back. I know we made a promise that we never promised, but… God, how can it be over?

How can you not form some kind of emotional attachment after almost two years of screwing around?

I just…have this *feeling* that something could be different. It says something if he's coming to say goodbye, right? Like maybe it's not a goodbye.

NFL players travel. He's not going to Mars. We could still see each other.

An unexpected chime from my phone has my arms flailing, and I nearly drop the device. Get a grip, Remy. Jeez.

Glancing at my screen, a text alert from Jamie has me tensing. Please don't tell me he forgot something or is going to prod me again to meet him out.

JAMIE: You are such a bad liar.

What the heck is he talking about? I text him back exactly that.

JAMIE: Either I hallucinated as I was driving away, or one very large tight end was creeping through our backyard and into your bedroom window.

What? Oh, my God! He's here!

Scrambling off the couch, I nearly drop my phone again. Fumbling it in the air, I'm glad Chris isn't here to see that I can't even catch a phone compared to his grace with a ball, but then a deep voice rumbles behind me.

"Remy?"

I let out a squeak. My phone clatters to the floor when I jump at the sight of a shadowed figure in my bedroom. Dropping, I palm my device and pop back up like I got shot out of a jack in the box.

"Chris! Hey! Hi. Hey there… Um, you're here."

"Is *Pajamies* gone?" His whisper filters through the open doorway.

"Yeah," I laugh breathlessly, as if I haven't embarrassed myself enough. Cologne can't cover up awkwardness.

That nickname he gave Jamie is pretty funny though. My roommate could never be bothered to change out of his pajama pants for the eight o'clock class they had together.

His wide frame steps into the light, his shoulders filling the doorway. Can you swallow your own tongue? It's really not fair how good he looks. There should be hazard tape wrapped around him.

I've always been proud of my self-control. I'm the only person in my family who doesn't complain about feeling like they've overindulged during holiday dinners. Whenever I go shopping, I ask myself if I simply *want* an item or if I actually *need* it when I decide on what to buy. Jamie teases that I've never even returned a library book late. I can withstand temptation, except when it comes to Chris Mightener. The man is a walking temptation.

I can tell he shaved for his trip to rookie camp. There's no trace of the dark scruff that usually frames that square jaw of his. He once told me it helps him look more menacing to his opponents, but I never saw it. I just saw the soft hair that felt incredible, tickling my skin. Right now, however, all cleaned up, he's even more of a vision than usual. His dark amber eyes finish his scan of the room and land on me. I like when they land on me.

"You did it," I let out, needing an outlet for my anxious energy.

A smirk ticks up the corner of his mouth, and he lets out a breathless laugh. "Yeah."

It's funny the things you realize at the most random moments. I've so rarely seen him smile. If I was giddy at the mere sight of him a moment ago, I'm not sure what to call the feeling that the joy in his expression gives me. He has two moods—serious and turned on, and both turn me on, so I've never felt deprived by not seeing him smile more.

"How…how were the draft and camp?" I babble, knowing it's a rare opportunity for us to talk. I can cool my jets. The physical will come later.

Blowing out a breath, he runs his hand down the back of his head over his close-cropped hair. My fingers itch to touch the way it spikes up a little, and yet it's so soft against my fingers.

"It's been wild. Negotiating the contract, meeting so many other players at camp, orientation—the whole thing. It still feels surreal to have been practicing on an NFL field."

The way his face lights up slices a pain through my chest. Every word puts more distance between us that I can't lessen. Many people would probably be satisfied with the fact that a handsome NFL player was standing in their bedroom doorway for a night of illicit desires, but those people haven't seen his nose buried in a book in the library countless times. They haven't seen him show up with broken knuckles and cracked ribs or placed kisses on them and then watched him go out and play again only days later. They haven't heard the special register his voice takes on when he whispers his most unfiltered thoughts into my ear. They don't know how beautiful his face looks after he comes. And after tonight…I won't know it anymore either.

"I'm so happy for you," I whisper against the thickness in my throat. "You've worked really hard."

Straightening up from the doorframe, he takes a step back into my darkened room. Gaze never leaving me, he reaches for the hem of his shirt and peels it over his head. He tosses it to the floor and then brings his hands to the button of his jeans, a coy smile playing on his lips.

"How about a graduation present?"

And like that, Chris Mightener manages to steal all the air out of my house. I swallow, moving with shaky steps around the couch to reunite with that view again. Stepping into my room, I blink at the change in lighting. Glancing at my mattress on the floor, he kicks off his shoes.

"My bed frame is packed up in the U-Haul," I digress absently, drinking in his profile.

I missed all that skin. That thick waist. The meaty globes of his ass. Even his stance—how he looks like a hurricane couldn't knock him over. I'm only about three inches shorter and have some muscle tone, but around him I always feel small…*less*, until he looks at me.

As his hungry gaze travels down my body, I'm no longer less. I'm everything he wants right now, making me somehow larger than the life force he is to me. His wanting gaze returns to mine, silently saying that my excess of clothing is offensive at the moment.

This is the part I've never mastered—feeling sexy. I don't know how he can look at me like I am, but I've become addicted to it. Drawing my shirt over my head, my nerves ring like tiny bells throughout my body, exposing my slighter frame.

"Last night," I let out breathlessly, flashing him a smile to lighten the words.

There's nothing light about them. They've already settled in the pit of my stomach, a lead weight as I anxiously finger my shirt in my hands.

He stares at me, his lips parted. I wait with bated breath, wondering what he thinks about the subject. If he'll say something to set me free of this anguish that I don't want and know I shouldn't have.

"Yeah," he concurs.

That one honest word signifies what I already suspected. I can't decide whether he looks somber or uncomfortable. I decide to go with somber, that he has respect for our time together. It's enough for me. I promise myself it's enough. He never promised me the moon after all.

Stepping forward, he moves into my space, angling his body between me and the door. The heat from his skin warms mine. It's the welcome comfort of a favorite old, worn coat, wrapping around me. His chest touches mine. Then our stomachs. Our pelvises. He moves forward, pressed against me, gaze hungry with intention. I move with him, snared by the heat in his amber eyes. It's like being hunted, but in the best way possible. With each step he takes, I take one back, living off the same breath and obeying his silent commands.

My ankle connects with my mattress, making me lose my balance. I latch onto his arms, but they move around me, and then we fall. I land with an *oof* from his weight covering me, which is immediately swallowed. There's no preamble to the kiss that owns my mouth, as I let out a moan. No hesitation in his hands as they roam and grip me.

Breaking away, he moves to my ear. "I needed this," he rasps, kissing the sensitive flesh there. "Fucking thought about it for weeks."

He's always carnal and unrelenting, but, God, this is another level. He's never been big on kissing. Whenever I try, I get a wary look like he's wondering if I'm getting too attached and trying to break our rule. It's for the best, I know, but if he'd always kissed me like he did a second ago, I'd probably be hanging onto his ankle while he tries to flee out the door, begging him not to go.

I try to keep up, raking my hands over the cords of muscles in his back and tasting the skin at his shoulder. The rough fabric of his jeans, accentuated by his erection, is pressing into the juncture at my hip through my thin shorts. I grind against it, hoping for more delightful confessions.

"Me too," I admit, and because you catch more flies with honey than vinegar, I add, "Going to miss this."

Maybe if he knows I won't be clingy, he'll give me another kiss like that. What I really mean, though, is *you. I'm going to miss you, Chris Mightener.*

His hand moves to the waistband of my shorts and yanks them down. Palming a scoopful of my ass, he squeezes it and sucks in a breath as he stares at my mouth. Grunting, as though he's battling with the urge to connect our mouths again, he buries his face in my neck and grinds up against my cock. I guess my confession was a bad idea.

Just live in the moment, Remy. Savor it.

I catch the soft stream of light filtering in from the living room, pooling on the floor as I hang on to him. It reflects off his muscles, highlighting his mesmerizing shape. It's the first time the door has ever been left open. It makes it feel like we're lovers—*real* lovers. Like two guys who live together and just barreled into bed after having been curled up on the couch, watching a movie. It's what I imagine being boyfriends would feel like and inspires my determination to not be the passive one this time. If it's just sex to him, I want him to know what he's going to miss. You're supposed to fight for the things you want, right?

Pushing to get him off me, his weight makes the feat difficult. I give up and slide out from underneath him instead.

"What?" he asks, turning onto his side, confused.

It's the perfect angle to give me the leverage I need to move a man of his size. Pushing at his shoulders, I cover his lower half with my body as he falls onto his back. I probably look like Jamie when he's raiding our cabinet on one of his snack binges with the way I attack his zipper. I want to blow his mind. I want him to stay or regret *not* staying. If I can't have either of those scenarios, then I want him to at least remember me.

There's one problem with my plan, however. I've never sucked his cock unless he's fed it to me, so I'm not entirely sure he'll be receptive to my boldness. I love his commanding presence. It makes my knees weak with every word, every unspoken message, and each firm nudge to drop to my knees or flip over on all fours. Yet, I want him like this just once. Tonight, I don't want to abide by the unspoken rules we've created.

I hear a soft chuckle as I finally yank his zipper down. Amused Chris is better than annoyed Chris, so I don't stop. His hips rise, making my heart flip. I grab the denim and the band of his underwear, yanking them down over the thick globes of his ass. The silky, warm flesh brushes against my knuckles. It's so soft, unlike the rugged image of him from a distance.

His cock springs free, looking as strong and solid as the rest of him. It fills me with pride knowing *I* did that to him. I stop when I get his pants down to the tops of his thighs, unable to wait any longer.

"You want that, huh?" he taunts, gripping his base, just as I lower my mouth and take his tip in. "Oh, fuck," he hisses. He arches his hips up, his muscles going rigid beneath me.

I made the Dean's list and don't give a damn right now. *This*—laving my tongue around Chris' head and hearing his sounds of approval—is an achievement I'll take to my deathbed.

His fingers graze my scalp, weaving through my unruly mess of brown hair and turning my flesh taut. His familiar salty essence has my tastebuds salivating, so I use it to my advantage, lathering him up as I take more of him in.

I don't realize I'm moaning until I hear his voice. "You like sucking a football star? Seeing me on TV and knowing you had your mouth on this cock?"

I can't say I blame him for being hyped up over his achievement, but it's the corniest bedroom talk I've ever heard, and so *not* what I was thinking. Yet, it draws an embarrassing groan from me as my cock knocks against his thigh. What is wrong with me?

Jamie's right. I *do* have a problem. He'd better not come home early. Problem or not, I will cut him if he interrupts us because I don't want to stop. Either I *do* have a famous football player kink, or Chris can just say nothing wrong in my eyes.

The hand in my hair moves to the back of my head and is joined by another one. My pulse skitters, hopeful and curious. I know how to give him the perfect blowjob because he's taught me exactly what he likes.

'Just like that.'

'Lick it.'

'Yeah. Now, suck on the tip.'

His self-assured commands always leave me throbbing in wait. It's a delicious agony I've become addicted to. Glancing up, I do what he likes, proving that I know him. That I don't need direction. That I'm a perfectly good *'special friend'* who shouldn't be thrown away. Except his hands follow my head as I take him deep, and then I feel pressure, urging me further. The look that crosses his face is sex drunk.

"Can you swallow it all?" he whispers, hopeful and maybe even a bit desperate.

Oh, hell. I've given him ideas. Just thinking about it has me closing my eyes and suppressing a moan. Exhaling through my nostrils, I relax my jaw.

"Oh, fuck yeah," he gasps.

His fingers swirl through my hair, and then something touches my upper lip. Opening my eyes, I see not just his nest of dark curls in front of me, but one of his fingers. The tip traces my slobber-coated mouth. I can't imagine how I must appear right now, cheeks burning.

"Look at this mouth all stretched around me," he murmurs reverently, turning my self-consciousness into an accolade.

I shouldn't. I know I shouldn't. I'm already about to gag, but I want this first to be with him. Closing my eyes, I swallow. His tip bumps the back of my throat. I hear him gasp again just as I gag and pull back, eyes watering. Stifling a cough around him, I make a few shallower slides, hoping it will distract him from the chuffing sounds I'm making.

"Shit," he whispers. "Did you like me in your throat?"

How does someone even answer that? Instead, I drop back to his tip, sucking on it the way I know he likes.

He lets out a contented sigh and shifts his legs, kicking off his jeans. I reach down and help. When I lower my shorts the rest of the way, he bends a leg, hooking one of his feet into them. Tugging them down, he kicks and sends them sailing somewhere behind me. I feel his insole glide up my bare calf and his strong fingers knead my shoulder, loosening knots I didn't know I had there. I'm pliant and spun up all at once.

God, I want him. Right now. Want to feel him pushing into me. Reaching underneath me, I give myself a stroke, unable to hold back.

"Don't."

I couldn't have heard him correctly, but when I look up, he repeats his warning. "Don't touch it." Slipping his leg between mine, he pushes his thigh against my cock. "Touch *me* if you need to."

And then he cups my face, holding me at his tip. I stare, disbelieving, but move as he guides my head up and down over his glans. We've never been face-to-face for this long during sex. Granted, his gaze is fixed on my mouth on his cock and not my eyes, but it's so sensual. I shudder and have to close my eyes, getting lost in the feel of his glans passing over my lips. The soft hair on his leg, the warmth—it's too much to resist. I start rocking against him, grinding myself shamelessly on his thigh.

"Look at you. Did you wait for me?" he pants, his guiding hands becoming more unsteady.

The answer is that it shouldn't even be a question. There is no one else but him. I didn't wait—I *pined*, but that's too embarrassing to admit.

"*Did* you?" he asks again in a tone that brooks no debate, his thumb tracing my lower lip as his thigh presses tighter against me.

A mewling sound escapes my throat, spilling all my secrets. He pulls me off his tip with a grunt, breathing hard, and gives himself a squeeze, teeth bared. For a second, I think he's angry, but then I realize it's something entirely different in his eyes.

Oh, fuck. He's going to pound the shit out of me tonight.

Rolling, he swipes up the bottle of lube I leave by my pillow each time he comes over. It's another grain of salt in the wound.

See, I want to tell him. *The familiarity between us has reached this level of convenience. No one else will adore you the way I do.*

Rising to his knees, he watches me wipe my mouth with the back of my hand as he slicks himself up with the liquid. My breath catches when he shuffles forward. I slide my hands up his chest in anticipation of another precious kiss to stow in my memory bank. He circles an arm around me, pulling me close, but his mouth moves to the side of my neck, sucking on the skin there. His fingers slide between my cheeks, lubricating a path and then circling my ring. I tense, wondering if he can tell that I prepped, even though his gesture is thoughtful. Slipping a finger inside, he groans against my jugular. I grunt and close my eyes, gripping onto him and savoring the vibrations of that noise.

Did he dream of doing this with his teammates? Was I just a convenience to save him from outing himself in the world of his precious game?

The jealous thoughts are too ugly to give credence. I need to hold fast to Jamie's sage advice earlier. I'm young. I deserve a night of recklessness that I may never get again.

"I'm ready."

Pushing against him, I have half a mind to flop down onto my back. Would he look at me like I'm being strange by wanting to do it while facing each other for a change? I don't have the heart to try, and I honestly don't care at the moment, as long as he's in me. As long as he's mine again one last time.

Dropping to all fours, I feel the mattress dip as he moves around behind me. His calloused hands glide across the small of my back, making me shiver before one latches onto my hip.

"You want it bad tonight, huh?" he says, but it's not a question.

For some reason, I'm not ashamed to admit it, arching my back to spread myself open to him. "Yeah."

I can hear his intake of breath behind me. I wouldn't have thought a guy like him needed any kind of praise or reassurance when he gets it all over campus and from the press. Maybe he's never heard praise from someone he wants to fuck. When he grazes his tip up and down over my hole, I have to fight the urge to push back onto it. I wanted the evening to last as long as possible, but to hell with drawing anything out anymore.

"Fuck me, Chris."

His fingers grip my hip tighter, and he presses against and through my ring in one go. Sheets balled in my fists, I swallow a cry and gulp for breath.

"Shit, Remy," he grits. "Shit."

He must understand that expression about the mind being willing because he makes a pass over my ass with his warm palm while I wait for my body to relax. He said my name. That helps. I love it when he says my name. Dropping to my elbows, I bask in the scent of him, of *us*, in my room. This empty space of memories. All the clutter and trinkets I acquired—none of them mattered. All I ever needed, apparently, was this mattress and him. Nudging my hips backward, I take more of him in. He lets out a guttural breath and grips my hip again, gently this time, as though he doesn't want to interrupt my plan.

"You're a slut for me tonight, aren't you?"

He doesn't wait for an answer, thank goodness. I'm not about to admit that truth, but maybe I do anyway because, when he thrusts to meet me, I moan long and loud.

"Aw, yeah," he concurs, sliding back and doing it again, hedging deeper this time.

We create a chorus of huffs, grunts, and groans—my body thrumming from head to toe—until his soft thatch of hair brushes flush against my ass. I am consumed completely. It's a touching and yet overwhelming sensation.

Chris retreats a fraction, and I discover it's so he can bend down over me. His palms land on either side of mine, his thick arms pressed against my own. Lips brushing against the side of my neck, he just stays that way, breathing heavily.

I know, I want to tell him. *All the things you won't or don't know how to say—I know.*

And then he moves like he can't stand the deafening silence any longer than I can, his animalistic side taking over. The side of him that chews up and spits out anything resembling feelings and weakness. It's the side that made him a winner and me a total slut for him, apparently.

He must know by my sounds when he's found the best rhythm to tease my gland, because he shortens his thrusts. He rocks back and forth over it several times, reducing me to a mess of whimpers and groans. The man may have started out as a terrible top, but his dedication to perfecting game plays has paid off in the bedroom over the last two years.

"Is it good?" he huffs, warming my heart that he's asking for a change. He's been doing that more in the past few months.

I'm panting so hard my lungs are burning. Why is he trying to make me speak?

"You know…it is," I get out, hooking my pinky over his index finger, not caring if the gesture is a penalty in the Chris Mightener rules of affection book.

He murmurs something, sounding almost annoyed, but there's no way I imagined it. "Shouldn't…think about this ass…so much."

He thinks about me? About us? *This*?

Groaning, I push back onto him, not caring if it's going to make me sore tomorrow. He curses under his breath and picks up his pace. Each slap of our skin nudges me forward until my arms give out. I sink onto the mattress, trying to hold my hips aloft so we won't lose our connection.

His beautiful, heavy weight, settles onto me. He's crushing me, but I'm in heaven.

Breathing? Who the hell needs to breathe when they can feel Chris' pecs and abs brushing against their back as his cock repeatedly lays claim to their body?

I mumble into my pillow, needy, drunken-sounding syllables, and press my hand to the wall. He clutches my wrist and nips at my ear-lobe. The friction from my bedsheets isn't helping my wish to prolong this. Reaching beneath me, I find my cock and wrap my hand around it. Something bashes into my elbow, and I feel rough fingers on my arm. If he tells me not to touch my cock again, I'm going to have to find a way to ignore him. He doesn't, though. Instead, his hand wraps around mine, grazing against my stomach in the confined space.

"Come. Wanna feel you milk my cock one last time."

I cry out—and possibly cry a little inside too. I do exactly as he asks, my body a servant to his desires. Fire rises up my legs. I feel the terrify-ing pressure on my bladder, and then I come. With each pulse, I clench around him.

I've seen game playbacks of him growling at opponents and decid-ed I could no longer watch them without getting aroused. He makes the same sound into the top of my shoulder, his heat erupting inside me. Our flesh rubs together with each jerk of his body. His open mouth moves to my cheek, panting against it. Damn, he smells amazing. I lean into the touch like it's an umbilical cord giving me life.

Graduation is supposed to be a time for celebrating. I can't, though. How am I going to give this up?

Closing my eyes, I absorb every sound, every breath, each beat of his heart against my back. I want to stay pressed into this mattress like a leaf in a scrapbook. After several moments, however, he slips free from me. It leaves behind a cruel mix of dizziness from my comedown and hollowness from his leaving.

Rolling to his side, the mattress dips next to me when he lands on his back. I turn my head and watch him search for something to clean up with. He finds the pack of baby wipes I left on the floor and catches me staring at the cock that was just inside me.

"That was overdue," he says with a sigh.

Clearing my throat, I roll over and take the package from him. "Yeah."

Gone is the appreciative excitement from earlier. A heavy silence falls over us.

"Your room looks strange, empty like this," he comments, glancing the other way when I clean myself off. "When do you leave?"

"In the morning. Home for the summer to work, then I start my doctorate in the fall."

I hear a disapproving grunt. "More school. You're a glutton for punishment."

I could say the same to him about football, but I don't know how to *un-glamorize* the life that's waiting for him. Suddenly, he sits up, covering his lap with his hands.

"Shit. We left the door open."

"It's fine. Jamie will be gone all night." That seems to put him at ease, but I no longer have any patience for our rules if getting caught is more important than us parting ways. "Besides, it doesn't matter anyway. He saw you crawling in the window earlier."

"Shit."

Okay, *now* I feel guilty, but can't he see how ridiculous this total secrecy has been? Maybe I'm just bitter from feeling so raw right now. Like if I can't have him, can I at least have the truth not be so thickly veiled?

"He won't tell anyone," I assure him. "He never has. He caught you doing it last year, actually."

"And you didn't *say* anything?"

Of course, I didn't. He might have been so freaked out that he'd quit seeing me.

"He won't talk," I reaffirm, hating how downtrodden my voice sounds as I ignore the alarm in his voice. I sit up and grab my shorts. Glancing over, I can see the gears turning in his head—the possibility of a dream he's worked for years for being shattered by his secret. My bitterness softens, and I take pity on him. "He knows I wanted my privacy."

He processes my ruse of taking the blame and nods. "I should go." Getting up, he pads over to his pile of clothes. "My parents are having a thing tomorrow."

A *thing*. Not a graduation party. Not an NFL inception party. Not a boring lunch to celebrate nothing in particular. No further explanation needed for his secret hookup. The barrier tape is back up between us— that damn agreement I made two years ago when I was drunk on the fact that he was even speaking to me. I've lowered myself so far into the pity party well that I didn't realize he's already dressed and getting into his shoes.

Shit. This is it.

Rising, I don't know if I'm doing a good job of not looking like my heart is in my throat. I'm never going to see him again unless it's on network television or I go to an NFL game. Lately, I've been wishing that I'd told him two years ago how stupid I was for him and scared him off then instead of letting him get his hooks this deep into me.

Our gazes lock. He shifts in place, the corner of his mouth ticking up anxiously. Maybe he doesn't know how to say goodbye either.

"Well…good luck with everything." I force as much enthusiasm into the words as I can because I *do* wish him well. From the bottom of my breaking heart.

"Thanks. You too." The words are at least soft and sincere. He even gives me one of those rare boyish smiles of his.

He *does* care. Some part of him. I knew I wasn't wrong.

I raise my arms to hug him and lean in, hoping this kiss will be my shooting star, changing a fate that only magic can. One of his heavy arms wraps around my shoulders, and the next thing I know, my face is practically smashed against his clavicle. He gives me a squeeze and ruffles my hair with his other hand.

Okay…that was…awkward.

"And thanks for the arrangement. I don't think I'd have gotten through the stress of the last two years without it."

Arrangement? As in…the sex?

When he lets go, I don't even have a chance to ask him to clarify or tell him he can call me whenever he wants. He's already headed to my bedroom window. Opening it, he straddles the sill and slips through without a backward glance.

He's…gone. He thanked me for our no-strings-attached sex and then left.

It's me or football, and football has won again. It always does.

Right…

It's done.

I repeat the words to myself again. *It's done.*

I glance at my mussed sheets on the mattress which probably smell like him now. Would wrapping myself in them do me more harm than good?

I decide not to take my chances. Taking a leaf from Chris' playbook, I leave the room without looking back. I need to see this for what it was— just a chapter of my life that's now over. An agreement where I bit off more than I could chew.

Curling up on the couch, I close my eyes and cradle my arms around me. I also have a future I've been working toward that starts tomorrow. One that will be just as wonderful as I imagined it would be before I met Chris Mightener. I hold on to that assurance. I grip it even tighter when a tear slips down my cheek.

CHRIS
chapter 1

It's going to rain. The unimpressed look I flash Colin Bentley, the local weatherman on the television above the bar, doesn't seem to convince him. Smiling, he waves his hand over the map of San Antonio.

"We might see a few clouds, but this low pressure system is going to move south of us. You can expect nothing but sunshine for the rest of the week."

The schmuck.

"Shut the fuck up, Colin," I mutter into my gin and tonic.

I'm not being salty. He *is* a schmuck. I've run into him plenty of times while I was reporting sports events, but that's beside the point.

Sunshine? My L3 through L5 vertebrae know better, and my knee and ankle second their motion. They're the reason I'm sitting at Mahoney's right now, medicating. I'm a walking barometer.

Throwing back the last of my drink, I close my eyes and weigh the state of the throbbing in my bones. It's down to a dull reverberation—thank God—numbed enough that it isn't shouting at me anymore. A fourth round would give me a better night's sleep for the joyous outing I have tomorrow with Dad, but contrary to what he thinks, I *have* learned a lesson or two in the last decade and a half. I could be popping painkillers right now instead of downing liquid arthritis silencer. The fact that I'm not drinking beer, which tastes much better, is proof I'm not here for enjoyment, but there's no telling him or Mom that. So, my odorless friend gin it is when Mother Nature crawls out to screw with me and Dad drives down to screw with my life.

An upheaval of laughter erupts over by the pool tables near the door. Anything is more interesting than Bentley's inaccurate weather report, so I glance at the commotion as I wave to the bartender for my tab. The gray and black letterman jackets are instantly recognizable—Leopards, football players from the local high school. I need to stop coming to bars that serve food where minors can get in during kitchen hours, even if it means the bar is conveniently located three blocks from my house. I know too many of the players' names from covering games for the paper. I want to watch them play football, not watch their social lives.

Despite myself, and because I refuse to look back at the television for the weather recap that's sure to be repeated, I study their youthful faces. Soft skin, hardly any signs of facial hair yet, smiles oblivious to the unknown the future holds. I both envy and pity them—little kings of the hour in the tiny bubble they know as their world.

"Twenty-seven, Chris," Mike tells me, wiping down the wood where my glass left a ring of perspiration.

Tugging some bills out of my wallet, I toss them down and thank him. Gripping the bar, I rise, slowly letting my weight settle onto my joints. I stuff my wallet into the front pocket of my pants. The lump looks odd there, but it's better than having to twist to tug it out of the back one once I get in my truck.

My gin-infused muscles cooperate, giving me smooth sailing. What a bit of liquor can do for stiff joints and a throbbing back. I should sleep like a baby. Maybe a temperamental one, but still a baby. No bags under my eyes tomorrow while Dad, no doubt, tries to make a spectacle of me. He promised he's just coming into town for some quality time, but I'm not about to hold my breath. I wish he'd devote all his time to living vicariously through my nephews, but as his only son, I'm unfortunately obligated to receive a turn now and then.

The toe of my shoe connects with something hard near the end of the bar. The scrape of metal against wood and the shift of an empty stool to my right tell me what I got caught on. I flinch and stutter my steps to a halt to keep from toppling forward so I don't snag it.

Wrong move. Wrong fucking move.

The quick, jerking motion shoots a blade of pain up my spine, stealing my breath. I dig my fingertips into my lower back in a death grip to stop the assault, but it owns me already. I stagger to my right and grip the bar, begging my knees not to drop out from underneath me, and let out a garbled cry. There's a loud clatter in front of me that silences all the chatter in the bar. I know it's the stool without even having to open my eyes, but it's the least of my concerns right now. Huffing, I exhale through the sensation of jagged metal stabbing my spine.

"Shit. Chris, you all right?" I hear Mike ask from the other side of the bar.

"Y-yeah," I grunt, hating that someone has to hear how I can't even get out a one-syllable word when this happens. Sucking in a breath, I try again. "Yeah. I'm good. Just…need a minute."

"Hold tight. I'll get the stool."

"No," I stop him, grateful I'm able to lift my hand from the bar. "I can get it."

Damn it. There went my twenty-seven-dollar cure for the evening.

The commotion of conversations resumes around me, blending into background noise with the low music playing from the speakers in the bar. Good. I hope it means the *crippled guy* at the bar is forgotten. Just the way I prefer it.

When my stomach muscles stand down from their preservation response, I bend down gingerly at the knees in a squat to retrieve the barstool. At least, Mahoney's is a little hole in the wall that doesn't get much of a crowd. Not that anyone knows me anyway, besides Mike.

"You know who that is?" I overhear one of the kids by the pool table whisper at bar volume.

"Should we?"

I grip the frame of the barstool tighter than necessary and grit my teeth as I set it upright again. They're too young, I chide myself, but then I hear it.

"'The Mighty' Mightener," the first kid whispers. "He played for the Panthers years ago. He had over a thousand receiving yards and over a hundred receptions each year he played."

"You and your stats-encyclopedia brain, Quinn," another kid snickers.

"*He* was a Panther?" the first buddy asks, sending a different kind of pain through me than the one I'm already in as I keep my head down and slide the stool back into place.

"Yeah," the stats nerd confirms. "He got drafted first pick to the NFL, but only played one season. He got in a car accident and broke his back."

In three places, I mentally note. *And his knee and ankle.*

The history lesson doesn't even bother me. It has about as dull an effect on my pride as when a weight bar's perforation digs into a tough callous. Frankly, I'm impressed the kid knows his shit. *I was* that kid.

It's the final remark from his buddy that does it, though. It's just a four-letter word, but the delivery of it—disbelief and a hint of pity—sobers any buzz I achieved.

"Damn."

Swinging my gaze toward them, I watch the gaggle's spines stiffen in guilt. Their baby-faced jaws drop. A few go red in the face and look away.

I'm not glaring at them, just letting them see the truth they were so curious about. *Enjoy it,* I tell them silently. *Enjoy it while you can, and don't be fucking stupid.*

Turning away, I hobble to the door, unwilling to stomach being an exhibit of broken dreams a second longer. *The Mighty.* What a stupid fucking nickname. *I* didn't pick it. Whoever came up with it should have thought about what it might be like to live with it after a person can't embody it anymore.

The humidity outside hits me with the force of a sucker punch. My nerve endings tune in to the barometric pressure, a veritable equivalent of the squelch of a radio signal trying to break through static. Something wet hits my cheek. Looking up at the evening sky, not a single star greets me through the overcast. Another droplet hits my nose.

And what do you know?

It's fucking raining.

REMY

chapter 2

"Give me a second to unlock the door," I tell Jamie, pinning my cell phone to my shoulder with my cheek while I sort through my keys.

"I still can't believe you bought a house."

"What? Why?" I laugh, side-stepping a stack of boxes in the entry-way that my mother sent. "*You* have a house. Why can't I?"

"Because you've either lived in someone else's or rented since I've known you."

I know it's just his perpetual honesty and not meant to be a dig, but I don't need *that much* honesty. Grimacing, I toss my bag on the side-board and kick my shoes off.

"Yeah, well, it was time for a change."

At that, he cracks up. "Don't get me wrong—I'm proud of you for ending it with Winston, and glad you like your new job, but I hope you're not becoming a *change addict*. What's next? Get a new best friend? Because if that's the case, then I might have to fly out there and stage an intervention."

And like that, my mood is restored. Leave it to Jamie to amuse me by making everything about his neediness.

The hardwood floor creaks just the right amount as I make my way further inside. I know the memories it's seen weren't mine, yet the broken-in sound effects are a balm to my soul. It feels like a home already, one that's housed lives before and is now passing the torch to me. I still want to kick myself for not having done this sooner. It only took me six months of—yes—renting again after my breakup to work up the nerve, but I did it. I bought my first house all on my own. I've only been in it for a month, but I've gotten more fulfillment from being a homeowner than my last relationship ever provided. I didn't cave in to my indecisiveness or let a partner make the call for me. *I* did this. On my own.

It would be an insult to my ex to call our four years together a waste, but, seriously, how did I stay for so long in a situation that was…nothing? Jamie used to tease me that I was looking for something that didn't exist—a fairy tale. I'm not about to admit it to him, but I think he might have been right.

Six months ago, as I stared into the living room at the man on my couch watching television, I realized Winston might as well have been a stranger, not my boyfriend. I cared about him. I still do. He's a nice guy, but…I should have felt *something*. Right?

Hell, maybe I actually have learned nothing and am still holding out for a fairy tale.

"Is a guilt-trip your housewarming gift?" I counter. "If so, that's not going to fly. You've been cheating on me with Janessa for years now."

"Oh, come on. That doesn't count. She's my California bestie."

"And so what? That makes me your Texas bestie? Nice to know your loyalties only go as far as state borders."

"No, you've got national bestie status. I gave you the good recliner when she was over here when you visited, remember? You'll always be number-one."

Smirking, I withhold any further comment and start toward my bedroom. He could move to another planet, and I still wouldn't be able to get rid of him.

"Ah! Mother fluffer!" The yelp that comes over the line is so loud I have to hold the phone away from my ear.

"Are you all right?" I try to hold back my amusement over the censored expletives he's adopted since his sister and her kids moved in with him.

"*No!* I just stepped on a *LEGO*. *Why* is there a LEGO in the *bathroom?*"

Hitting speakerphone, I kick out of my khakis and try not to laugh at his rhetorical question. It's difficult not to find humor in the one thing that's finally given my oldest friend a run for his money. Gripe to me as he does, he's a model uncle and brother. I am curious, however, what his breaking point may be. I've been getting calls like this for weeks now.

"How's '*Uncle Jamie*' life treating you? I don't suppose you're ready for a vacation and going to come visit soon?"

"No, I wish. I've still got to help get Meg and the kids sorted. My ex-brother-in-law is turning out to be a prime *duck*head. Sorry."

Wincing, I shrug into a pair of soft old shorts. Last time we talked, he told me his unfaithful brother-in-law had yet to visit the kids since Meg had come to stay two months ago. I'm guessing that hasn't changed.

"It's fine. I understand. I'm glad they have you. It's really sweet how you're helping them out."

He groans, and I hear footsteps like he's moving through his house with his one speed—chaos. "Yeah. Apparently, *helping* means tripping over toys, cleaning muddy handprints off my walls, and listening to Meg either cry or rant about Jason. There is nothing sweet about my thoughts. So, save the compliments. What about you? Is it weird yet being back on campus? Do the athletes look like little kids now that you're an old man?"

"They look like *patients*. And it's not just college students. The center treats alumni, faculty, and even the local high school teams."

"Blah, blah, blah. Yeah, I know. You told me already. Whatever. Congratulations on trying to perfect the already elite of the human species. I still vote you should have stayed at the military hospital and found some hot Army guy who'd deploy every other year. It would have afforded you the perfect opportunity to come visit me more often."

Rolling my eyes, I head back to my entryway to unpack the boxes Mom sent so I don't have to dodge them anymore. He's impossible, dismissing the fact that the rest of the world doesn't have his convenient work arrangement.

"I'd have still had to work forty hours a week, Mr. Life Advice."

"Jealous," he taunts, not even trying to conceal his smugness.

I'm jealous of his freedom, not his career. I wouldn't know how to come up with continual content for the gay men's column he writes. Repeatedly reaching for and missing a fairy tale hasn't exactly left me wiser. Experienced, I suppose, but not wiser.

Speaking of experience…

"So, I ran into Miles Keller last week," I say casually.

"Who?"

"He worked for the same company that David did."

"David?"

Cringing, I elaborate, "David as in two exes ago."

"Oh. Okay. So, who is Miles? Did I meet him?"

"I think so. Remember when you came to see me that one summer, and you went to that hibachi grill with me and David and some of his work friends? Miles was there. He was the one with wavy blond hair."

There's a pause, and I don't know whether he's processing or distracted by his surroundings until he chimes in with, "Wait, was he the one who said, *'you know?'* after, like, every sentence?"

Frowning, I try to recall something so trivial and yet oddly specific. However, I think he may have actually said that the other day when I ran into him. "Maybe?"

"Oh, yeah. The curly-headed fucknugget."

"What?" I bark out a laugh. "Why was he a fucknugget?"

"He just was. He had *fucknugget* written all over him. Why? Don't tell me you're going out with him."

Great. So much for this segue. "No," I insist, but it sounds guilty. "He gave me his number, though, and said he'd call the next time he was in town. He asked to go out for drinks."

"Ew. Total fucknugget behavior. Throw it away."

Laughing, I pick up the top box, setting the phone on top of it, and haul it to the living room. "This isn't 1997. No one writes their number on a matchbook anymore. It's in my phone."

"Then delete it. Enjoy your freedom or at least get some good sex and then never answer his calls again, but don't date him."

Rolling my eyes, I round the couch. "Maybe I will. He's good-looking and funny."

"I don't remember much about him, which tells me he's not that funny *or* good-looking."

"You think that, and yet you told me to have sex with him. Wow. That's…amazing advice. How do you keep your job?"

"Atlas! What is *that*?" he shrieks, yelling his youngest nephew's name. "I can *see* that it's a cat. The problem is that *I* don't have a cat, and neither do you, so why is there one in the house?"

Oh, boy. Maybe that breaking point I wondered about might happen sooner than I thought.

He's still traumatized over his grandma's cat he inherited along with her house when she passed away years ago. He was grateful she'd left her house to him. The cat? Not so much, and I was the one who had to hear about it. I do not miss those phone calls. He'd rant. I'd tell him to put it up for adoption, and then I'd get a lecture about how you can't abandon a deceased relative's pet. I never thought I'd be relieved when an animal passed away. I didn't think that thing would ever reach its ninth life.

I set the box down on my new coffee table. Well, new-to-me. The big oak-framed piece with its glass top will be a convenient footrest when winter comes, and I want to stare at the fireplace in my fuzzy socks. Winston preferred modern furnishings. I never complained, but thought they made our townhouse feel like a showroom. It wasn't warm and

inviting. Perhaps I was just projecting the lack of warmth from our relationship into the space.

"O-kay," Jamie cautions on the other end of the line. "Is that my oat
milk? You *cannot* give a cat oat milk."

"But you said it's healthy," a small voice replies, and I have to bite my
cheek to keep from laughing.

"He's right, Jay," I chime in, cutting the tape off the box. "You *did* say
that." I've lost track of the number of health kicks he's taken up over
the years.

"Shut up," he mutters, which I assume is directed at me. His voice
goes muffled again, though. "It is, but we should take it outside in case
he has any friends that might want to come by if they're hungry."

Oh, Jamie, I want to warn. You're opening yourself up to
more trouble.

"Hey, man. I'm going to have to let you go," he returns, but then
switches to a stage-voice tone, "because Uncle Jamie needs to go im-
part some *life advice* to the little people who are *pillaging his house.*"

"Blah. Blah. Blah," I mock in retaliation for earlier. "Have fun with that,
but just remember—you were young once, too."

"I'm *still* young. My '*sweetness*' has just robbed me of
my independence."

"Good luck, cat daddy." I hang up before he can hear me snickering.

Pulling some crinkled old newspaper out of the box, I think his mis-
fortune did me some good. With any luck, I'll be like him in a few weeks
or months—so comfortable living independently that I become annoyed
with the slightest deviation from my routines.

What am I saying? I don't plan on being a confirmed bachelor like
Jamie. Thirty-seven, never been tied down, and I wouldn't doubt he still
goes to go-go clubs.

My hands still in the box, wondering what that makes me. Am I just
holding out for another elusive fairy tale that's never going to happen?
Does Miles only seem appealing because I'm that desperate to have a
happily ever after?

No. Absolutely not. I'm just…easing into accepting that it's okay not
to hang on to relationships that aren't working like a felled rider who
refuses to let go of the reins. Having a drink with a guy doesn't mean I'll
dive into another doomed relationship.

Setting the packing materials aside, I find something lumpy and
solid wrapped in more paper. I have no idea what's in this box. Mom
must have been serious about turning my old room into a crafting room
if she shipped me my childhood memorabilia. It makes sense. I do
have a maybe-forever place now. Why shouldn't I house all my worldly
possessions here?

I know Jamie insists that we're still young, but I can't say I've ever
felt more like an adult than these past few months. I literally have no
one to rely on but myself now. Winston and I may have lost our spark,
but there was a comfort in being able to split day-to-day tasks with

another person. I took care of the laundry. He took care of the meals. I paid the utility bills. He did the grocery shopping. Holding a piece of my past in my hands and knowing there's no one to share it with hits differently suddenly.

I'm not lonely, so why am I even thinking about things like that? Shaking my head, I peel the paper off, knowing I did the right thing where Winston and I were concerned. Maybe it's just all the changes I've made this year that have a twinge of regret creeping in.

I ended a stable relationship with a decent man, left my job of ten years at Brook Army Medical Center, and then bought a freaking house. That's…a lot. For me, anyway. Being in relationships for the past decade was a good cover up for my indecisiveness.

Sometimes at night, when it's quiet and I'm alone with my thoughts, though, I get this sickening feeling that none of the decisions I managed to make this year will save me from failure. Am I going to get my hopes up the next time I have a nice conversation with an eligible man and end up in another lukewarm courtship that goes well past its expiration date?

I mean, I hope not. That was the reason I made so many changes: to break away from my bad habits. Because clinging to relationships as a sense of security *is* a terrible habit. Before Winston, there was Caleb. Before Caleb, there was David.

But you have to keep trying. Right? Either that or be like Jamie. God, I love him, but I'm not built like he is. I tried the hook-up thing in my early twenties, and it wasn't for me. Yet, what the hell did the alternative get me? Playing house?

Maybe it's what Winston said before I left that has me so rattled. I know without a doubt that he didn't feel the chemistry anymore either, but he still looked upset when I told him I wanted to end things.

'Did you ever think that maybe you're not capable of falling in love?'

His question still haunts me like an agitating jingle you can't shake from your brain. He knew my entire dating history—that's the kind of stuff you joke about and divulge over the years when you think it's all behind you. When you trust someone. They're mistakes you revel in knowing they were the road that led you to the person you're with. I never thought he'd use that information as a weapon to rattle my self-image.

Maybe I'm *not* capable of falling in love. Maybe a false sense of security is all I'm capable of falling into.

The packing paper falls away, revealing a ceramic coffee mug. Why did Mom send me a coffee mug?

Turning it, I stare at a familiar logo on the opposite side. *The Sunshine Diner.*

"Oh, my gosh." I let out a laugh, instantly seeing flashbacks of drunken breakfasts with Jamie in college.

What a blast from the past. I didn't even know I had this. I should send it to him for Christmas. It's a relic now. That place closed a long time ago; I would know. He went on to see the world, while I never left San Antonio. The thought of ever moving back home to Kansas makes me shudder as much now as it did back then. Not only are there fewer opportunities there, but I'd be subjected to being near my parents, the most in-love couple on the planet. I don't want another reminder that the candle is burning, and I might die alone if I never meet someone.

Setting the mug aside to take to the kitchen later, I fish a mini photo album out of the box. The plastic pages stick together momentarily when I open it, but give way.

Oh, wow.

There's Jamie's stupid face and those old, round-rimmed glasses he used to wear. He wouldn't be caught dead without contacts now. I guess I won't be completely alone after all. Except being stuck in the same retirement home with Jamie might be too much for me.

"Blackmail photo," I declare, turning the page.

There are others of us goofing around with our nerdy friends. One of Jamie, looking up, enamored, at a go-go dancer that he *still* wouldn't stand a chance with.

Jeez, it seems like a million years ago. I remember driving through this neighborhood back then. It's still surreal to believe I'm now living in it. I spent all my years in San Antonio living on the opposite side of town, east of the Army hospital.

Turning the page, I expect to find another silly photo. At first glance, it might appear so to Jamie, who I assume took the photo. It's me, packing up my nearly empty room in the duplex we rented together after we moved out of the dorm. The look on my face is unenthused by his intrusion, but the sight of my mattress on the floor behind me reminds me it was so much more than that. The memories hit like a tidal wave and keep coming.

It would be a big, fat lie if I said I never thought about Chris Mightener after I graduated that semester. It would be an even bigger one if I said I didn't think about him for a long time after that. God, I had it so bad.

If Winston thought our calling it quits was heartbreaking, he should see this photo. I looked absolutely miserable, and it had nothing to do with college ending. I can't even say how I made it through my finals that last semester, knowing my time with Chris was coming to an end. I was so infatuated with him that it's still mortifying to think about.

He was everything to me, and then he was just…gone.

Flipping the album closed, I stare at the box dumbly, the ambition to unpack it now gone. I feel like I suddenly have an answer to Winston's uncomfortable question. I *was* capable of falling in love. Once. Falling hard.

Obsessed, Remy, my conscience corrects. *You were obsessed.*

I can't even argue with myself on that one. I knew it then, and I still know it now. My first year of graduate school was a depressing fog of going through the motions. Just when I thought I had gotten into a new routine that didn't include seeing Jamie every day and having Chris sneak through my window at night, I heard about *the accident*. It was covered quite a bit in San Antonio, considering Chris was a Panther alumnus—they were proud of him. I don't know if they were proud of him after that, however, but news is news.

Setting the album back in the box, I cart it to my bedroom, deciding it can sit in the back of my closet for now. Everyone keeps a few things stored in boxes in their house, right?

Drunk driving. Critical condition.

It still makes me sick remembering the words I read in the paper. They even showed his smashed-up flashy sports car on the news. It was so crumpled and distorted; I don't know how he survived it or how they got him out. I can't imagine what he looked like or the injuries he sustained. I sigh and set the box down, scooting it to the back of the closet with my foot. The age-old questions come back like a nightmare. I went over this in my mind a thousand times back then.

Why was he drunk? Why was he drinking and driving? He was so strict about keeping his nose clean back when I knew him. I assumed maybe he was celebrating or trying to keep up with his new team-mates—anything that took the blame off my precious image of Chris. Finally, I decided it didn't matter. What I thought, what happened, what we were or weren't—none of it mattered. All that mattered was that he lived. I only know because I never read about him dying.

I'll be honest—when I got offered the lead position for the new sports rehab facility Cameron University at San Antonio built, he flitted across my mind. I assured myself it was natural to think about old memories of a place. I shrugged it off, though, and didn't let it play into my decision to take the job. It was a great opportunity. Chris wasn't the only person who went to Cameron U. And it's not like he's here now. For all I know, he's a plumber back in his hometown or selling sports equipment some-where in Colorado, where he was signed. Maybe he made a full recov-ery and is a personal trainer in New York City, living his best life out and proud. Maybe. Not that it matters…

I should eat something. I've hit the ground running at the new physio center ever since day one, sometimes refusing to stop for lunch. Tearing my eyes away from the box of doom, I pad to the kitchen, admiring the endless wraparound of white cabinets. I haven't done nearly enough cooking in this beautiful space. Maybe I'll buy some cookbooks and try out new recipes.

Grabbing a leftover Cubano sandwich out of the fridge, I plate it. Like a bad dream, however, I remember how many times I hoped Chris would ask me out to dinner, even though I knew that wasn't possible at the time. Putting my plate in the microwave, I spend the minute it heats assuring myself that I wasn't in love. Maybe he was just my first fairy tale that didn't come true.

The microwave beeps, pulling me from my soul searching. I grab a glass of sweet tea and get situated with my plate at the table, telling myself it doesn't feel strange to eat alone. It's no different from the silence of having nothing to talk about with someone else. In fact, it's better.

There's a soft tapping sound against the patio door that overlooks the back of the property. I take a bite of my sandwich and watch the iridescent droplets of rain dribble down the glass. No doubt it will help feed the weeds I've seen sprouting up around the previous owner's shrubs. Flipping through my mail, I search for the gardening catalog I'd spotted the other day. I should do something about the yard. The landscaping is a bit unkempt, and the stones in the walk up are cracked and crumbling. I've done nothing more than cut the grass since I moved in, having been too busy situating things inside the house and possibly having an existential crisis.

The subconscious is a fascinating thing. I've studied the human body extensively—having had to in my work as a physiotherapist—but the mind always baffles me more than muscles and nerve endings. Are we ever really in control of our thoughts, or is there some little person inside our brains, controlling levers and pressing buttons? Because as I stare at a page of sundials, any focus I thought I had escapes me.

'Get some good sex.'

Jamie's words come back to me, and my first thought is of Chris. I've had enough sex now to know that Chris wasn't the most thoughtful top, which tells me he had as little experience as I did when we met. I was too sore plenty of times after our late-night encounters, but each time was pleasantly intense. It was the kind of scorching intimacy you can't wash away and wear the memory of it like a sore muscle for days. There was something incomparable about the connection I felt when we were together that I've never felt since. That memory leads to the next thoroughly depressing one.

I left him a voicemail after his accident. I don't remember what I said, but it was something along the lines of hoping he was okay and that if there was *anything* at all that he needed, I'd do it. I think I checked my phone a million times in case I missed a call from him.

And he…never called back. The end.

Shifting my gaze to my plate, I stare down at the last bite of my sandwich. I pick it up and shove it into my mouth, chewing mindlessly.

That's how it started, didn't it? My addiction to making relationships work. Calling a man who'd already made his decision about us well before that. A man who made me unwittingly set a precedent for a level of passion that exists only once in a blue moon.

Shoving away from the table, I cart my dishes to the sink and scrub them with resolve. No shame. Just resolve. I'm too old to beat myself up.

I have a home, a good job that I love, and a best friend who's always just a phone call away. I'm going to be happy being single while I work on myself. Maybe I'll let myself *'have some good sex'* now and then or not, and neither option will be some damning life sentence.

They say you find things when you least expect them. Who knows? Maybe I'll learn to be in a relationship without losing myself. Maybe I'll meet someone whose company I enjoy so much that life won't make sense without them. A spark that turns into a steady flame and doesn't burn out. I'm not asking for an inferno. I've learned a few things after all.

CHRIS

chapter 3

Inhaling, I hunker further over the press desk and bounce my knee to release the restless energy brewing inside me. My joints are killing me, and it's all I can do to focus on the game in this humidity.

He promised me he wouldn't. He fucking promised, but the joke's on me for believing him. I knew he was lurking in the back of the room, just waiting for the first opportunity to pounce on one of the line coordinators. I can hear him—that boisterous Vince Mightener laugh. He wore his damn college bowl ring today. I should have known.

Can't he just accept the fact that I'm lucky I'm even sitting here in the press box? I have. I will always be grateful that he and Mom brought me home to recover. Grateful for how hard they fought to get me the best care possible. I can't imagine what it was like for them to see me like that after I'd been so capable my entire life. But how much of what little I've accomplished after that, do I have to share with Dad?

I only started going to local high school games just to have an excuse to get out of the house when I was able to finally move on my own again. Writing about the games afterward became something to pass the time, a way to keep my mind sharp and prevent me from climbing the walls of that bedroom that seemed to close in more each day I was under my parents' roof. I knew I'd never play sports again, nor be well enough for any kind of physical labor. It's laughable how I put the cart before the horse back in college, majoring in communications like I'd be broadcasting NFL games after I retired from an illustrious career on the field. Sitting in that stupid hospital bed that my parents had put in my old room, a light went on, though. If I couldn't play the game, maybe I could at least write about it. I knew football. It's all I know, really. That and how to write articles for the press.

Overhearing Dad trying to talk me up to people who owe me nothing leaves a bitter taste in my mouth. He might have been a big reason why I fell in love with the game and how I learned the plays at a young age, but the writing? I did that on my own. *That's* mine. It's all I have left, and I hate that he's so disappointed in me that he's trying to pimp me out for more glory. Always pushing for more. Pushing for me to be a star at something else. It's fucking embarrassing.

"Chris! Hey, Chris!" he shouts from across the room, making the guy from the Houston Gazette next to me turn and frown at the distraction.

Pinching my eyes closed, I curse under my breath and set my pen down on my notepad. I *have to* go. If I ignore him, he'll just come over and draw even more attention to both of us.

Pushing up off the narrow counter that runs along the press box window, I get to my feet. The movement pushes my chair back, but not far enough. These workspaces are narrow and cramped. I prefer snagging a seat on the end, but Dad was lollygagging on the way up, so I wasn't able to get here early enough to secure a prime spot. Shuffling to the side, I make my apologies to a coach and reporter in the seats I have to squeeze behind to get to the end of the aisle. I'm a big guy. Getting injured didn't deplete my size. I've certainly shifted from some muscle to more fat over the years, since I can't work out the way I used to, though. Either way, I'm too big to be able to make a smooth exit, bumping into the backs of their chairs.

Glancing over, I give Dad a chin nod to let him know I'm coming. The last thing I need is his hollering across the press box again. By the time I make it up the carpeted, dull gray steps, I've worked some of the stiffness out of my joints from being squished behind the press workspace, so my movements are more fluid and dignified for the pony show he no doubt has planned. He's standing next to Glen Moriarty, an offensive coordinator, who's clearly analyzing footage. To top it off, I can see Glen communicating with someone on the field via the headset he's wearing, a standard practice during gameplay.

I flinch, watching Dad clap him on the shoulder. For God's sake. I know things have changed since he was in college, but he should know better than to interrupt one of the team coaches during a game. Just because the guy's in the press box doesn't mean he isn't working.

"Here he is, Glen. Have you met my boy, Chris?"

"Dad," I warn, giving my head a shake as Glen holds up a hand and says something into his headset. I can tell my plea will be all for naught, judging by the excited smile on Dad's face. Fuck. He's already in his element.

When Glen finally looks up at him, Dad gives me a clap on the shoulder this time, reverberating the ache in my back. "Chris used to be a Panther. Tight end."

As he rattles off my former stats like they matter at all, I want the floor to open up and swallow me. I'm pretty sure Glen already knows who I am. He's seen me up here a few times since I got on with the San Antonio Times and cleared to come to the press box. I've congratulated him and the other coaches on a few wins without dropping my past. Without bragging about the nothing I have to brag about. You know, kind of like a normal human being who isn't trying to get their kid a job? Besides, anyone who can read could look my name up on the internet if they read my articles, which I'm sure the coaches all do.

As Dad goes into way too much detail about my ancient training history and even some of my best plays, I clench and unclench my fingers at my side, trying not to twitch. He used to do this all the time when I was younger, and I'd just stand there like a dutiful son. A slab of meat, like cattle being auctioned off for the best price per pound. I always appreciated how proud he was of me, but I can't say I was ever comfortable not having a voice while he tried to get me into the best schools, and later, the best agent.

As Glen's confused gaze shifts from him to me and back, I can't take it anymore. The poor guy is probably trying to figure out where this is going.

"Dad…" I try to interject, angling my chin toward the press window that overlooks the field. "We've got to get back to the game."

"Went all the way to the NFL," he continues, unfazed. "Now he covers the games. You should see his articles. Hell, he probably knows the plays better than half the coaching staff."

Jesus, I fucking can't anymore. He's trying to get me into coaching. I know it. He's been going on and on about it since the first time I brought him to a press box. Does he think insulting the guy is the way to get my foot in the door? It's not like Glen's in charge of hiring anyway. Why does he put me through this shit?

Gasps and sounds of horror erupt around us. I turn back toward the window, but all I can see is everyone standing on their feet, a few with their hands to their heads. Shit. What did I miss?

A guy with his arms up drops back into his seat, and I can see a still shot of the Panthers' quarterback lying on the field, gripping his knee. Oh, man. Not Kinnion. He's the best QB they've had in years.

I move to start back toward my seat when Dad's hand grips my shoulder. "Chris, wait."

"We're working. We'll talk later, okay?" I assure him even as I hope there's some way I can avoid doing so.

Without waiting for an answer, I spin back around, but my foot snags on something. Just as I spot Dad's backpack strap hooked around my foot, I falter and go down. I reach out to grab the end of the nearest workspace counter, but I'm already in motion, my weight causing too much momentum to stop the inevitable. My ribs bash against the side of it. My knee hits the hard floor. The descent of the stairs makes for an incredibly unkind downhill landing pad, the edge of one step hitting me square across the chest. The scratchy carpeting grates against my cheek as I skid.

"Oh, shit," someone gasps a second after the *thud* sound my body makes.

"Who in the hell put that there?" I hear Glen ask as someone untangles Dad's bag from my foot.

"Chris? You all right? Did you hurt your back?" Dad's worried voice calls at my side, his hands pawing at my shoulders to try to right me, twisting my spine uncomfortably as he huffs.

"I'm fine," I mutter, rolling over like a broken sea lion.

I feel hands under my arms as I try to get up. A covert glance around the room tells me Kinnion is momentarily forgotten since all eyes are on me—the awkward nobody whose father is vying to get him a job he doesn't want and who just face planted.

I shake Dad off as I get to my feet, but he gives me a slap on the back. "See?" he calls out to Glen, chuckling. "He can still take a hit."

A hit? I just tripped over my own feet in the middle of a crucial game play. My ankle is now throbbing because he left his freaking backpack in the middle of the damn aisle.

Glen gives me a wary look, but then his gaze flicks to the screen. His sense of duty clearly tells him that the game takes precedence over some washed-up old player and their obnoxious father.

"You good, Champ?" Dad murmurs that stupid nickname he gave me when I was a kid. "It's fine. Don't even worry about it. I think I can get him to go out for drinks with us after the game."

His nonchalant confidence is an electric pulse to my system. I can't tell whether I'm vibrating with anger or on the verge of a panic attack because of the dread coursing through me.

I shake my head before I can even get a word out. "No."

It's only a whisper—a desperate plea to not subject me to feeling more worthless than I already do. Cheers rise in the room, rattling my eardrums. On the screen, I watch Kinnion getting back on his feet. He waves as he walks off the field with a slight hobble in his step. Risen. Saved from the humiliation of the end of a career that's just being born.

"Hey, that's how these things work," Dad assures me. His urgent tone contrasts with the shouts of joy around us. "Someone puts in a good word with someone else. You *know* football. You could be coaching, not sitting here writing about it."

Not crippled. Not a disappointment.

I'm full-on shaking now, my lungs burning. I lock my eyes on the door as though it's my salvation because it is. If I stay here, I'll fucking explode or, worse yet, maybe even deck my old man. Angling around him, I dart a glance at the floor. The last thing I need is to wipe out again.

I can hear him calling after me as I shove through the door. The stifled air in the hallway reeks of concrete dust, beer, and sweat. It's not far enough away.

"Chris! Where are you going?"

"Home." I can't look back. If I do, I might say something I'll regret.

"Hey, it's fine. You just tripped. No one cares."

"*I* care," I grit grudgingly, and it strips a piece of me to admit it aloud. Can't he leave me with what's left of my dignity?

I resent how quickly his footsteps approach to catch up with me. He's nearly twice my age, and I can't even run as fast as my father. One of his thick hands clamps down on the back of my shoulder. My feet stop on instinct out of respect and duty, but I close my eyes, willing my breathing to go back to normal.

"Champ…come on. Look at me."

The part of me that remembers he's the man who helped get me up to go to the bathroom when I was laid up in bed for months wants to comply. The other Chris…the one who lives far enough away from his parents so they don't have to witness the fresh hell that is every waking moment of his life, doesn't budge. I must look like a fragile diva who's crying over a broken nail. It makes the sickening feeling in my gut worse. I concede, turning my head a fraction.

"I know it's hard," he prefaces.

The four words soften my resolve, hearing that he might understand all the sleepless nights I have, the constant pain, the numerous disrupted functions that most people take for granted.

Sitting. Walking. Standing for prolonged periods. Sleeping. Hell, even keeping an erection sometimes. Not that it matters. I don't make a habit of entertaining company often enough to worry about my performance issues. Whether he knows or cares to accept which gender I want to perform for still remains a mystery, another bullet point on the list of things we don't talk about. At least he and Mom have given up trying to set me up with a *'nice woman.'*

"You made it to the top and had your whole life ahead of you, only to fall all the way to the bottom of the ladder, but that doesn't have to be it." The words congeal in my veins but he keeps going. "If you just had a little bit of confidence, you wouldn't have to hole up at home writing about junior leagues and scrimmages."

And there it is. The great divide between us is so expansive, we might as well be from different planets. I swear, whenever he looks at me, he sees old Chris. His *champ*. When I look in the mirror, however, I see reality. The thing is, though, it doesn't feel like I've settled by being a sports reporter. I actually enjoy it. Aside from fiddling around my yard when I have good days, and playing fetch with Gale, it's the only enjoyment I've got. I get to give young athletes hope and a sense of pride in their accomplishments. Words to memorialize their endeavors—ones they can hopefully look back on more fondly than my own brief success.

"I *like* writing."

"Oh, come on. That was fine when you were getting back on your feet, but you're hiding. I hate seeing you like this. You could be coaching. You could have a life again."

It's such a brutal accusation that a disbelieving puff of breath passes my lips. *A life?* If he can't see that's what I've been trying to carve out for the last decade and a half, he's never going to understand. His version of a life involves trophies, accolades, and publicity. I reached for the stars once, and I don't know how to tell him that, broken body or not, I couldn't give a damn about ever getting within touching distance of them again. You can't live vicariously through your kid if they smash into a guardrail and break their back in two places.

Shaking my head, I start down the hallway to the stairwell. My skin is as tight as armor two sizes too small. The perpetual ache in my bones echoes louder, a resounding drumbeat now that he's ruined my distraction from it through watching the game.

"Chris! Chris," he calls.

My eye twitches, a telltale sign of an impending tension headache. "Just go home, Dad. I'll call you next week."

He hollers something chipper about leaving it to him, not to worry, and that he'll set something up with Glen. I can't walk fast enough to get away from his delusions.

It takes a long walk of shame to my truck, a fifteen-minute drive to the club I decided on, where I can hide from him in case he goes by my house, and five shots to silence his pipedream speeches. The music at Dooley's thumps around me. Welcome noise that the conveniently located sports bar near my house can't afford. Following the handsome cowboy I just met into the men's room, I blink through my haze as I stare at the tight fit of his jeans over his ass.

Self-medicating—the warning from my stint in rehab years ago whispers in my ear. I can tolerate the whispers. They're better than my screaming demons and body aches I've managed to silence. Shots aren't pain pills, I tell the whispers. I feel too good right now, too alive to give a damn about how buzzed I am. Hell, it's the most human I've felt in a long time. I'm not even limping as I follow the smiling brunet into the nearest open stall. Alcohol lets me be an imposter. Too bad

I'll probably feel worse in the morning than I normally do, but that's a tomorrow problem.

I barely get the stall door closed when he grips two handfuls of the front of my shirt and smashes his mouth against mine. His stubble grates against mine. His insistent tongue is sloppy, and he tastes like whiskey. It's not a good kiss, but it's physical contact. A warm body against my own. I give back, feeling some of my tension escape into the kiss as I back him up against the opposite wall. His cock, thick behind his jeans, digs into my thigh, and he moans, yanking my shirt up. Rough, cold fingers run across the layer of pudge above my hips that I never imagined having at this age—or ever. I'd care if I actually gave a shit about whoever he is, and I don't have any room for vanity right now. I haven't been touched in forever. Anyone will do. When his fingers slip to my back, I feel them grate over my surgery scars, half-dead to sensation, half-sensitive in other places.

Gripping me, he pulls me tighter against him and murmurs against my jaw as he bucks his hips into mine, "Fuck me."

I remember hearing those words when I was younger and in my prime. The thrill they used to give me over the stolen moments doesn't surface. My half-hard cock starts deflating, and if I'm being honest, I don't think it's from my pinched nerves cutting off circulation to where I need blood right now.

'You could have a life again.'

Dad's words surface, sticky, midnight oil. The scent of urinal mints lingers in the air, mixing with my companion's whiskey breath. Did I ever even have a life back when I was playing ball?

As the years have crawled by, I've sat at and tuned into countless football games, a blister of jealousy and regret deep in my chest as I jotted down highlights. For some reason, it occurs to me like a bolt of lightning that it's not the playing that I miss. It's the unspoken promise of how all that playing was supposed to make me feel—like I was king of the mountain. How all those years of work from peewee league, even to the NFL, were supposed to leave me reeling in a glow of victory and joy. Yet, even when I finally made it, I still felt like I had something to prove that first season after I went pro. Like the climb had started all over. The worry was back in my gut to be better. To always be better. How could I have forgotten about the pressure?

Winning games always gave me a high, but like the opioids that got under my skin after my surgery, the sensation would fade until my next fix. I've done nothing with my life since then but mourn a loss that wasn't as fulfilling as I thought it was.

A bubble of morose laughter gets caught in my throat. Fifteen years later, and I'm still searching for the sensation of being alive. It's just another kind of pain I'm trying to bury this time.

"Come on, stud. Come out to my car and fuck me." He cups my fly and gives it a squeeze, then pulls away, glancing down.

I blink at him, just now noticing that he has three very distinct freckles on the right side of his nose. They're incredibly off-putting for reasons I can't even say. His goatee has hints of auburn mixed in with the brown hair, and there's a dimple in his chin that does nothing for me.

Staring at my fly, he strokes me through my jeans with a placid look on his face. It's about as intrigued an expression as one might have while deciding between two different brands of laundry detergent in the grocery store.

"Want me to suck you first?" he asks, off-handedly.

My stomach roils, my cock instantly telling me it's no longer in the mood. *Suck me? Fuck him?* Then what? I'm clearly the only one of us who's hung up on the part after the major event.

My hands-on experiment portion of the evening has officially crashed and burned. Dad and I may not have the same idea about what having a life looks like, but I know this isn't the one I want. I want more than just getting off or silencing my demons with a quick orgasm. I want someone to look at me like I'm worth as much as I was in my heyday. The closest I've ever come to that was when it wasn't possible to even entertain the idea—covert moments at night during college. A sexy, eager young man who let me do whatever I wanted to him and looked at me like I hung the fucking moon. God, that feels like another lifetime. In truth, it was.

After I went pro, I was too terrified of being recognized to seek anyone out. At least one positive about ruining my career is that it doesn't matter who knows about my sexuality now. I've done the hook-up thing over the years when I was desperate to be touched by someone other than myself. Apparently, I'm not as desperate as I thought because the need to see deeper longing in my partner's eyes feels like it's the only way I'd get my dick to come back to life. Suddenly, I feel worse for having his hands on me. Worse than I know I'll feel tomorrow, because the only thing worse than a hangover is a hangover while you wallow in the reality that no one will ever look at you again like the sun rises and sets because you're in the world.

Swallowing, I consider my options for another second. Maybe I'm just being too emotional and all up in my head. As the guy leans in and sucks on my neck, however, I can't muster any enthusiasm to even pretend. I'd rather be at home with Gale, my overweight Rottweiler. She gives better kisses and presses up against my spine in bed when she knows I'm hurting.

Shaking my head, I pull back and draw his hand off my cock. I move to leave, but bash into the stall door, compounding my utter foolishness of enticing him to come in here with me. I want something that doesn't exist—someone to wake up next to who doesn't mind what I am. Or rather, what I'm not. And I want them to look at me as more than some mundane decision on their shopping list.

For the second time this evening, I stagger away from a man shouting at my back. Fumbling through the crowd on the dance floor, I burst out of the club door, where the humid San Antonio air greets me. The *sewage-y* smell from the Riverwalk blows on a soft breeze as I lumber down the sidewalk and punch in a request for an Uber ride. I'm already kicking my ass that I'll have to come back tomorrow to pick up my truck for no other purpose than I was hiding from my father. The cab smells like vinyl and stale incense, hitting every pothole on the way to my house. Gale yips as I fumble to get my keys in the lock. The sound warms my heart. I give her some ear scritches and watch her pityingly as she zips outside to do her business. What did a good dog like her do to get stuck with someone like me?

Still, I stubbornly reject Mom's worried claims that I wouldn't be able to take care of a dog when I told her I'd brought a puppy home from an adoption event a few years ago. That animal has helped me more than any therapy I've tried.

"Come on, girl. Let's go to bed."

She looks at me warily, ears back. It's like she can tell when I've been drinking, and I hate it. All of a sudden, her head whips to the right, and her spine goes rigid.

"Ah, shit."

I blink, making out the distinct colors of a skunk in the neighbor's yard. Gale lets out a deep *woof* and starts toward it. I take a step and call out to her, but my porch gives way. Logic tells me it can't give way. It's concrete, but as I step into nothing but air off the side of it, I know just how bad of an idea self-medicating was tonight. My hips shift uncomfortably, and the harder I try to stop falling, the more awkwardly I topple over, my feet getting snagged against each other. My spine twists. There's a popping noise, and a sharp sensation shoots up my back and down through my tailbone. I hit the ground two feet below as hard as a tackle. Mouth open, a broken sound comes out that doesn't even come close to representing the paralyzing pain. It's so debilitating that it steals my breath. All I can do is pant and lie in a snarled heap.

Something wet and rough laps my cheek. Gale whimpers and nudges me with her nose. She doesn't smell like skunk. At least there's that. I let out a pained laugh through the tears in my eyes and squeeze her shoulder. Flopping down in front of me, she licks my forearm like she knows.

"Yeah…" I pant. "Yeah, I think I'm good and fucked this time."

REMY

chapter 4

Well, I totally called that. Shaking my head, I chuckle at Jamie's cry for help text on my phone.

I'll be there Friday evening. If you don't have a guest room ready, I'll sleep on your couch. I don't care. I need to get out of here for a few days.

To give him credit, he lasted longer than I thought he would. I'm an only child, so I can't say I'd be able to handle having five additional people under my roof either. I shoot a reply off to let him know I will have the royal treatment awaiting his pampered ass whenever he arrives, and then pocket my phone to get back to work.

I barely get it tucked into my pants when Adam, one of the center's PTAs, comes flying through the doorway of my office and makes a beeline for the trash can on the other side of my desk. Clutching his stomach, he drops to his knees and latches onto the plastic receptacle in a death grip.

"Oh, my God. Are you all right?"

I realize it's a foolish question, given how pale he looks. There's a sheen of sweat across his forehead, and his grumblings earlier about the new restaurant his wife wanted to try out now come back to me.

"No." He lets out an unholy gagging sound. "Fuck. It's food poisoning. I know it. Oh, God. I'm gonna die."

He doesn't die, but what happens next makes me forget about thoughts of going to lunch any time soon. I manage to get him up on his feet and help him to the bathroom. There are half a dozen patients in the center, but fortunately, they're spread out in the large open space. Still, his retching sounds aren't a pleasant soundtrack for an atmosphere where people need to either let their bodies relax or their minds focus.

"I'm sorry, Jeremy. I think I'm going to have to go home," he pants, now leaning over the sink in the bathroom.

"Yeah, definitely. Man, I'm sorry. Do you need me to call anyone to give you a ride?"

"I'll call my wife if she's not sick. I swear that woman has never so much as had a stomachache in her life, though." He pauses for a moment to catch his breath and lets out a few more desperate moaning sounds, splashing cool water on his face. "Shit. I've got someone in number four. I was just hooking him up to the TENS unit."

"It's fine. I'll finish up for you. Just worry about yourself right now. Okay?"

"Thanks," he heaves a breath of relief, and I have to say I'm grateful to have a reason to leave him in his misery. I've never had a weak stomach, but the power of persuasion is real.

"Just TENS therapy?" I clarify, heading toward the door. "Do they need heat for post-exercise or anything?

"No. Just TENS. Broken screws in the lower lumbar spinal surgery. And he had a fall recently."

"Shit," I mutter under my breath, feeling a twinge of sympathy for more than Adam now.

I hit the hand sanitizer pump on my way out.

"Christopher," Adam calls.

"What?"

"His name is Christopher."

"Oh. Okay. Thanks."

Heading toward the drawn curtains of therapy table number four, I mentally go over my knowledge of such severe cases. I'll have to see if

Dr. Sanders, our resident sports medicine doctor, allowed for any other treatment options in the man's file if the patient doesn't respond well to TENS.

Drawing back the curtain, I see a pair of sneakered feet hanging off the end of the table. The TENS unit is lined up next to the table, most of the wires still sitting on the cart with their leads.

"Hi Christopher, I'm sorry for the delay. Adam's a bit under the weather, so I'm going to finish getting you set up."

"Chris is fine," a deep timbre calls, muffled by his face-down position. "Whatever you've got to do, just as long as I don't have to lie like this all day."

Whipping the curtain closed behind me, something familiar about the sound of his voice has me spinning around quickly. I jerk to a halt when the patient comes into full view, or rather, the view of his back from feet up. He's too big to fit on the table, explaining why his feet are dangling off the end of it. And for that matter, he's almost too wide. I haven't seen shoulders that wide since...

I swallow at the close buzz of dark hair at the back of the man's head and give myself a mental shake. Jesus. It can't be. And so what if it was? I'm at work and...well, it just can't be. I'm just being paranoid ever since unpacking that box from Mom last week.

Walking around to the TENS unit, I glance at where Adam placed the first two leads—on either side of the L3 lumbar vertebrae. It's an easy map going off the long surgical scar that runs from L1 down to L4, where the waist of the man's jogger pants is folded over. It was a lot of work, I can tell. To top it off, there's another incision scar several inches above it on his thoracic spine.

"Adam said you have broken hardware? Is it all in the lumbar?"

"Yeah. They broke years ago. I had the nerves burned off, but they're growing back. I can usually manage it, but I fell off my porch last week and torqued it."

I have to bite my cheek from uttering an expletive over the horror that must have been. Swallowing, I place a lead in the next position, absorbing the reverberating sound of his voice. As I do, I can see my hands trembling.

The center has three distinct scents—hand sanitizer, sweat, and rubber from the floor mats. The whiff I catch, however, is a mix of shower clean and a soft natural musk. I've dreamt about that smell thousands of times. I smooth my fingertips over the next lead to ensure it sticks, and can't prevent touching a bit of his skin when I get to the edges. A tingle shoots up my arm. I do a double-take at the TENS unit to make sure it isn't on by mistake, but the panel is asleep. Try as I might to convince myself of some logical explanation, the thickness in my lungs tells me the truth as I stare at the two lower back dimples I remember tracing countless times.

It's *him*. It's Chris. *My* Chris.

Raking my gaze up his back, I take in every inch of bared flesh. Arms bent at the elbows, his large biceps frame the back of his head. I swallow when I stare at his hands, loosely closed above his head, a familiar, distinct disfigurement to a few knuckles that I know he broke during college. My mouth waters, remembering how they so easily took me apart.

His body shifts, and I hear a soft grunt, jolting me from my stupor. He's clearly in pain, making me see his casual comment about not wanting to lie here all day in a different light. Trying to get my breathing under control, I move to the panel on the TENS unit and press the power button.

"Um…all right. I-I'm going to start at a low level and work my way up," I manage to get out, rattling off my usual speech from memory. I can't even think straight right now, staring at the controls like I've never seen them before.

I've heard people say that if you ever meet your celebrity idol, it ruins the appeal for you. Similarly, I've heard the same is true for running into your youthful crush. I know for a fact that whoever thinks that has obviously never crushed the way I did on Chris Mightener because he has the same effect on me right now that he did fifteen years ago, if not more pronounced. My stomach flips, and I have to will my body to stop trembling.

"You'll feel a tingling sensation. Let me know when it gets too intense."

I bite back a delirious laugh. *I feel a tingling sensation and it's way too intense.*

He grunts in acknowledgement, and I realize he's likely done these before, having played sports and gone through all the things he has with his back. Flipping the switch to initiate the current, I turn the dial from one to two and then from two to three. He says nothing. He doesn't even move to indicate he's feeling the prickle of the electric current, so I inform him as I move the charge higher to each subsequent number.

"All right," I pause. "That's six."

"Okay," he says, sounding unfazed.

And so it goes for the next few iterations until I get to nine. Ten is the highest you can go. The more damaged and irritated the muscles are, the less likely a patient is to feel the effects of the current. Not many people make it to a nine before crying uncle.

"And here's ten." I wait for a reaction, a word, anything. "Can you feel that?"

His response is delayed as though he's considering. "Mm," he grunts, stirring too many memories I don't need to think about right now. "I guess there's kind of a faint tickling sensation."

I was starting to worry I'd done something wrong in my distraction, but a glance at the monitor shows the pulses are still being administered. It should come as no surprise that he's got that much swelling and pain, considering what his back has been through.

I take a wobbly step back now that there's nothing more for me to do. Have I even breathed in the last five minutes? Leaning against the counter behind me for support, I take in his profile, still trying to wrap my head around the fact that he's here. He's still real.

I used to think he was larger than life. I'm not sure how it's possible, but he seems even larger now. He was all carved muscle when we were younger. I always thought he was too perfect. My face washes in heat as my eyes roam over his broad shoulders, less defined than I remember, past the skeletal patterns of scars, and down to the soft padding above his hip bones. Drooling like a creep, I can't find a single thing to deter me from thinking any differently now, even if his composition isn't the same. A tug of longing stirs deep in my gut. If he looks at me right now, I might incinerate into a pile of ash on the floor.

What would I even say? Will he even remember me? Do I want him to? Of all the days I had to stand in for one of the PTAs.

There is no way I can stay in here during his treatment, not that I need to. I'm going to have to come back and unhook him when he's done, though, but I need to get it together before I do. I can't let my first interaction with him be while my mind and nerves are all over the place. I survived my embarrassing behavior fifteen years ago, but I don't think I'd recover from it this time.

"You're set for ten minutes, so I'll leave you be. Just holler if you need anything. Okay?" I ramble, making my way to the curtain to escape.

"What's your name?" he mumbles from his prone position.

"Remy," I blurt, but it's not until my hand freezes on the cloth barrier that I realize it came out as an indignant croak, as if my brain wanted me to say, *'Your Remy, of course.'*

Dashing like a haunting spirit through the curtain, I speed walk through the center, oblivious to anything around me. I can hear my heartbeat in my ears and a scolding chant in my head. *This is stupid. So stupid.*

I'm thirty-seven years old, and I'm practically hyperventilating over the sight of a guy I fantasized about more times than is healthy. I stop when I realize I've fled all the way out to the hallway between the main physio center and the therapy pool. I'm at work. I can't just run into oblivion like Forrest Gump to hide from my feelings.

"Feelings," I mutter under my breath and let out a puff of laughter.

What a joke. They weren't feelings. It was just lust and wishful thinking. Leaning against the wall, I let my head fall back with a *thump*, hoping it will knock some sense into me. Have I learned nothing?

Maybe this is what I do, what I've always done. Get giddy about a guy until I date them, and then everything loses its fizzle. I never dated Chris, so perhaps that explains why the fizzle never went away.

A part of me that I'm not proud of suggests that maybe it's just because he's so physically attractive. Both then and now. Please tell me I'm not guilty of lookism. I can't be that shallow.

No. Despite his lack of romantic overtures when we were younger, I was drawn to his personality. Except, I don't know the first thing about fifteen-years-later Chris. He could be a horrible, awful person. He could be married. The shot of nausea that stirs gives me pause.

Did he ever stop hiding? Did he marry a woman and have three kids? Does she know what he used to do with me in college?

Jesus, listen to me. I sound just as obsessive as I did back then.

Why? Why am I like this? What is it about this man that made and apparently continues to make me so irrational?

I had just gone three full days without a single thought of him after opening that Pandora's box Mom sent me last week. Because yes, that's how long it took to shake off the memories that her package unearthed. For crying out loud, I've been texting back and forth with Miles a few times since then. It's been nothing more than chit-chat over what both of us are up to, but I'd started feeling a flicker of curiosity that it might go somewhere when he comes back to town. Now, I couldn't care less. Because that's what Chris Mightener does—makes me forget that any other person in the world exists. I think it took me a year and a half before I stopped ignoring anyone who tried to flirt with me after my senior year, holding onto false hope and one-sided heartache.

"Enough," I whisper, shaking my head against the wall.

Scrubbing my hands over my face, I let out a sigh. I'll just go back in there, and maybe I can turn my back so he won't even see me. I don't know why I didn't say, *Jeremy*, when he asked my name. The staff and I have all settled into the new facility well enough, but only half of them call me by my nickname, probably because I'm their boss.

I can act indifferent. Hell, I've done it without even realizing it after a while during my past few relationships.

'Hey, Chris. Remember me? The guy you used to fuck in college? How've you been?'

Pinching the bridge of my nose, I groan. If Jamie were here, he'd probably backhand me so hard I'd see stars right now. I kind of wish he were. A good smack might set my brain right.

Dropping my hands to my sides, I open my eyes and blow out a breath. Fairy tales, I remind myself. Chris was nothing more than a fairy tale that didn't come true. Probably not even that, if I'm being honest. He was just the sexiest fucking knight in shining armor I've ever seen.

This really is ridiculous. I didn't even see his face. Maybe it didn't age well. Maybe if I saw it, I wouldn't be attracted to him at all anymore, and that phenomenon about meeting your idol being a disappointment would finally occur.

Sucking in a breath, I push off the wall and turn to head back down the hallway. I make it one step when an invisible force stops me in my tracks. That force is the unexplainable chemistry I've been trying to shake for the last fifteen years as I stare at the knock-me-down-and-fuck-me gorgeous face looking back at me.

Shit. Jamie's going to have to do a lot more than bitch slap me to get the sight out of my mind.

CHRIS

chapter 5

This shit isn't going to work. I did TENS therapy after my surgery, but that was before I broke the hardware in my lumbar when I thought I could move a new refrigerator into my house to save a few bucks on delivery fees. Whatever. At least there are no co-pays for alumni here.

The new guy's fingers are at least softer than whoever started working on me earlier. I can tell he's younger than the last man by the sound of his smooth, skittish voice. I have half a mind to beg him to just massage my back with those agile fingers, but I've found I like being touched less and less over the years. It's like living in skin and a body that aren't your own. My mind is thirty-seven, while the shell it inhabits feels seventy. After my idiocy last week, I've decided to stick to the comfort of my own hand, my heated massage recliner, and muscle rub gel. Wild nights ahead of me. Yay.

"You're set for ten minutes. I'll leave you be. Just holler if you need anything. Okay?" the guy rattles off, his steps heading toward the privacy curtain.

There's something pleasant about his voice that relaxes me, making me mind less that I'm stuck lying on my stomach, the worst thing for back pain. On that note, however, I know I'm not going to want to wait here if he's breezing away to fuck off and forget about me.

"What's your name?" I call, my lips half smashed against the therapy table.

"Remy."

The name sticks out like a carnival game sign popping up after a ball hits the target. *Remy.* Really? Of all the names. There's a soft waft of air and a rustling sound from the curtain, telling me he's slipped through.

I've only heard that name once before. It brings back a flood of memories. Satisfying, hot memories that make my belly burn deep down in the pit of it. A wash of heat runs up my neck and into my cheeks, remembering the sound of it on my own lips. *Remy.* I guess it's not entirely true that I've only heard it once before. I remember saying it many times like a prayer that was pulled from my throat as I released into a beautiful, firm, lithe body that hugged me to the point of delirium.

Shit. Wrong thing to think right now. Somehow, the blood flow to my cock doesn't seem to mind my uncomfortable position at the moment.

Closing my eyes, I take a deep breath and try to focus on the little tingles from the leads around my spine, willing them to work magic. The memory of the man's fingertips, however, and the sound of his voice hover like a distraction.

'Um…all right. I-I'm going to start at a low level and work my way up.'

Am I clouded by old memories, or did he sound nervous the way Remy used to? My Remy, who always seemed so irresistibly drunk at the sight of me.

Okay, so he wasn't exactly *my* Remy. We never made it into anything it wasn't. He was just there and willing whenever I wanted. The perfect arrangement to get me through the stress of college and a budding football career. So fucking perfect. My first drug, if you will. One that never left my insides crawling afterward. Two years of the blissful sensation of walking on air and feeling like I could take on whatever was next. Maybe in that regard, he *was my* Remy.

Huffing a laugh, I silently gloat over the fact that I don't think he sought out any extracurricular activities aside from me the entire time. We had an agreement to show each other new test results if we ever hooked up with anyone else, but he never did. I don't get much to gloat about these days, so the memory is good for my ego. Sometimes, when I need to jerk off to forget about the pain, I pretend I'm back there in his room. Agile, limber, strong as an ox, with him on his knees looking up at me the way he used to. Him under me, moaning the sexiest sounds no porn has ever been able to replicate earnestly.

Snorting, I turn my neck and bury my face deeper into my forearms. He wouldn't fucking look at me like that now.

I wonder what happened to him? He was roommates with that obnoxious guy from my journalism class who always showed up in pajama pants and had something snarky to say that had the professor sighing, an exasperated noise, while everyone laughed like minions. Remy only had bio with me that I had to take as a requirement, while he ate it up because he was going to become a physical thera—A…therapist. A *physical therapist*.

The confident, unaffected voice when the therapist entered the room, the peculiar shift to skittishness, and rushed speech after I told him my name. The way he rushed out of here. It can't be, but…what are the odds there would be another Remy who's a physical therapist at a center connected to the college we both attended?

Was it him?

Hell, it's got to be.

That heat in my belly returns, expounded upon by a live-wire charge that tightens my mid-section. It's not a rogue current from the TENS unit. It's a delayed reaction to knowing whose hands were just on me.

Oh, God. That means he saw me.

Remy saw me. Like *this*. Like *me now*.

The machine lets out a monotone beep, signaling the end of the treatment course. My pulse kicks up, galloping away from me, snaking tension around my lungs. He'll come back in, and I'll have to get up. He'll have to see me crawl off this table like a drunk grizzly bear. Hear me grunting and my joints cracking as though I've been in extended hibernation. I can feel my love handles sticking to the vinyl fabric of the therapy table. Love handles that weren't there fifteen years ago.

Fuck.

Fingers twitching, my mind races for a way to escape. Why though? Why do I care?

He's probably married or in a committed relationship with someone by now. That's what happens to nice guys like him. That's what happens to everyone but me. He could probably care less about recognizing me, if he even remembers.

My stomach swirls. A sour sensation creeps up my throat. I can taste the reason for my panic, clarity in the form of stomach bile. He *was* a nice guy, and I…was a total asshole.

Suddenly, those longing looks he used to give me that I've lived off during wet dreams over the years don't feel like something I can gloat over. Not when he's minutes from being in the same room as me, face to face. It all comes back to me—the hearts in his eyes, the way he used to nibble his lower lip, and how he'd stutter when he'd get too flustered. The way he'd look at me like he wanted to kiss me all night was just a bit too on the far side of intimacy for me at the time, and yet always so tempting I had to rush out his window to stop myself from giving in. I think I knew it then, but what did I do? I repaid the closest thing I've ever received to devotion with frenetic dickings and reveled in the way my bossy bedroom commands could bring him to his knees.

There is no way I'm letting him see me like this after the way my cocky, amped-up-on-adrenaline ass used to talk to him. No way. I'd rather live with the delusions of my memories than see an ounce of disappointment in his eyes. The memories are all I've got. I'll be damned if life is going to take those away from me, too.

Reaching around behind me, I yank the cables off the leads. Only half of the sticky patches come loose, but I don't care. I can pry the rest off when I get home.

Peeling myself off the table, I ease to the side until my feet touch the floor, and I grunt from the stiffness after lying down for so long. Spinning around, I locate my shirt where I discarded it on a chair and tug it over my head. Shoving my arms into my zip-up, I flip the hood up and peek through the slit in the curtain. If there's a check-out process, they can figure that out after I'm long gone.

Hustling through the center, I keep my head down. Hood pulled low, I probably look like I'm evading capture after a robbery. With each heavy step, my footfalls reverberate not just the pain of my weight to my worn-out joints but a message of shame. *I did this to myself.* Both my accident and how I'm fleeing right now from a reunion with my college hookup.

Shoving through the door, the smell of chlorine from the therapy pool across the hallway that leads to the exit stings my eyes. Did he know it was me? If he didn't, will he find out later when he's going through records?

Why the fuck did I wear these bummy old jogging pants and let my ass get so fat? Gale really needs to stop letting me eat Rice Krispies Treats. It's one of the few non-chocolate snack foods I enjoy that aren't harmful to dogs. It doesn't seem as funny now, blaming her when I reach in and feel the bottom of the box while we binge-watch TV together. How have I not noticed the feeling of my ass jiggling when I walk until this moment?

Glancing up, so I don't end this walk of shame by running into someone or the exit door, I stop in my tracks. My sneakers squeak to a halt, ass fucking jiggling from the force like I haven't been mocked enough by my life choices today. It is Remy. Definitely *my* Remy.

My God, was he always this handsome?

His arms fill the sleeves of his blue button-up, tucked neatly into his khakis. My eyes rake over the lines of his torso—slim, yet solid, with more meat on him than I remember. Sleeves rolled up to the elbows, his forearms are speckled with hair that I imagine would be soft to the touch. My mouth waters watching his throat undulate, remembering how it felt under my mouth. I used to graze my lips across his jaw, which is now covered in a light layer of dark stubble that adds a sexiness to the years he's acquired.

He scrubs his hand across his forehead. It's oddly fascinating to see that his bangs don't fall into his face the way they used to, back when guys all had longer, messier hair. They're shorter, combed back. Both stylish and yet unassuming, with flecks of blonde like they've been kissed by the sunlight from time outdoors. Head leaned back against the wall, eyes closed, he blows out a breath like he's trying to calm himself.

The distress on his face pierces the bubble of my mini fantasy. It doesn't take a genius to put two and two together. Is he…out here because of me?

Part of me wants the floor to swallow me up, knowing that would mean he was dreading having to face me. Who in the hell wants to leave that kind of impression on someone? But if he's out here having a moment because of me, does that mean…

Turning, he takes a step, and those blue eyes of his damn near pierce me to my soul. "Chris," he blurts, sounding breathless, like he hit a brick wall.

My mouth moves, but nothing comes out. Nothing goes in either. It's like I've forgotten how to breathe.

"Remy?" I croak like an inquiry even though I know damn well and good he's real and standing right in front of me.

He lets out a puff of air, as though he's suspended in the same disbelief. "Yeah."

The view of him head-on is just as good as his profile. Better even with those bewildered eyes on me. Maybe I'm just imagining things, but they scan me from head to toe like he's done so many times before. Something instinctual kicks in, making me want to take a step forward, back him up against the wall, and claim him the way I used to. Press my chest and pelvis against his. Breathe him in and find out if he still has a hint of that sweet scent that used to cling to his skin underneath his cologne. Run my lips down his neck and suck on the base of his throat to hear him whimper those sounds that made my nuts draw up. God, how am I just now remembering that little detail?

I knew him once. Or at least my body knew his.

Would it still be the same? Would his still know mine?

"Are…are you done?"

My gaze snaps to his, feeling caught. "What?"

"I mean, I can see that you're done. Is…everything all right? I'm sorry I didn't disconnect you. I lost track of the time."

His words register, humbling me more than the idea of getting caught ogling him. Right. I'm just a patient. He's not here waiting for a fuck or to drool over my broken body, thirty-pounds-heavier ass, and useless, doesn't-always-work-right cock.

"Yeah."

Everything is *not* all right, but I don't know what else to say. Looking past him, it would only be a few short, awkward steps to go around him and get to the door, but despite the urge to flee, I have questions. So many questions. Things I need to know before I bolt and piece back together a new version of my wank fantasy fodder to get me through the next fifteen years.

"You work here?"

"Yeah," he answers with a breathless laugh, stuffing a hand into his pocket.

Cringing internally, I shift in place. Of course, he fucking works here. Man, I'm smooth.

"I was at BAMC for about twelve years," he elaborates, "but when I heard they were opening this center, I thought it might be a nice change."

He's been in San Antonio for *twelve years?* This whole time?

Shit. We could have…

Could have *what?* What the hell am I saying?

I spent most of my savings on a house in a decent neighborhood that put me smack in the middle of all the colleges in the area, so I could easily get to all the games. I doubt there would have been any appeal in an unemployed guy on disability who was just coming off a pain pill addiction and spent his time sitting in the bleachers like a lost puppy.

"Um…did you want to schedule another session?"

"What?"

"For your back," he says delicately, gesturing to me.

My back. My back, which he just saw. My back, which makes it obvious to anyone that I can't play football and haven't for a very long time. Does he know what happened?

Hell, the whole world knew. I was all over the national news for two weeks and then forgotten. Of course, he probably does.

There is no way to even fake the bravado I had back then that was so appealing to him. Dropping my gaze, I shake my head and shuffle around him.

"No."

"Well, I… If you…" he stammers behind me as I reach for the door handle, but then blurts, "Take care!"

Take care. There's a polite brush off if I've ever heard one.

It's official. Whatever appeal he once found in me has worn off. Maybe he was only stammering because he was worried some ex-NFL player he used to screw, who got drunk at a fancy party he didn't fit in at, and then smashed his car into a guardrail, would make things awkward. I push outside and tromp across the parking lot to my truck, hating myself a little more than I thought was possible.

REMY
chapter 6

Flashing red and blue lights whir past my car down Route 281 as Jamie and I head home from the restaurant we stopped at near the airport. The traffic up ahead slows down.

"Great," he enthuses from my passenger seat.

I love him, but I can only handle his complaining in small doses. Getting stuck in gridlock after listening to his adventures in Unclehood over dinner will require a little more focus than I'm currently willing to give at the moment. Luckily, we approach a turnoff, and I follow other like-minded travelers who have the same idea as me.

"We'll take the scenic route," I inform him.

"Are you up for finding a watering hole on the scenic route?"

I snort, noticing how some of the animation has gone out of him now that his belly is full. After a few blocks, I turn down a street that should eventually cross the one that runs to my house. As we ride in companionable silence, I take in the contrast of the houses to my own. I realize it's the Monte Vista neighborhood, easily identifiable by the rows of large trees lining the streets and the spacious yards. I always loved this area for the unique architecture of the homes. They're a mix of historic brick structures and European revival. There is nothing wrong with the craftsman I snagged, but, hey, a guy can admire beauty.

We settle on a quaint but well-kept-looking little bar called Mahoney's, since it's the first one we see in the predominantly residential area. Once inside, it's clear that if the place has a theme, it's a sports bar, judging by the many posters and signs on the walls and the number of televisions.

"Ah, beer and testosterone. Perfect," Jamie sighs and heads toward an open high top in the back. Once we're seated, he rests his elbows on the table and scrubs his hands over his face. I shouldn't find so much amusement in his misery, but he's razzed me enough over the years, I can't help it.

"Are you going to live?"

Huffing a laugh, he picks up a sticky-looking drink menu tower. "Yeah. I feel better already. Thanks for picking me up."

"Well, I'm pretty sure TSA would have called me if I'd left you at the airport for too long."

I get a kick in the shin for my remark, but he snickers and calls me an unkind pet name. As I rub my leg, he drops the menu and folds his arms, glancing impatiently around the place.

"I'm guessing this is one of those classy joints where you have to go up to the bar and wait for the bartender to notice you."

Rolling my eyes, I get up. "I'll go. You are my guest after all."

"Mighty kind of you."

Leaning back on his stool, he threads his fingers behind his head. Judging by his smug expression, he has no problem being waited on. I'm not sure why I missed him, but it's good to see him in person again.

Luckily, the bar isn't crowded. Only a few patrons occupy spots along the worn wooden structure. I slide in between two empty stools and glance down the bar to wait for the bartender.

My gaze snags on a bulky frame one stool down, a presence that's too big to avoid. Just as I go to look away, I do a double-take. I'd know that profile anywhere.

Except, it's not his profile. Chris is staring right at me, like maybe he noticed me first.

My mouth falls open, as usual. How many times have I just sucked in air for ten seconds each time I see him?

God, he looks good. His snug jeans are doing him lots of favors right now with the way they're molded to his thighs. The black T-shirt he's wearing is stretched across his back and tight around his biceps, revealing every detail of his shape. He's bigger than he was when we were younger, a little thicker. I don't know why that makes him seem even more human to me, softer. A different level of sexy. He looks just as good with a shirt on as he did without one the other day after he high-tailed it out of the center, leaving me wondering if I dreamt the entire encounter.

Shit. I'm staring.

Say something, Remy.

Licking my lips, I have to swallow before I can form words. "Chris... Hey."

I swear his gaze stays fixed on where I just wet my lips before it flicks up to my eyes. "Remy," he says my name like a warning. "You following me?"

"What? No! I...I have a table," I assure him, hooking my thumb over my shoulder, hoping I'm pointing in the right direction.

He doesn't even glance to see where I'm aiming. His mouth ticks up at the corner, and he turns on his stool to face me.

Wait...was he just messing with me?

"So...you live in San Antonio?" I realize that's probably obvious, so I amend it as though I only get a limited number of questions before he disappears again. "How long have you been back here?"

"About ten years."

Ten years? Chris has been here almost the entire time I floundered through hapless relationships? How is that possible?

Wait. Maybe it actually makes perfect sense why none of them ever stuck. Maybe there was some cosmic force interfering because we were still both within the same breathing space.

Yeah... Because *that* sounds totally plausible.

Jesus. Now I need a drink as badly as Jamie.

The bartender stops by, saving me from further gawking. I ramble something to him, hopefully an order for a hundred proof sensibility with a shot of erasing verbal diarrhea. When I dart a peek at Chris, my breath catches. I swear he's...checking me out? His gaze flicks up to mine with something intense in it. I'm sure of it because I have the urge to clench my ass and groan.

"What are you doing tonight...*Remy?*"

"Just...having a drink with..." With...who the hell am I with? Turning back, I spot Jamie arching a brow at me curiously.

Yeah...him, I think to myself. That annoying guy I call my best friend, who will no doubt have a heart attack if he sees you.

This time Chris' gaze does look in that direction. I watch his expression morph into one of terrifying displeasure. He lets out a snort and leans his arms back on the bar.

"Is that Jamie?"

"Um...yeah."

He doesn't seem to share the enthusiasm I put into that confirmation, picking up his pint glass and throwing its contents back with a scowl. What's the deal with that? Did they have a beef in college that I didn't know about?

Glancing back, I catch Jamie giving me a wide-eyed look. His mouth moves, forming words I clearly decipher as, *'Chris? What the fuck?'*

The only thing worse than listening to him bitch for the last two hours about how his family has invaded his personal space would be him reminding me of how depressed I was for months on end after senior year. If he thinks he even saw a flicker of interest in my face while I was standing here, this is going to be the weekend from hell. One I probably could use to whip some sense into me that I've clearly lost, but still hell.

Grabbing up the drinks I ordered, I try to act unaffected for both him and Chris. Except my feet don't want to move away from the bar. What if this is the last time I see Chris?

We've lived in the same city for a decade and have never run into each other. What's to say that we never will again?

"It was nice to see you again. I'll talk to you later?"

It takes zero courage to make that sound like a suggestion as I turn away and hurry back to the table. I blame serendipity and a curiosity that feels like it just got reinvigorated. *Just* curiosity, I tell myself again as I refuse to make eye contact with Jamie when I set our drinks down.

"Hoooolyfuckingshit! Was that…"

"Uh-huh," I mumble, sipping the head off my beer with my full concentration.

"Oh, my God. *Why* did you pick this bar?"

Is he serious?

"Because you fucking told me to pull over!" I remind him in as harsh a whisper as I can, still silently freaking out.

"What did he say? Wait. What did *you* say?"

Jamie isn't exactly quiet, but I doubt Chris can hear him over the noise of the TVs, the patrons, and the music. I tell myself that's why I glance back over at the bar.

I catch him looking back at me, half-turned in his stool. His expression is equal parts curious and perturbed. Did I say something to piss him off?

Pulling my gaze away, I shake my head. "Nothing. I…I don't know."

Jamie groans, putting his face in his hands. "Ah, fuck. He's already scrambled your brain again."

"What?"

"Dude, do you remember what a Chris addict you were? You think I didn't know each time you were expecting a visit from him? You'd get all quiet, start super cleaning the duplex, and peeking out the window or pretending you had to '*study*' in your room. And then *after* graduation…you were this hollow, lost version of my friend, like a lamp without a lightbulb."

I glare at him. "That is a terrible simile. And I cleaned because one of us had to. You weren't the hygienic roommate you thought you were."

"Okay," he chortles. "Whatever. You know I'm right."

"You're not," I mutter petulantly, sneaking another glance at the bar only to find I'm still the center of someone's attention.

Why is he looking at me? And why do I not want him to stop?

"Fine. Then why are you acting weird? What was this '*nothing*' you talked about for a whole ten minutes?"

I snort because ten minutes is a complete exaggeration. I have to tell him *something*, though, or I won't hear the end of this for weeks. "I just..." Crap. I'm going to have to tell him. "I saw him last week. He came into the center to get therapy."

"What? And you're just telling me *now*?"

"Would you keep your voice down?"

If it wasn't apparent to Chris that I'm either talking about him or that I still have him on the brain, it most certainly is now as I glance back at the bar and meet his eye again. It's like being interrogated while you're naked. Shielding my eyes with my hand, I block him out so I can get through the details that Jamie thinks he needs to know.

"I didn't know it was him at first." I go on to elaborate about how I figured it out, hyping up how I waited in the hallway to avoid him as though I intended not to engage him. And then I explain the weirdness that came after when he saw me. The way he looked stunned and then just up and left like some damaged, closed-off version of the guy I used to know.

"So, when I saw it was him just now, I was trying to be nice and said hello," I explain, sneaking a glance at the bar.

The view I'm treated to this time is a full frontal of Chris' beefy thighs, spread open with his feet resting on the rungs of his stool. He's turned all the way around, openly watching me now as though he's trying to decipher something. I can't decide if I feel like the luckiest prey he's ever laid eyes on or the target of a soon-to-be murder.

"Why do you keep looking over there?" Jamie scolds.

"I'm not!"

I *am*. I'm literally still looking right at him.

"You are too! You're practically eye-fucking him."

That has me sitting upright on my stool to face my accuser. "What? I am not. He just keeps looking over here. It's...distracting."

At that, Jamie cranes his head around and catches the view that's making my stomach squirm. He groans dramatically, turning back around and rubbing his eyes.

"I'm in the middle of an eye-fuck sandwich. I feel so dirty. Gross."

My heart skips a beat. *Is* he eye-fucking me?

"There's no eye-fucking going on," I retort like I have an alternate personality from the one inside my head. "You're just...being *you*."

"You mean, observant?" he deadpans, cocking an eyebrow.

I can't fight the laugh at his confident resolve. So, I just shake my head and take a drink, making sure to direct my gaze to a safe area.

"You know what? Fuck it." He throws his hands up. Leaning back on his stool, he folds his arms over his chest. "You're finally single. I say go ahead."

"Go ahead, *what?*"

I cringe when he waves a hand toward the bar. As if I haven't drawn enough of Chris' attention to myself already.

"Now's your chance to fuck him out of your system after all these years. Maybe it'll be cathartic."

The way my body lights up at his suggestion has to show on my face when I peek at Chris yet again. I wish I could crawl under the table, but I settle for shielding my eyes again. "Oh, my God. I'm *not* going to fuck him. He barely said a word to me the other day, and not much more just now."

It's a ludicrous idea, even coming from Jamie. Me and Chris…fucking now.

My cock doesn't seem to think it's a bad idea, but what does my cock know?

The fizzle… I need to remember my quest for finding myself and the eternal fizzle, one that doesn't evaporate after dating.

"Besides, I've been talking to Miles," I throw out to change the subject and maybe even to distract myself.

"Who?"

"I told you about this last week. You know, *Miles.*"

"You mean fucknugget? No!" he wails, pinching the bridge of his nose. "Would you listen to yourself! He's already got you talking like him. *You know?*"

This again? Jamie must be mistaking him for someone else.

"Whatever. Well, he's coming into town next week, so…I don't need *complicated* right now."

"Are you dating him?"

"No, we're just going to get dinner or something. The center is going to have a fundraiser appreciation dinner, and he said he'd be my plus one for it."

"Then it's not complicated." He rolls his eyes and leans forward. "Listen to the expert here. Casual sex is never complicated. Dating is. You are a free, healthy, *youngish* man with lots of options." He gestures toward the bar, making me cringe. "Exhibit A—screw your college demons away." Moving his outstretched hand toward my phone, he adds, "Exhibit Fucknugget—get a free meal and some terrible conversation, followed by, perhaps, a night of very boring sex."

He ignores the unimpressed look I cast at him, sitting back and picking up his drink again. "However, if *I* were you, I wouldn't do them in that order. Always save the hot, anger-bang sex for last."

Closing my eyes, I take a deep inhale. I'm not even going to argue why sleeping with Chris wouldn't be an anger bang because I don't feel any of the hostility that situation would require. How does my friend make a living giving advice like this?

"How many followers do you have again?" I ask dryly.

"Six hundred thousand."

"Baffling. Besides, I can't believe you're encouraging me to hook up with him after all the shit you gave me when we were in college."

"You were a shy little sex zombie then."

"Wow. Thanks. And now?"

"Now, you're a successful, confident homeowner who doesn't have to settle for fucknuggets or jocks that crawl in through your bedroom window."

I scoff to assert my annoyance, but I can feel my face heat. Of course, he had to remember that embarrassing detail.

"As those are my only two potential suitors at the moment, apparently I do."

"You're missing the most important element. They both want you." I make a disbelieving face, and he rolls his eyes. "They do. You're a catch, Remy. Just remember that you have the power to say no to commitment after dessert. There is nothing wrong with getting a little D without all the baggage that comes with it."

Frowning, I absorb how that sounds a lot like having casual sex and no long-term plan. He must see the conflict on my face.

"Hey, all I'm saying is that it's okay to get sucked by a few frogs without co-leasing before you find your prince."

I must be immune to his analogies at this point. Either that or I'm so used to them that they're starting to make sense because my gaze drifts to Chris again. Could I really sleep with him again and not be haunted by visions of him moving around my kitchen with me or curled up on my couch? Ugh. I'm hopeless.

"What if…I don't know how?" I ask warily, swallowing against a lump in my throat.

"Fuck." Jamie sighs, pulling my attention back to him. I flash him a pained, yet appreciative smile for understanding the mess that I am. "All right, let's get out of here."

I nod, knowing deep down it's probably for the best. Jamie throws back the rest of his beer and rises. I hear him curse softly under his breath, and then a deep voice rumbles to my left.

"Can I buy you a drink?"

My eyes work their way up the snug black T-shirt that's now right in front of me until I'm staring into the determined-looking face of my weakness. It feels like a moment as we look at each other. A very loaded moment. Something inside me celebrates. He came over.

"Hey! Chris!" Jamie cheers, jostling me from my haze when he throws an arm around me.

"Hey," I add, breathlessly, suddenly conflicted by my friend's cock-blocking. "Um…I think we were just leaving."

Chris' nostrils flare. I swear his gaze moves to where Jamie's hand is squeezing my shoulder before looking back at me like I've committed a crime. Is he...jealous?

"Long time no see," Jamie adds with more feigned enthusiasm, and I can detect a hint of saltiness over being ignored. Typical Jamie.

Gaze shifting, there's no less agitation in it as Chris looks at my friend. "Jamie," he grunts.

My pulse is on double-time, which I absently realize is silly for a thirty-seven-year-old man, but I can't help it. Especially as Chris' gaze crosses mine for an instant before he turns and walks away. Was that a flash of hurt in his eyes? What just happened?

"Wow, yeah. We need to leave," Jamie mutters. "Come on, Romeo."

His slap on my back brings me back to the present. I nod and take a gulp of my beer to wet my throat. Standing up, I dig my keys out of my pocket. When Jamie starts across the bar ahead of me, I take the opportunity to locate Chris again. He's not at the bar, though. The sensation of loss that ripples through me fills me with regret. Is he always going to disappear from my life like a wispy cloud on a strong wind?

As we near the door, I see it swing shut, a wide frame ambling through it. I nearly run into Jamie's back. I can tell he's slowing down on purpose, but I fiddle with my keys to play ignorant and walk around him. Something urgent in my steps for one last sight of Chris.

Outside, I'm surprised to find he hasn't made more ground, descending the last step from the bar entrance. He sways for a second before moving forward across the gravel lot.

"Is he driving?" I murmur to Jamie as I watch Chris tug a set of keys from his jeans pocket.

"Hopefully only a bumper car at a carnival."

It's not the answer I wanted to hear. As we stall at the doorway, a sense of protectiveness prickles my skin, watching Chris' fame shift further to and fro.

"Shit," I hiss, remembering that horrid image of his fancy car on the news. I move without further thought, ignoring Jamie's groan behind me. "Chris? Can we give you a ride?"

His footsteps stop abruptly, and he swings around, looking suspicious. His gaze flicks to Jamie and then back to me, frowning.

"Why?"

"You just...look like you shouldn't drive."

"Or..." Jamie chimes in, coming up beside me and throwing his arm around my shoulders again, "We can call you a cab, and then Sugar Britches and I can get home and snuggle."

I've never seen a look more full of disappointment. "You married *Pajamies?*" Chris says accusingly.

What? Is that what he thinks?

"No!" I insist, appalled at the very idea, at the same time Jamie declares, "Yup!"

I whip my head to Jamie and flash him an aggravated look. I know he's trying to save me from my own stupidity, but this is about a man's safety, and…well, I don't want Chris to think I'm married. Because…lying is bad. Shuffling out of Jamie's grasp, I take a step forward.

"No," I clarify, shaking my head. "He's just in town visiting from California."

"Oh, my God. You threw away a perfectly good out," Jamie grumbles and starts around me toward my car as though I'm a lost cause.

"And is…*still* Jamie," I add with an awkward smile when I'm left facing Chris' befuddled face.

His eyes narrow at Jamie like he's piecing things together. When he looks back at me this time, it feels like I just got put on his dinner menu again.

"I'd *love* a ride."

I stand stock still, trying not to cum in my pants as I watch him turn on his heel and start toward my car. Chris, Jamie, and I all together in public, with Chris about to get in my car. Is this real?

"*Rem*," Jamie whines next to my passenger door, arms hugging himself. "Unlock the car, will you? It's freezing here."

Right. I can't just stand here having an out-of-body experience while his delicate California coast self and my ex-crush are waiting. Raising my key fob, I aim at my car and hit the unlock button on the remote. It chirps just as Chris approaches Jamie.

He reaches across Jamie for the passenger door handle. I watch my friend's face morph into shock like someone just brought another cat into his home.

"Hey! Shotgun," he demands, shuffling forward like he's going to slip in through the now open door.

One of Chris' big palms covers his face, though, pushing him away and making me nearly swallow my tongue on a delirious laugh as Jamie rears back from the unexpected move. Chris uses the opportunity to angle his big body in between Jamie and the opening, plopping down inside. His hungry gaze latches onto me again as he closes the door.

I snap my mouth shut when Jamie looks at me and huffs, "If he fucking calls me Pajamies again, we're kicking his ass out while the vehicle's moving." Grumbling, he wrenches the back door open and folds himself inside like a pouting, overgrown child.

Jesus, what am I getting myself into?

As soon as I get behind the steering wheel and shut my door, the tension is evident. I'm partly to blame, unable to avoid noticing how Chris' knees touch the dashboard of my car. His thick thighs are spread to accommodate his size. I haven't felt thighs like that since…well, since his.

Pressing the ignition button, I don't need to look over at him to know he's watching me with that same loaded look from earlier. I want it to mean what I think it means and to follow Jamie's ridiculous advice. Except, I don't just want one night of sex. I want…to talk. I want to hear about his life. I want to see his easy smile again and wonder if fifteen-years-later me can still be the cause of it. I'll need to get his number if I plan to do that, but I don't have the guts to ask for it in front of Jamie.

"Okay, I didn't flee California to drive around all night," Jamie drawls from the backseat. "Where are we taking you, Your Royal Highness? I've got a date with Remy's spare room, which has the supreme luxury of being devoid of the sound of any of my nephews, and I plan to enjoy the shit out of it."

He gave me an out earlier. I know that's not what he's trying to do now, but I see a new one and take it.

"Um, I can drop you at the house first," I suggest as though I'm being a considerate friend without any selfish motives. "Is your place far, Chris?"

"*Very* far."

Why did I look at him? Wrong move. That is *definitely* eye-fucking.

I hope Jamie didn't hear the little noise that just squeaked out of my throat. I nod and shift into drive.

"Let me guess," Jamie mutters. "It's in the *Cockholm* neighborhood."

Gritting my teeth, I apply more pressure to the accelerator. I need to drop my friend off at my house as soon as possible. It's the right thing to do. Clearly, he needs some sleep to get over his grumpiness and jet lag.

The silence in the car has my nerves skittering. I have Chris Mightener in my car. We both have our clothes on. I'm a grown-ass man, not some starry-eyed college kid. I can do this.

"Do you think you'll come back to the center for another treatment? There are other things we can try if the TENS therapy doesn't work well enough."

"Feeling adventurous?" he smirks, and my heart flips over in my chest at the suggestiveness of the comment.

"Just north of Dickadilly," Jamie wagers, mumbling a new unhelpful zing about Chris' address.

If Chris heard him, he doesn't show it. His attention, solely focused on sending me unspoken signals with his eyes.

"Um…there's another electrical stimulation method that uses steroid treatment—iontophoresis."

"I don't like drugs," he clips, jaw ticking as he shifts his attention to the windshield.

Shit. Why do I feel like I touched a nerve? I was just trying to be helpful, but I guess he didn't ask me to solve his medical problems.

Glancing over, I catch him doing the same. His fists unclench on his thighs as his gaze rakes up my legs.

"What other kinds of *stimulation* do you do?"

Jamie groans from the backseat. It's a splash of cold water to the heat creeping into my mid-section. He adopts his best impression of a sat nav narrator. "Turn left at Uranus, Missouri."

"Heat. Ice. Light therapy. Exercises," I blurt out as though it will erase my obnoxious friend's commentary from my car. "Massage."

"You give massages?" Chris raises a brow, sounding intrigued.

"S-sometimes. If…if the person needs it."

"Welcome to Sphinctershire! You have reached your destination!" My *ex*-best friend mumbles from the backseat like he's talking to himself, because at this point, he is.

I see my house up ahead and gun it only to have to slam on the brakes a few seconds later. "O-kay! We're here!" I feel a sliver of guilt over how that sounds like *'get the fuck out of my car right now,'* so I tone it down as I unclip my house key from my keychain and hand it to Jamie. "I'll be back in a little bit."

Snatching it from my hand, he leans forward between the front seats. Without looking at either of us, he delivers a monotone, "I expect you alive and present for breakfast." Glancing at Chris, he adds, "Goodnight, *Kermit*."

Fucking hell. I need a new friend. Leaning my head back against the seat rest, I close my eyes until I hear him get out. When the door slams shut, I let out a sigh and shift back into drive.

"He hasn't changed," Chris says dryly.

"Not one bit."

Look at us. Agreeing on things already. He stays quiet after that, and I realize I don't know where I'm going yet.

"Um, so, *where* is your house?"

He directs me to turn left twice and then stay on the new street until he says otherwise. Offhandedly, I realize this will send us back in the direction we just came from, but the silence that follows doesn't let me dwell on it. I'll find out soon enough where he lives, and then this peculiar encounter will be over.

"Do you ever think about college?" he suddenly asks quietly.

"No," I blurt insistently, but cover it up by clearing my throat. "Er, sometimes." When he doesn't respond, my nervous energy shifts to rambling. "My mom actually sent me a box of my old stuff the other day. There was this mug in there that I think Jamie stole from the Sunshine Diner."

"I remember that place."

"Yeah." I laugh for some reason, but a twinge of regret reminds me that Chris and I never went there together. "Um, the box had an old photo album in it. That brought back a few memories." I fidget in my seat, wondering if he's being unusually quiet or if I just have no concept of time at the moment. "There was one from when I was packing up my room to leave after the semester we all graduated."

Shit. Why am I telling him this? Glancing over, I see him look away like he's uncomfortable. Here I am being all hung up on my own memories when he has an entire set of his own. I suppose that time in our lives isn't an easy one for him to remember. It wasn't long after that his dreams were upended.

"I…tried to call you after your accident. I heard about it on the news. I mean, I'm sure everyone did." God, that's probably not a comforting thing to say. "Anyway, I just meant, I called and left you a message to see if you were okay or…or if there was anything I could do, but…I'm sure you had a lot to deal with." I adjust my grip on the steering wheel, feeling like I've both said too much and yet not enough. "I'm sorry about what happened to you. That must have been horrible."

We go a full block in silence. I want to pull over and bang my head against my dashboard.

"You called?"

"Uh…yeah. Or…sent a text. Or both." Holy shit. Shut up, Remy. "I don't remember," I mumble, begging my mouth to stop speaking.

"I didn't get anything."

"Oh? Um, well, I did. I was worried about you. I mean… I felt bad."

The upholstery on his seat creaks, and I feel him shift. There's curiosity in his eyes when I glance over at him.

"Why?"

"Because…" Because I was over the moon for you? "Because I… I don't know."

He shifts his attention back to the road, and it feels like I lost something. Why wouldn't I feel bad for him? Why wouldn't anyone?

"Nobody called." The admission surprises me as much as the fact that he answered at all. "I got a few cards. One from my high school coach. I don't think anybody felt bad for a guy who got so drunk he almost killed himself and could have taken out a family of four." The naked honesty bubbles up a well of pity in my chest. "Can't say I blame them. I wouldn't have blamed you either."

I'm glad that he realized the severity of his poor decision, but people make mistakes, especially when they're young. As long as they learn from them, that's what matters. I don't think an error in judgment should strike them from receiving compassion when they probably needed it the most.

Frowning, I assure him, "Well…I did," but judging by his following silence, I can see that he has nothing further to say on the matter. "Anyway," I blow out a breath, hoping it will take the heaviness out of the air for both of us. "Um…where am I going?"

Leaning forward, he squints at a street sign up ahead. "Turn left in two blocks."

Our surroundings look familiar. When I make the turn he requested, we pass the bar that we just came from. Did he…accept our ride to keep me around longer, or is he just disoriented?

"What would you have done?" he asks.

"What?"

"You said you called to see if I needed anything."

"Oh."

"What would you have done if I'd answered and said I needed you?"

Anything is the first word that comes to mind.

"I...I'd have done whatever I could have, I suppose. I was back in school, working on my doctorate at the time, so I don't know—"

"Stop!" he barks out.

I flinch, wondering what I said to set him off. Does he have some type of mental illness that I didn't realize?

"Sorry."

"No, stop the car. You just passed it."

"Oh. Shit. Sorry."

I back up to where he's pointing and then turn down the street to the house on the corner he's indicating. It's a white one-story home in the revival style I've admired, offset by a large front yard with a beautiful walk-up of paver stones. It's not as large as some of the loftier houses in the Monte Vista neighborhood, but it's idyllic and would likely fetch a much greater price than the one I just bought. I'm glad the price he paid for football got him something.

"Well," I sigh, knowing our time has come to an end.

This is so awkward. Would it be weird if I asked for his number? Do I even want his number? Of course I do; I just don't know what I'd do with it. Type and delete a bunch of messages.

He opens the door and starts to get out, splashing me with a wave of foolishness. I guess all we had left between us were a few flirtatious moments. Maybe he only doled them out as payment for a ride home.

"Um, goodnight. It was nice see—"

"If you come in, you can meet Gale," he interrupts, motioning with his head toward his house before closing his door.

What? Unfounded jealousy seizes my lungs as I stare after him and whisper maniacally,

"Gale? Who the fuck is Gale?"

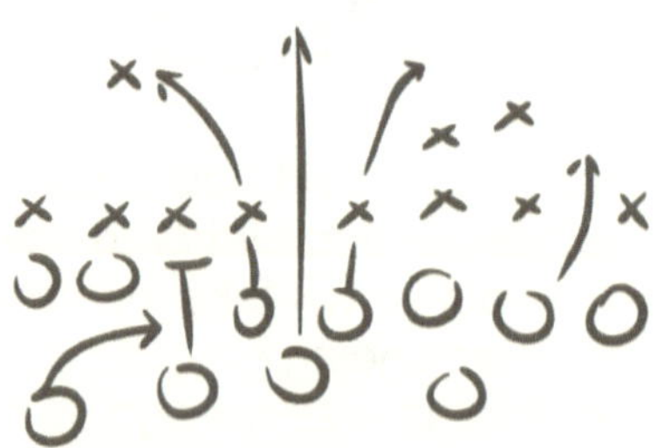

After hesitating up a path of beautiful mosaic paver stones and landscaping that puts my neglected yard to shame, I follow Chris inside and stop short at a skittering sound. Gale turns out to be the most adorable Rottweiler I've ever seen in my life. Stocky, broad-shouldered, and slightly well-fed like her handsome owner, whose cheek she's currently peppering with doggie kisses while he rubs her belly. In short, I want to be Gale.

With each rumbly croon of "Did you miss me? Did you miss me?" I can't stop myself from silently shouting, *yes*. Maybe I'm just overjoyed at learning Gale didn't turn out to be a wife or girlfriend.

Tearing my gaze away from his bent-over backside, my eyes adjust to the dim light coming from a lamp in his living room. The first thing I notice is an oversized brown leather recliner. Given all the controls on the arm of it, my guess is that it's not just a piece of furniture, but a much-needed form of therapy. The cluttered end table next to it speaks volumes. Its top is littered with menthol gels, creams, and even a discarded ice pack. There's a stack of *Sports Illustrated,* too, and several remote controls, telling me his massage chair is the lucky recipient of many hours housing Chris' ass.

When he straightens up, a soft grunt leaves his lips as he sends Gale on her way. She trots over to the couch next to the recliner expectantly, as though to ask if he's settling in for their usual routine. It paints a picture without the need to ask questions. My greedy eyes capture a few more details as I hedge deeper into the room behind him.

The floor-to-ceiling bookcase on the far wall extends all the way to the front of the room, where a big-screen TV sits on a stand. It's filled from top to bottom with what looks to be a heavier dose of nonfiction than fiction. Books on football, no surprise, but also on every other sport. What's peculiar is that there are biographies of famous people from all walks of life, history books, some on accounting, auto mechanics, masonry, cooking, and…pottery?

"What do you read?" I ask when I catch him looking at me.

Brow pinching, he glances at the shelf as though it's merely a decoration and shrugs. "Things I should have learned years ago. Things I'll never use."

"I see you still keep up with the local games." I nod toward the newspaper on a desk, open to the sports section.

"I have to. I cover them for the SA Times."

"Oh, that's cool."

He's a reporter? He majored in journalism, but I always saw it as an afterthought.

Hands stuffed in his pockets, I notice now that he took his shoes off. I still can't believe I found him, let alone am in his home. His house *smells* like him. I never want to leave. Would it be too weird to ask him if I can bottle up some of the air to take with me? That might be easier than figuring out what comes next and if it will have life-altering consequences.

"Do you want a drink?" He motions with his head to his kitchen. "I think I have a beer in the fridge."

"No, I'd better not. I've got to drive back."

Smirking, he takes a step closer. "That's why I walk to the bar."

Maybe I should be embarrassed hearing that I was duped, but instead, I laugh. "Smart."

He stops a mere foot away from me. If I were a candle, I'd have melted to this spot without my wick even being lit.

"Long time, huh?" he asks, voice low, but it's not a question.

"Yeah." I clear my throat when the word comes out in a near whisper.

He gives me a slow perusal from head to toe, easing his hand out of his pocket. Is this it—the part where I'm supposed to leap head-first into Jamie's terrible advice? If so, how come I find myself backing up a step and bumping into the wall? It's difficult to discern if I moved at all because Chris is still as close as he was a moment ago, closer in fact. He reaches up, making my pulse skitter. When his palm rests on the wall next to my head, I want to laugh at myself for being so spun up. I haven't felt like this since…him. I didn't think it was possible.

He leans in, his gaze scanning my face mere inches away from his. There's a pleased curve to his mouth as he utters my name in wonder, as though he still can't believe that we've found each other again, either.

"Remy."

"Chris," I whisper, my voice drunk to my ears.

His chest presses against mine, and all the air floods out of my lungs along with a desperate little sound. He makes a noise that sounds like relief, and the next thing I know, his lips are on mine. Soft and hard. Both hungry and appreciative at the same time. I grip onto him so I don't slide down the wall and make a puddle on the floor. He's solid and warm as his bittersweet flavor bursts across my tongue when he silently asks to taste my mouth. I keen and feel my eyes rolling back in my head. Kissing—why did he have to start with kissing?

He lets out a moan like someone who's starving, which makes my head spin, squeezing my arm and then sliding his hand down to my side. I'm practically hanging onto him, my fingers gripping the back of his shirt in two tight handfuls. The kiss goes on and on, even as I try to prepare myself emotionally for it to be over. With each slant of his mouth and brush of his tongue, it feels as though the world is spinning.

It's Chris. *My* Chris. I want to celebrate the return of this piece of me that I thought I'd never get back, and yet, at the same time, the arousal in me feels foreign, as though it's being stoked by a stranger, a Chris imposter.

Breaking away for air, I hope the flood of oxygen will help me untangle this swirl of conflict. Chris smirks and takes a step back, peeling his shirt over his head and throwing it to the floor. I gape at the expanse of exposed skin as he reaches for me and slips his fingers under the hem of my shirt. The brush of his fingertips makes the flesh on my stomach go taut and my cock tingle. Yet, the bubble of panic expands in my chest. It's like we're in a time machine, right back in my old room. I know what happens when we're done, and I don't think I can live with that anymore.

It's just sex, some horny part of me reminds. The me who's been learning how to spend quiet nights alone at home, becoming a man who doesn't depend on the consistency of a relationship, however, cautions that this will disrupt the shred of peace I've found.

I believe Jamie's exact words were that I should do this to exorcise my demons. That it would be cathartic. For the life of me, I don't think I have any demons about our past. I was young and enamored. And then maybe I let those feelings become a standard I strived to achieve in other relationships. Maybe a prolonged fizzle isn't possible, but fucking Chris right now…I don't see how that's going to change anything. Sex can't change me or wipe my memories.

Did Jamie mean I wouldn't see Chris the same way that I used to if I had sex with him? Because I don't need to do the deed to know that. I can tell he's different. Hell, I'm different. That's what life and age do to people.

There's an edge about him and scars on his torso and by his eye that weren't there before. If either of us has demons, it's him, not me. I don't want him to be my catharsis any more than I want to be his. I think I just want what I always have—to know all of him. And I get the feeling, he's not willing to be that naked. Frankly, I don't know if I am either.

"I don't know if we should," I gasp just as his lips are inches away from mine again.

"What's the matter?" Straightening up, he smirks, trailing a hand down his chest before stopping at the button on his jeans and popping it open. "Not as good as you remember?" he asks like a challenge, and he's daring me to lie.

There's a jagged horizontal scar above his right hip and fewer divots defining his abs. He's thicker and softer, but I still wouldn't use *soft* as a word to describe him. There's just *more* of him, and I could never not like more of Chris. My head shakes dumbly as the sound of his zipper lowering seems to fill the room. I realize my rattling skull might have been misread when his smile falters, so I swallow and answer honestly.

"Better."

He snorts as though he doesn't believe me, but then smirks again. "You *like* what you see?"

It sounds like another challenge, not delivered with the same confidence I remember. Did I only imagine it back then, or was he just as vulnerable as he appears now, and I didn't see it?

I resist my instinct to answer his question, too terrified to encourage him with more truths. His gaze rakes down my body, and his expression softens to something more innocent that makes me want to hug him.

"*I* do," he whispers as though he's confessing a secret.

Reaching out, he slides his hand along my jaw. His palm is just as rough as it used to be, but warm and reverent. I close my eyes, pulled under by the heady lure of it, and let out a rush of air as he traces my lower lip with his thumb. Leaning in, his forehead presses against mine.

"You're still so fucking sexy."

The surprising whispered words ghost my lips. I close the space without thinking, capturing his mouth to thank it. With each slant, he lets out noises that sound like grateful sighs. His hands go to my hips, pulling them against his and punching my gut with arousal. However, a flurry of questions mutes it to a dull roar.

He thought I was sexy all those years ago? What else did he think? And why does he think so now? I'm caught in a snare, trying to connect the past to the present.

These probably aren't the things you're supposed to think about for one night of casual sex. I could follow him into his bedroom and let him fill me the way he used to, cry out his name, ball the sheets in my hand as he writhes against me. I could go home with a pleasant feeling in my ass and the high from an orgasm. I could, but I'm me. And this is Chris. I'd want more.

Because this is what I do. Every freaking time. I make out with someone and then end up in a relationship without even dating. I put a roof on before I've even built a foundation.

Is Chris capable of dating now—or even willing to? If there's a remote possibility that's something he's interested in, I'm not about to fuck it up with fucking. I want to know who he is now first. I want to build four solid walls so the ceiling doesn't come crashing down on me. And if he has sweet things to say, I want to hear them without alcohol on his breath.

"I have a date next week," I blurt when he abandons my mouth to suck on my neck.

"Cancel it. I'll make sure you won't be able to walk," he purrs, squeezing my ass and nibbling at the base of my throat.

Shivers run up my spine even as I laugh breathlessly. Drawing the tip of his nose along the cord in my neck, he moves his lips across my jaw as his hand snakes under my shirt and up my back.

I think he's going to kiss me again, even though I exaggerated about calling my upcoming meet-up with Miles a date. I don't want it to be a date, and I want Chris to stop being so damn magnetic.

I'm unbelievable. He's finally kissed me with abandon, the way I always dreamed he would, and I want him to stop. I can't believe I'm going to do this, but given his state and the mess that my head is in, I know it's the right decision.

Pressing my hand to his chest, I tilt my head away, heart hammering from two opposing wants.

"And then what?"

His hand freezes inside my shirt, and he draws back slowly. I'm not sure who's more shocked by my question.

"We've done this before," I remind him, blushing at how it sounds like I don't cherish those wonderful memories. "I just… I can't. I'm sorry."

Realization dawns in his eyes, which don't look the least bit glassy now that I'm so close and staring right into them. I don't think he's drunk at all. Buzzed maybe, but my level-three alarm looks like it just killed that.

Releasing me, he steps back. Gone is the softness in his expression and even that edginess, completely shuttered. He gives a single nod, turns away, and pats his leg. Gale hops off the couch, races over, and follows him.

"Thanks for the ride."

I scramble for words to call out, some way to segue into what I wanted to say next. I still don't even have his number. As he ambles down a darkened hallway, I feel like an utter fool for numerous reasons. He's not swaying because of alcohol. That's just how he walks now, painfully rigid and stiff-jointed, his torso leaning to the right from a misaligned spine. Does that mean he really wanted me? With a clear mind? As Chris of the present?

The well of hope that rises in my chest drains as quickly as it burbled. I just shot him down, and I don't currently possess the words to figure out how to make him understand why.

Somehow, I end up back in my car after walking in a shaky haze across his lawn. The slam of my door has a finality to the noise as images from the evening flash through my mind. Clenched fists, scowls, the tick of his jaw. Last week, when he was at the center, the way he put his head down before he hurried out the door—he's not the same Chris I knew. Sometime over the last decade, life robbed him of his confidence that used to make me feel like a guest in the presence of greatness. I have a sickening feeling that my rejection may have done more than just halt our foreplay and that I won't be getting a reprieve. The funny thing is that I want one now more than ever. I want to know the Chris who gives his dog kisses, reads random books to learn things, and was sitting at a raggedy little sports bar all by himself on a Friday night.

Dropping my head against my steering wheel, I groan. What happens in a fairy tale where the prince comes in hot and heavy when you aren't ready for it?

CHRIS

chapter 7

Unloading the last bag of pea gravel by my garden shed, I stow my hand truck inside the little building for the day and wipe the sweat off my brow with the hem of my shirt. The wind chills the damp skin on my belly, making me shiver now that I've stopped moving and the sun has moved behind the clouds. My knee gives a throb as though it's shouting at the cold to stay away.

If my body and the weather cooperate, I should be able to finish the pathway to the oak tree in the back corner of the yard this week. One last project before a long winter of holing up inside and catering to my arthritis. It doesn't get as cold here as other parts of the country, but

I'd probably move to a less humid location if it weren't for the amount of college teams in the area. At least my sunporch is insulated and heated, so I can work on my mosaics and watch Gale out the back window when I give her yard time. Three cheers for brooding being an effective motivator.

Locking up the shed, I turn to head toward the gate that opens to my front yard, where I backed my truck up to unload my bounty from the hardware store. One more bag and I'm calling it quits for the afternoon. The ache in my joints from the full day of manual labor is proof that anger can only fuel the stamina required for overzealous distractions for so long. Surveying my house, it looks like a crime scene when I think about what went down in it over the weekend with Remy.

I can't believe I just assumed he'd be down for a repeat of our college activities. Instinct kicked in, some meatheaded alter ego that used to work for me in college, and I ran with it.

Gale races over, nudging a stick against my hand. Wrangling it from her, I give it a toss deeper into the yard. She zips down one of the paths I set a few years ago and then does a ninety-degree turn to dart into the grass where the stick landed, her usual eccentric flight path. I can read dogs, apparently, but not people.

I thought he looked at me like…

Shaking my head, I sigh and start toward my truck again. I had myself convinced that he was avoiding me and just being polite when I left the center last week, but then I came home and marinated in it. Shallow breathing, wetting his lips, the way he gets all jittery like he can't even form a sentence—I started thinking that maybe I just got all up in my head. That maybe there was something still there.

When I saw him walk into Mahoney's with fucking pain-in-the-ass *Pajamies* of all people, the cloud of jealousy and petulance that hit me was an eye opener. I have no claim on him. It's not like he wasn't free to be as stupid as he wanted to be and end up with Jamie, even though I didn't know it wasn't the case at the time. I swear, when he walked up to the bar, though, he gave me *that look*. The one he used to give me each time I showed up in his room. It was like I was the best thing he'd ever seen. I haven't seen that look in fifteen years. Needless to say, it made me go a little savage, instantly determined to pull out all the stops. I needed to know if it was real. When he told me he wasn't with Jamie, I thought I won the damn lottery. There was no question—Remy was going to be mine for the night. Again. Just like we used to.

He wanted to be too. I was sure of it. Until I wasn't.

Stopping at the tailgate of my truck, I reach in and grab the bag of *Sakrete* I bought. Dragging it to the end of the bed, I stare down at it blankly.

'And then what?'

I asked myself that very question recently, so I couldn't even feel slighted about it. How can you begrudge a guy for passing on casual sex with an old hookup?

It's just... Was it because of the way I am now? I want to shout, '*I object!*'

Disabled people are more than their disabilities. I just wish in my case that were true. Ugh. I sound like a damn incel. Poor me and my broken dick and back. Pinching my eyes closed, I curse under my breath, disgusted with myself on a whole new level.

Something black whirs past my periphery. I open my mouth to shout at Gale over whatever she decided to take off after, but then snap it shut at the sight of Remy in my front yard as though my moping summoned him. A burst of hope inside my chest goes off like a firework, taking me aback. He looks so good in the light of day. Good on the eyes, good to see him, and just good in general. There's something pure and honest about him, a what-you-see-is-what-you-get type of vibe that's a breath of fresh air. I've spent the last couple of days blaming my obsession on my lack of interaction with people. Breathless and tingling, I know now it's so much worse than that. I like what I see. I like it a lot, and I have a snowball's chance in hell of having it. The hesitant look on his face and slow, cautious steps give me the feeling that I'm about to be treated to a pity party.

"Hey," he calls.

"Hey."

"I hope it's okay that I dropped by. Have you got a minute to talk?"

A minute? Yup. Pity visit. Called it.

"I'm surprised you remembered where to find me without your sat nav."

Hoisting the bag of concrete mix onto my shoulder, I bite back a grunt at the pressure it puts on my spine. It would be nice to look like something he should regret walking away from for this minute. Apparently, my petulance still has teeth.

"No," he chuffs. "He flew back home yesterday."

This time, I grunt on purpose because I don't know how to do whatever small talk this is. Turning on my heel, I start toward the backyard. The urge to hide is strong, but that's not the impression I want to leave him with either. Glancing back twists my hips the wrong way, though, making me instantly regret it. I wince, sucking in an involuntary breath between my teeth.

Remy hustles a few steps forward. "You're in pain."

I'm not in the mood to air my updated biography with him, so I continue on my path without looking back again. If he follows, he follows. It's not like it's a requirement that you have to be face-to-face with someone when they come to add another layer to their rejection with a polite explanation.

"What else is new?"

The grass crunches behind me as I head toward the sunroom door. I guess it was too much to hope that he'd just run off again like he did the other night.

"Your yard is amazing." The compliment has me preening, but then he asks, "Did *you* do all of this?"

"It wasn't that difficult." That's a lie that I can't hide behind now that he has a full view of me hobbling along in front of him. I worked my ass off on this yard for years, picking good days to get shit done. Powering through bad days when I was so desperate to get out of the house that I refused to let the pain dictate my life. "Slow and steady wins the race."

"Have you looked into getting the broken hardware in your back replaced?"

Pleasantries and reminders that I'm not what I used to be. Great. I wish he'd just get on with whatever he came to say. I guess this is the price I have to pay for acting like a Don Juan.

I set the bag down on my workbench in the sunroom, regretting now that I'd left the door propped open earlier when I find Remy standing in it. Is this the universe's cruel way of making me pay for realizing fifteen years too late that I was an absolute heathen toward him back in the day?

"Yeah. Several times," I try to say without sounding curt, sweeping off my bench for something to busy myself with. "But apparently, spinal surgeons aren't keen on doing surgeries that could potentially paralyze the patient. Can't say I am either."

"Well, that's why I stopped by."

My hand stills with the dustpan brush in it. Please tell me he doesn't have some *miracle* suggestion like every single one of my parents' friends that they tell about *'Poor Chris.'*

"You're a spinal surgeon now?"

"No." He kicks at a kernel of dried cement on the floor with the toe of his sneaker and then immediately blushes like doing so vandalized my home. That blush of his really isn't something I needed to see right now, warring with my attempt to appear aloof. "I wanted to ask if…you'd like me to show you some exercises that might be able to help, in case you don't want to come back to the center."

That's why he's here? Not to give me some further explanation about why he shot me down? I did call it right. He is here out of pity, just not for the reasons I thought.

"I think I manage just fine." I use some of the anger boiling under my surface to heft my newest paver stone off the bench and set it on the stack of the ones by the far wall that I finished. "I kind of gave up on exercising a long time ago. I count this as a workout when I can." I gesture to the general area of my sunroom and the backyard.

"You made these?" he asks, the wonder in his voice soothing some of my nerves as he inches forward. I nod, dreading what it will cost me to do so, but he surprises me, letting out a breathy sound. "Oh, my gosh. They're beautiful. Like…that's not even the right word."

The look of awe and appreciation on his face as he reaches out and traces a fingertip over a design in one of the stones has me wanting to puff my chest out. I don't know why it's so important to me to impress him. I've gotten used to people either ignoring me like I don't exist, throwing curious glances as though they wonder what happened to me, or worse, looking wary because of my size, like my broken gait must have been caused by violence.

"Just…wow," he chuckles, the sound seeping into and warming my skin. "How do you know how to place all the pieces so perfectly?"

"I watch a lot of YouTube."

Smiling at me, he makes a mystified noise and shakes his head. Gale trots past me and stops at the door to go inside, giving an impatient huff.

"Excuse me, Your Highness. It's not my fault you didn't finish your lunch."

Opening the door of the house, I let her run inside. I don't think anything about reverting to the casual conversations I have with my dog until I hear a soft laugh behind me.

"She's cute. Why *Gale?*"

"Sayers," I say plainly, not expecting him to understand.

"You named her after a football player." He chuffs, nodding with his head down as though he's embarrassed he didn't guess sooner. I didn't need to discover one more reason why I like clothed, older Remy.

"She runs like the wind and can stop on a dime," I babble matter-of-factly.

His smile is warm when he meets my gaze. It feels like sunshine to my soul. I want to move closer to it like a starved houseplant and let it heal the empty parts of me.

Clearing his throat, he shifts in place.

"So…about the exercises."

Nothing like a splash of cold water on an out-of-body experience. Scrubbing my hand down my face, I glance out the window.

"I told you. I can't do all of that anymore."

"I don't mean like you used to…"

The warning look I flash him is a dare to finish that sentence with the deprecation I'm sure is about to follow. Mom is always telling me that people don't think about the impact of the words they choose, which I translate as my being sensitive. It's difficult not to be when people have no concept of what your day-to-day life is like.

"You know how to work out better than I ever would, Chris." The confusion I find on his face isn't what I expected to see, nor is the sincerity in those words. "But maybe you don't know how to work out with a broken back. There are still some things you can do that might help with your quality of life."

"If this is a peace offering for the other night, don't worry about it. I'm a big boy. I can handle it."

A rush of pink tints his cheeks. His mouth parts, but then he presses his lips together and shakes his head. "It's not about the other night."

I believe him, but damn, that rubs an entire bag of salt in my self-in-flicted wound. An awkward explanation would have been better than this reality check. Shoving my hands in my pockets, I face the wall of windows, my pride refusing to let me look at him anymore.

"Well, newsflash—I've tried it all. Surgeries. Nerve ablation. Hot tubs. Hot stones. Massage chairs. Therapy pools. Acupuncture. If there were a fix, I'd have found it by now. And excuse me if I don't sound grateful, but if you came all the way over here just to make me your pity case, then you can scratch me off your list and keep hunting for a different project."

I wait for the sound of his feet to scrape against the floor and make his exit. They scrape, but the noise comes closer. Why is my body still so in tune with him that I can sense his presence at my back?

"It's *not* pity," comes a subdued voice, and yet there's conviction behind it. "That's not why I came, but I get it. You don't want anyone to feel sorry for you."

I will never understand how this fractured shell of mine that fails me almost every single day can also be as strong as prison bars, holding in the boiling pressure of my endless frustration. Sometimes I think I could combust from having no outlet for my misery. I count to ten, hoping it will make the air easier to breathe and keep the moisture in my eyes from turning into tears.

My silence and complete lack of acknowledgement must be the breaking point for Remy to give up on his offer. The sound of his shoes crunching over the concrete grit on the floor comes as he heads out the door. Will it be another fifteen years until I see him again—or never? Friday night was probably as awkward for him as it felt for me afterward. Common sense tells me that a person would actually have to truly care about someone else to come all the way over here after an uncomfortable meeting like we had. I don't ever remember him being a liar. If I never see him again, the least I can do is leave him with the truth.

"No," I call out. "I don't want to feel sorry for *myself*. That's more dangerous than what anyone else thinks."

The understanding in his eyes when I turn around both releases the pressure in my chest and has me feeling gutted. Hedging a few steps back in my direction, he stops at a safe distance as though I'm a frightened animal caught in a trap.

"I don't know if anyone but yourself can help you with that, but if you let me, I think I can help you feel at least a little better physically." I want to say yes just so I can find out what he's been doing for the last fifteen years, but it's difficult not to see it as charity. "And," he adds, doing that blushing thing again and stuffing his hands in his pockets, "I wouldn't mind the company."

He flashes me a nervous smile that clearly required some courage on his part. Am I really seeing this? If his idea of good company is a man who makes involuntary grunting noises every time he moves, I almost feel sorrier for him than I do for myself.

"You must have some pretty tiresome friends then."

Screwing up his face, he shrugs. "Well…have you *met* Jamie?"

I snort because I'm still not capable of laughing at the moment. My reward is the smile that cracks on his face.

"I go for a jog at six o'clock every morning, or…if afternoons are better for you, I get off work at four."

I'm too baffled by the hopefulness in his tone to form words. He wants to help me…just because. And he's what? Lonely for company? Who wouldn't want to spend time with him? I want to say yes, but doing so would commit me to subjecting him to more of *me*. He's only seen a fragment of this Chris. If I show him more, he might stop looking so excited about the prospect.

"I'll think about it."

REMY

chapter 8

Is it acceptable to be grateful for your new job and also wish that the fundraiser banquet you were required to attend was over with like two hours ago? Granted, I know this big to-do is a one-time thing, but it doesn't mean I'm miraculously comfortable trying to sound like a subject matter expert for the people who funded my place of work. I've felt like I had to recite my resume all night, leaving me with a dirty wash of insecurity. I managed to answer everyone's questions about the center, the staff, and our available methods of treatment so far, though, so I hope my doubts are just a case of imposter syndrome. Luckily, some of the school's athletes who've sought treatment with us are here to help schmooze with the donors, letting them know their money went to a good cause.

After answering questions about the equipment we have for a middle-aged couple who run a law firm in the area, I thank them again for their contribution before they move along. Something nudges my elbow, and I mentally cringe that it likely means I won't be getting a breather in between conversations. When I turn, however, I find Miles smiling at me, holding out a flute of champagne.

"Thought you could use this."

"Thanks."

I'm not a big fan of the stuff, but I have to say, he's been thoughtful and attentive all evening. He's interjected smooth comments here and there that I suspect were meant to be confidence boosters whenever I downplayed my role at the center while talking to guests. I take a drink of the bubbly alcohol, the tart liquid bursting over my tongue, and nearly choke on it when I feel an arm slink across my shoulders. His contented smile and relaxed posture might lead anyone to believe it's a natural gesture. With his thick head of blonde hair and striking green eyes, he's fetching in his suit. There's this unabashed presence to him, making him look like he belongs in this fancy banquet room. As his Rolex digs into my shoulder, however, I know that calling the way he put his hand on the small of my back each time someone approached me earlier wasn't attentiveness. I was too distracted to give it more thought and was trying to think polite thoughts. Now that there's a lull and we're alone, I'm keenly aware of the way his thumb is tracing circles over my arm. I think I'm in danger of slowly being claimed when I thought I made it clear that this was just a work function, not a date.

"You know, the Westin is nice," he points out, looking like he's admiring the sleek design of the bar back near us, "but wait until you get a load of Porter Plaza. If you come out to visit me, my company holds a lot of its functions there. We could hit up this jazz club nearby afterward. It's not far from my house."

Maybe a few weeks ago, I might have felt the lure of possibilities over that comment. Right now, a sleeve of suffocation wraps around my neck. I just started getting good at being single, or at least, getting used to it. The thought of hitching my wagon to anyone only makes that sleeve cuff tighter. My quest for an eternal fizzle doesn't seem as pressing anymore. I have my yard to clean up and cookbooks I want to read. My entryway looks a bit outdated and could use a new coat of paint. What if I want to go visit Jamie? What if Chris decides to show up to work out?

And if he doesn't… I'll need time to be depressed about it. Alone and at peace. *You know?*

It's been four days since I worked up the nerve to go over to his house. What was born as a nerve-wracking shot in the dark to repair any potential confusion my hot/cold signals from last Friday night may have caused ended with a revelation. He's hurting in more ways than one. It felt like he opened up to me. I've delayed my jog every morning since then, peeking out my window with my heart in my throat. I really thought he might show up.

That sticky feeling of being watched again prickles my skin. I catch Miles looking at me.

Right. I should probably act like I'm at least listening to the conversation since I invited him here to tag along with me.

"Um, I don't get out of town very often. I work so much, and the new house has been keeping me busy with projects."

"Hey," he reassures me with a squeeze to my shoulder. "It's all right. I'm not going anywhere. You know?"

Fuck my life. I owe Jamie a drink for calling that nuance.

I manage a smile, but direct my gaze anywhere other than at him. The last thing I need is to accidentally give him more encouragement. It turns out to have the opposite effect I hoped it would, though, because I feel his lips press against my cheek. It's just a quick peck. It shouldn't elicit instant nausea, even if I'm not interested in him. Add in the fact that I find Chris staring at me from across the room, however, and I'm well on my way to becoming fully ill.

What is he doing here? How long has he been here without my noticing?

He's standing near a table in the far back corner of the room in a black dress shirt, the top button undone, and gray dress slacks. I spot a woman from a local news station who spoke to me earlier sitting at the table with her camera crew, and it all clicks.

Crap. I knew there were members of the press here. It escaped me, however, that this is technically a sports-related event. One that Chris is apparently covering.

He shifts his gaze away abruptly, walks to the nearest table, and sets down what looks like a glass of water. Turning on his heel, he starts toward the nearest exit. A sense of dread tells me something is wrong and that I might be the cause of it.

Whatever Miles is saying, I don't comprehend. Squirming out of his hold, I mumble off an excuse without waiting for a reply, "Would you excuse me for a minute? I'll be back."

I'm moving before I can think better of it, fueled by a sense of dread, concern, and my Chris Mightener obsession. By the time I make it to the lobby, I'm breathless from my nerves and from hurrying after him.

The look he flashed me was so cold, weighted with disappointment. When I see his wide frame pushing through the exit door out to the street, I call out to him. Either he didn't hear me or pretended not to.

Cursing under my breath, I practically sprint across the lobby. It felt like I made one step forward the other day at his house. Tonight, whatever he thinks he saw, seems like it could set us two steps back. Unless I'm just being conceited, and his scowly mood was about something entirely different. Outside, I catch him bounding down the sidewalk like a man on a mission.

"Chris!" He stops, and a fountain of hope springs up in my chest. "You're leaving? I think they're going to announce some—"

I don't get to finish my lame excuse as to why he should stay before he cuts me off. "I think they'll survive without some washed-up football player."

His jaw is set so hard you could break a brick on it, and the wall of the hotel appears to hold more of his interest than I do right now. Did someone piss him off or make a comment about his accident?

"Are you okay? What's wrong?"

"Why are you following me?" He snaps, sounding exasperated.

"Because... I care."

"*Care?*" He snorts, turning to fully face me and holding out his arms. "*Why?* We don't even know each other."

Sucking in a breath, I muster the courage to say what I didn't get to last week.

"I know, but I'd like to, though."

He scoffs, and his shoulders go slack. The quick dismissal stings. Does he really only care about the physical? He's still so drop-dead sexy he could get anyone he wants. I wish the way my pulse skips around him would stop if all I ever was to him and still am now is a piece of ass.

"What do you want to know?" He gestures with his chin, taking a step forward. "That my social life consists of a Rottweiler? That if you see me at a bar, it's not for a night of laughs. It's because I'm afraid that if I keep alcohol at my house, I'll use it way too often to help me get to sleep. Did you want to know that I had to learn to walk again and have my parents help me wipe my ass for months? Or that shortly after I could again, I spent six weeks in rehab for a pain pill addiction?"

Wetting my lips, the picture he paints is brush-stroked in lead, the heavy, dark colors adhering me to the spot. Kicking a leg out, he stuffs a hand in his pocket as though this is some casual conversation that doesn't mirror the barely checked anguish in his expression.

"How about how they don't advertise that if you get a career-ending injury in the NFL, you only get the rest of the season's salary. And that I'll be on disability for the rest of my life. Or how even though I've saved and invested what I could over the years to make sure I can keep the roof over my head, I still worry in the back of my mind that I won't be able to manage it if I live to be a hundred. And while it doesn't seem to satisfy my father's visions of grandeur, the only thing I'm good for now is sitting on bleachers at high school and college games, writing articles about kids who hopefully won't fuck up the way I did."

The portrait turns into a cannonball that was just lobbed at the center of my chest. Each rise and fall of his chest creates new cracks in my heart.

"That's not you. That's just what happened to you."

Running his fingers through his hair, his derisive noise tells me my words fell on deaf ears. He paces back and forth like a wild, injured animal, making me wish there was some way I could ease his wounds. When he finally comes to a stop, he levels his stormy eyes at me defiantly.

"What about *you*? Who are *you*?"

Me?

It's a simple question. So, why can't I think of an answer?

Shit. I didn't think this conversation could get any more difficult.

CHRIS

chapter 9

I'm being a dick again. Why he's still standing here after I just purged myself of that disgusting biopic is beyond me. And after I told him about my aversion to self-pity the other day, nonetheless. Now I get to add hypocrite to my long list of faults. I just keep racking up the points with him, don't I?

I need to move. To get off this sidewalk away from the freaking Weston. Get far away from the stifling air of exhaust and swampy Riverwalk water. And even farther from his stunned expression. Fantastic. I broke his innocent face. That's what I do. I broke my innocence and have been stomping through life like a clumsy ogre, bumping into walls ever since. Now, I've broken a person. I graduated from a *drunk driver* to a car crash on two legs.

Huffing against the tightness in my chest, I turn in the direction of my car. At least, I think it's this way. I don't care if I have to walk around the block at this point, as long as he's not still out here with that crushed look on his face by the time I hobble back around.

"I'm a mess who's been chasing fairy tales his entire life."

His distraught voice calls out behind me like a skywriting message you catch when you didn't even mean to look up. Both my fight and flight responses defuse, stopping my retreat. I turn back slowly, wondering if I imagined it.

He's still there, looking more handsome than ever, but way over-dressed in my opinion. I'm partial to the memory of Remy in a Panther's hoodie and sleep pants. Remy in just his boxers… or Remy without clothing, underneath me, looking up at me like I'm his North Sstar.

His Adam's apple bobs, and he shifts in place. Eyes wide, his gaze pings all over my face. Is he scared of me, or of what he's so clearly having difficulty saying?

"I don't think I've ever really dated… Each time I've made out with a guy, I end up in a relationship with them that doesn't work out. It's the first time I've lived on my own in almost fifteen years, and it still kind of terrifies me even though I know how pathetic that sounds. I'm a grown man who stresses about everyday decisions," he rambles like a list of self-grievances in quick succession, stopping momentarily to catch his breath. "I…love my job. I've never been injured aside from a broken toe and a sprained ankle. My idea of weekend entertainment is to try out a new recipe and binge-watch old TV series." Glancing down, he plays with a button on his jacket, half-muttering, *Dawson's Creek* and *The Vampire Diaries* are impeccably timeless, just for the record."

Knowing more about him is so much worse than merely regretting that I didn't before. God, I want to wrap him up in a blanket, throw him over my shoulder, and carry him home. I find myself inching forward, hoping it will encourage more of this emotional torment.

Glancing back up, he tries to square his shoulders as though he's found some confidence or just doesn't give a damn anymore now that he's rolling. "I've had the same best friend for seventeen years because even though he's a pain in the ass and gives me terrible advice, it lets me know to do the opposite of whatever he suggests, and he's loyal. I jog every morning so I can eat whatever I want without feeling bad about it, and…" he hesitates, looking away while he bites his lower lip. "And I didn't want to say no to you last week, but I didn't trust myself to say yes. I'm a weapon of mass destruction when it comes to my love life, and I don't want to be anymore."

I want to tell him he won't break me any worse than I already am or himself, and that I won't break him, but I honestly don't know if that's true. Raising my hand, I reach to cup his face, hoping it will encourage him to find some miraculous answer to what we should do.

"Remy? Is everything all right?" a man's voice calls near the doorway.

Fuck. This fucking guy…

Who the hell is he? Is this the date Remy mentioned last week?

I divert my hand's intended path, resting my palm against the wall of the building instead. Anyone who isn't an arrogant prick might move away to defuse a potentially uncomfortable situation, but my pride won't let me. It won't let me because even though Remy goes rigid, he doesn't move away from me either. That's got to count for something. Plus, I may be broken, but I'm still bigger than Mr. Fancy Pants.

I could take him. Probably. Worst-case scenario, and slightly less gallant, I could sit on him with my Rice Krispies ass.

Remy clears his throat. "Yeah. I'll be there in a minute."

The guy either doesn't believe him or doesn't like being dismissed while I'm around. I cock an eyebrow at him, glad that Remy can't see. At least my tackle face still works. He lets out a little huff, nods, and heads back inside, but takes his sweet-ass time. If my foot were closer, I could help him hurry that along.

Once he's no longer an eyesore, I glance down at Remy, wondering what he sees in the man. Why does that guy get a *yes*, and I get a *no?*

I might be blunt, but at least what you see is what you get. And I sure as shit wouldn't walk away and leave my date out on the street with someone else. It doesn't seem fair that he gets to spend time with *my*…

Pushing off the wall, I drop my hand. He's *not* yours, I remind myself. You just insisted you don't even know each other. Remember?

But we did once, I tell that voice. Or at least I wish we had. God, this is hopeless. Isn't it?

"I guess you'd better get back to your date," I mumble, the words painful to say.

"It's not a date." He shakes his head, sounding drained.

I broke my back, not my eyes. Maybe it's not a date to Remy, but it's definitely a date to the other guy. Just the thought of them finishing their evening after I piss off back to my house to curl up alone with Gale has a torrent of unfounded jealousy flooding my system.

Is Remy going to tell *him* how he binges old TV shows? Will he look at him the way he used to look at me? I've suddenly never felt more inadequate. Inadequate, and like I'm losing something I just found. I want it back. Want *him* back. I want a do-over where I tell football to fuck off and stay in that room with Remy. Maybe we can go out and celebrate graduation together, and then take a cross-country road trip, laughing, fucking, and exploring like in the movies.

Helpless against the pull of his presence, I crowd into him, chest to chest, my palm back on the wall. The way his face goes flush and his gaze flicks to my mouth has me wanting to rub my scent on him like an animal so everyone else will stay away from him. His breath mingles with mine, and it's all I can do not to lean forward the remaining inch.

"Can he make you moan the way I used to?"

It's bold talk I can barely get out. I know I can't fuck him, but I hope like hell that guy can't either. I don't want anyone else to even touch him but me.

His breath ghosts my lips. He leans in a fraction, mouth parting. I hold as still as possible, understanding that something from his speech earlier means he needs to be the one to initiate, or I'm in danger of crashing and burning again.

Like a wind snuffing out a flame, he sucks in a breath and draws back. My heart plummets to the pit of my stomach. Lines of conflict etch his face as though he's discovering something about me for the first time.

"I don't want a guy who used to crawl in through my window. I want one who comes to the front door."

The testosterone and adrenaline I was flying on burn out, coughing clouds of black smoke. If it weren't for the apologetic tone in his words, I'd take them to mean he's choosing Fancy Pants over me. Maybe I took too many hits to the head back in the day, but I think he's casting a generalization for what he deemed his destructive dating behavior. There's regret in his eyes, but there's fear too. I tried to see what I wanted the other night, but I can't miss it now. I'm still a stranger to him. He liked parts of the ghost of college past, but the ghost of dumpster fire present is a little too precarious to bet on. I can't hold that against him.

Drawing back, I give him space. It wasn't a no, but it wasn't a yes either. It's a murky and terrifying space in between. As much as I'm dying inside, I'm also grateful that it puts me somewhere still in his orbit.

Hell, I could be reading him all wrong, but I think I have a new window to crawl through, one of opportunity. If I don't, I'm going to have to find a way to shove my foot in it to keep it open.

I nod a silent goodnight and stuff my hands into my pockets so I won't look like a horny, threatening heathen.

"Good thing I know where you live now, so I don't get them mixed up."

Turning, I start down the sidewalk to head for the comfort of home, my chair, Gale, and my books. As the darkness and sounds of downtown swallow me, I silently hope that there's at least one book on my shelf about how to be a better man. If not, I'll have to buy a very strong crowbar, metaphorically speaking.

REMY

chapter 10

Chocolate-covered cake balls. I stop at the recipe in my newest dessert cookbook, deciding they sound like an appropriate breakfast food. I've already sworn I'm going to live in these sleep pants for the rest of my life, or at least the weekend. Since they have an elastic waist, I should be able to accommodate the entire batch.

The coffee maker beeps that my second cup is ready. Hopefully, the machine conjured magical powers over the last hour and brewed more invigorating properties into this cup than the last one I had when I gave up on sleeping. You can only lie awake in bed watching so much Dawson's Creek before you're in danger of getting bedsores.

Side note, that show really *is* timeless. I'm just as impulsive and indecisive as Dawson.

Dropping my face into my hand, I let out a groan. God, I can't believe I actually pitched old TV shows in my *About Me* speech to Chris last night. *That*...among other embarrassing things.

Additional side note: never speaking again.

Picking up my Sunshine Diner mug, I clod over to the coffee maker. I'm glad Jamie showed no interest in taking it when he visited. I wish I could be more unattached to memories like him. For now, however, I'll just cart it around the house with me like a scarlet letter. Maybe doing so will remind me of my terrible decisions.

Eyeing the cookbook, I decide my ambition meter isn't quite full enough for baking. They say emotions go into cooking. If that's true, it can't be wise to do so while you're disgusted with yourself. No one likes disgusting balls, cake-filled centers or not.

A survey of my living room makes the couch look tempting, but I know if I sit my ass down on it, I'll end up binging the life and loves of Sookie Stackhouse because fuck Dawson right now. Except, watching hours of horny vampires having sex probably isn't a wise choice either.

Crap. What's a healthy alternative to watching vampire sex?

Sunshine?

Vitamin D is supposed to be a mood booster. And can you really say you're part of a neighborhood until you've been seen in your pajamas drinking coffee on your porch?

Despite my cynicism, I'm grateful the sun is barely up as I step out my front door and breathe in the morning air. The only sounds I hear are the chirping of birds, telling me that my neighbors are normal people who sleep in on a Saturday rather than spend a Friday evening toying with the emotions of their former college crush. Tromping toward the rocking chair and little patio table I bought, I take a small comfort in the fact that I'm finally going to put them to use.

"Morning."

A deep voice I'd know anywhere has the hair on my neck standing at attention. I spin around so fast my coffee sloshes over the side of my mug. I let out a yelp at both the throbbing sensation in my hand and the sight of Chris at the bottom of my steps. The mug *clonks* to the porch flooring, spattering my stocking-clad feet with lava before cracking into at least four different pieces.

"Shit!" I hiss, but I'm not alone in uttering the expletive.

"Sorry," Chris adds, lumbering up the steps. "I didn't mean to startle you."

"No, you—" I'm about to say he didn't, but I'm still startled. What is he doing here? "Hey! Hi. Um...good morning."

"Are you all right?"

Lines of concern etch his face as he gestures to my hand. I shake it out, flinging droplets of coffee off it and schooling my features.

"Yeah. I'm fine." He frowns down at the mess between us, so I try to make light of the situation. "But I guess my Sunshine Diner mug has seen its day. Just, uh, wait here a second and I'll go get a broom and the dustpan." Tiptoeing over the fractured pieces, I do a double-take as he gets to a knee. "Careful you don't cut yourself."

"It's just a few shards. I'm really sorry."

"It's fine."

I talked myself into thinking his whole *good thing I know where you live* comment was just talk since he hadn't bothered to show up earlier in the week. Now that he's here, though, I'm not sure what to do with at-my-front-door Chris. At-my-bedroom-window Chris—no brainer. But this is what I asked for. Wasn't it? And he delivered.

"Are you going to keep them?"

"Huh?"

"The pieces." He gestures, setting another into his cupped palm.

"No. I don't think any amount of glue will fix that."

He nods, frowning at the collection of fragments in his hand as though he's mourning the loss of my mug. Looking up at me, his face is comparable to a child asking for forgiveness.

"Do you mind if I take them?"

"You want my broken coffee mug?"

"That's what I use for my mosaics. Broken dishes, ceramics…"

"Oh! Right. Yeah. Sure. Go ahead. Um, let me go get you a grocery bag or something."

Hurrying inside, I slide into my kitchen in a very *Dumb and Dumber* version of Tom Cruise's move in *Risky Business*, windmilling my arms to keep from face-planting.

Bag. Bag. Bag, I chant silently. Fortunately, my brain starts working enough that I locate a freezer bag that should serve as a viable means of transport.

I stop sprinting in time to prevent myself from running smack into my door and walk back outside at the speed of a calm adult. He drops the pieces inside while I hold it open. My skin prickles with gooseflesh when his fingers brush against mine.

A stilted smile shapes his mouth, and he takes the bag, raising it momentarily. "Thanks."

"No problem."

I smile back because I don't know what else to do. That, and I hope it's the equivalent of a white flag of peace. Remy, threat-level zero. I can appear in control of my emotions and drama-free… as long as he doesn't touch me or, as Jamie so eloquently put it, *'eye-fuck'* me again.

Shifting in place, he scratches the back of his neck and glances down at my pajama pants. I wish I'd worn sexy pajama pants…or *owned* sexy pajama pants. Not that I want to have sex. Sort of. But looking sexy is better than looking like you're having a midlife crisis.

"I take it you're not working out today? I'm sorry I just showed up unannounced. I guess I should have asked for more details."

I take in his attire, similar to what he wore to the center that day—gray sweatpants, a faded blue T-shirt, and worn tennis shoes. *That's why he's here?*

Okay. I can work with that.

"No!" I blurt so loud he flinches. "I mean, yes. Yes, I was just about to get ready."

Side note number three—I am a liar. A dirty, dirty, pajama-pants-wearing, Dawson's-Creek-watching, crying-over-cake-balls liar.

"I don't work on Saturdays, so I got moving a little slower and decided to have some coffee first," I explain, but that sounds like a horrible way to hydrate for a workout. And I wonder why he never took an interest in something more when we were younger.

His shoulders relax despite my verbal diarrhea, and I get another flicker of a smile. "Okay, great."

"Um…why don't you come on in? Just make yourself at home, and I'll go get changed."

I leave him in the open space between my kitchen and living room with an awkward wave before I try to walk at a leisurely pace to my bedroom. Closing the door softly behind me, I think I breathe for the first time in minutes as I scramble over to my dresser, kicking my pajamas off on my way.

"Chris is *in* my house. *Chris…is in…my house.*"

I should probably shut up until I find out how soundproof my walls are. Where is Jamie when I need a slap? Maybe he could air one to me via video chat.

No, he's an hour behind me, and there is no way I'm telling him about this. I'll just have to slap myself.

After triple-checking that I don't have my running shorts on inside out or backward, I make my way back down the hall. My steps falter at the work of art standing next to my island counter. Head cast down, the little smile at the corner of his mouth is the kind someone wears when they spot a baby babbling cute noises or an elderly couple holding hands. His face looks so much softer than recently. Fingering an earmarked page of my cookbook with one of his thick fingers, he handles it more gently than one would expect from hands his size. Does he find my love of making sweets amusing? Moving forward, I clear my throat, and he snaps his hand back.

"Okay! I'm ready. Thanks for waiting."

Working his jaw, he takes in my attire from head to toe—gym shorts and an old T-shirt. His grimace makes me wonder if I actually did put my shorts on inside out.

"I can't go far," he mumbles, bracing his hands on his hips and staring at his shoes. "I haven't jogged in years."

I'm over here all up in my head while he's wondering if I'm going to put him through physical torture. I guess I should have clarified.

"Of course not. Impact exercises are the last thing your body needs." There are exercises he could do, but we'll have to work our way up to them. I've seen this plenty of times before in people with permanent injuries. They go through their initial therapy, but there's no accounting for aging, and when they get back to their everyday life. "I thought we could work on some stretches in the backyard."

When I gesture to my patio door, he glances outside and then back to me. It must be degrading for someone who was once at the pinnacle of fitness to be taking instruction from a former wallflower like me. I'd take him to the gym down the street, but I have a feeling he's not up for an audience. When he nods, it feels like a small victory.

I lead him out onto the little deck and down the steps to my yard. It's a third of the size of his, but we don't need that much room.

"How long ago did you say you moved in?"

I follow his gaze across my weedy lawn with its bare patches where the grass has gone on strike, to the overgrowth of vines clinging to the wooden privacy fence. Right. He has his Mightener Serenity Garden, while I have the equivalent of Charlie Brown's Christmas Tree.

"I don't know what I'm doing." I laugh helplessly, holding up my hands. "And…well, I've got some really interesting cookbooks that don't require sweating in the hot sun. Priorities. What can I say?" Is that almost a smile I see? Wow. "We can go to your house next time, if you want."

"It's fine."

That wasn't a *no* to there being a next time. I guess we're doing this.

I have him demonstrate his range of motion to assess the capability of his joints. It takes me a minute to figure out if his stony expression is an indication of physical pain or his general discomfort at showing me what I assume he sees as weaknesses. I don't bother telling him that I don't view any attempt at adapting to living after injury as a weakness, however. I plan to do everything in my power to steer far away from repeat accusations of pity. As I watch him go through the motions of rotating his shoulders, hips, and neck, though, it lets me know that this is a *very* different Chris than the one I used to know, who's standing in front of me. How in the hell did he landscape his entire backyard like a botanical garden with such limited mobility? That must have taken a lot of grit.

Like many patients I've seen with back injuries, his arms are his wheelhouse and the epitome of his strength. His rigidity is indicative of only stretching for pain relief and not improved mobility—a trap most people fall into. Some days, I sure as heck don't want to go for my morning jogs. If I were in pain, I'd easily be able to talk myself out of going.

I get him started with some stretches that I think will help loosen up his spine and hips, since that seems to be where the brunt of his pain comes from. All the while, I find myself crossing my fingers that he'll remain patient since they likely seem basic to a man who used to train regularly. Gripping the railing of my deck, feet planted, I mirror the last stretch I showed him, keeping my chin to my chest to help extend the spinal column.

"You're lucky, really," I hedge, attempting to throw out some inspiration. "Most people who have gait interruptions usually end up dislocating their knees or getting hip or other joint fractures from the strain of walking with their weight distribution off-centered."

"Lucky, huh?" he grunts, keeping his eyes trained on the pitiful grass at his feet.

Nice, Remy. I swear I do this for a living.

"I'm sorry. It wasn't meant to put you down. I just always try to see the silver lining."

"I know."

After an awkward few minutes of silence, I move on to the lower body, showing him some adjusted lunges to help stretch the sciatic. He watches me like a trained sportsman, memorizing new plays. He even looks intrigued when I discuss the importance of inhaling and exhaling at key points and how it impacts the muscles. His attentiveness helps quiet my self-conscious anticipation of him calling it quits and leaving. Soon enough, we're just two guys stretching, amicably wordless.

That's why it catches me off guard when he asks, "Did I ruin your date?"

"It wasn't a date," I insist, shaking my head at myself for even entertaining the idea of Miles as dating material a couple of weeks ago. "At least to me, it wasn't. Anyway, it was doomed before it started, so Jamie will thank you for that," I joke. "Silver lining. See?"

I swear he snorts. I don't care if it's not actually a laugh and is at my expense, I'll take it.

"And what does Jamie think of *me*?"

Screwing up my face, I walk back to the deck railing to work on standing planks again. "Why don't we get back to the stretches?"

This time his snort is different from the last one. Look at me, fluent in *Snort*. I'm learning things about him already.

"Does he like anyone?"

"Me…sometimes."

He joins me at the railing and copies my stance. When he says nothing more, my mind begins to wander. Am I keeping him from anything? It's still baffling to me that the man whose attention I felt lucky to hold for brief moments at a time is spending part of his weekend with me without intimacy involved. Is this what pushing forty and neither hooking up nor dating look like? If so, I can't say I hate it.

"You know, you're not going to fix me."

The subdued warning surprises me. Face half hidden by his arm, I only catch a fraction of his expression. It's not defeat exactly, more so acceptance.

Straightening up, I nod and motion for him to do the same. It seems like a good place to stop today.

"We *can't* fix you," I agree. "But we can make you feel less pain and allow you to sit at the games more comfortably when you're reporting. Sleep a little better at night, hopefully."

Holding my breath, I wait for his reaction. I wonder if I'll ever stop looking at him like it's the last time I'll see him.

"That's more than I could ever hope for." The corner of his mouth ticks up for a second. The double meaning in that almost-smile softens my heart. I think I just got an apology that I didn't even need.

"I'll see you tomorrow?"

"See you tomorrow." He nods and picks up his bag of broken coffee mug pieces.

I watch him walk through my weeds around the back of the house until he's out of sight. And for the first time, I'm not afraid it's the last I'll see of him.

CHRIS

chapter 11

The Sunday morning sun peeks out through the clouds as I walk up
Remy's steps and knock on his door. Time for a second round of humility, because apparently, I'm a masochist. I hear the rapid thumping of
footsteps, and the door opens, bringing another ray of sunshine. How
does he always look so alive? Like he's breathing life into the universe
and not the other way around?

"Chris! Hey."

"You still on for…working out?"

The words sound foreign as soon as they leave my lips. What we did
yesterday didn't feel like a workout. Grandmothers in retirement homes

get more exertion with their walkers than I did, but after coming up short on how to exonerate myself from being the guy who used to crawl in through his window for a quick fuck, this is all I've got. Stretching my muscles won't make me a better man. I'm well aware. Scaring the crap out of him yesterday and making him break his coffee mug felt like a cryptic omen that this sophomoric crush I've been harboring is doomed no matter what. I can't be better, and all pursuing Remy will do is break him, despite how much I don't want that to happen.

So, why am I here? Well, I guess crushes take a while to die. And maybe, just maybe, if I don't screw this up, I can have him in my life. At least like this. Also, it's a bonus that our morning hour together will be that much less time he has to meet jerks who are as wrong for him as I am.

"Yeah, absolutely. Come on in."

I'm a little disappointed not to see him in sleep pants with bedhead again, but that's probably for the best. Stepping over the threshold, I pause once inside at the sight of a new decoration I don't remember seeing yesterday. I point at the skeleton on a stand next to the hall tree, where some jackets are hanging.

"*He* looks familiar."

"Wow! You actually remember Norman?" He laughs, patting the skeleton's shoulder and adjusting a small top hat on its head.

Of course, I remember. Norman isn't just bones. He's got a full musculoskeletal system and used to stand in the corner of Remy's room. I'm not about to bring up that I thought his exposed eyes always made him look like he was shocked by what we used to do in Remy's bed. It looks like Norman *still* remembers. Oh, Norm, I feel your pain.

"Jamie and I used to dress him up for holidays. One of my exes thought he was creepy, though, so he's been packed up for a long time." Suddenly, his cheeks go red, and he clears his throat. Rubbing the back of his neck, he starts toward his patio door. "Anyway, I thought it was cruel to make him live in a box any longer, so I dug him out."

Following him, I'm glad he can't see my frown. My sister, Alice, says it looks like I'm always brooding. I don't understand, though, how anyone couldn't appreciate his nerdiness. Is dragging Norman out of storage one of the everyday decisions he said he stresses over? Whoever this ex was that turned their nose up at his love for his skeleton needs a good kick in the balls.

"Good decision." The smile he flashes me over that morsel of solidarity warms the center of my chest, so I go for more compliments. "It's a nice place you've got here."

"It's not the Monte Vista neighborhood, and I've still got a little work to do, but I like it."

"If it makes you feel better, I couldn't afford what the houses over there go for now. It seemed like a good investment with what I had left from my contract when I bought it. And it was my escape plan to get far enough away from my parents that they wouldn't hover after my recovery."

I'm not sure why I admitted all of that, but when he turns to me on his lawn, his face doesn't hold any judgment. I've been geared to be on the defensive for so long, I don't think I gave him the benefit of the doubt when we first reconnected. Remy doesn't judge, though, does he? I don't think he ever did.

"Well, as you know, my yard certainly doesn't compare to yours," he rambles, wincing at our surroundings and looking adorably self-conscious. "I was actually going to work on pulling weeds later."

"It doesn't bother me. I used to go to the junkyard in my hometown to work out when I was in high school. The owner let me borrow an old tractor tire. I'd tie it to my waist and run with it to do some resistance drills during the off-season." I chuckle at the memory, surprised to have a good one for a change. "I must have looked like a psychopath."

"Or a roadside assistance worker," he suggests, making me snicker unexpectedly.

The mirth in his eyes suddenly makes me sad. Was he always this funny, and I never took the time to find out? I'm not going to delude myself that we're compatible, because what the hell do I know about relationships except for the girls I pretended to be into in high school? But…it would have been nice to have someone like Remy to talk to over the years.

We end up hanging onto his deck railing again, doing more planks and then some hamstring stretches. They're all things I could have easily been doing at home, and I kind of want to kick myself for not being more diligent. I woke up with soreness in new places this morning. It was enlightening just how much grandma stretches can make you remember muscles you haven't used in over a decade. The dull ache in my joints that's always there, however, was at a lower roar than usual.

At one point, Remy disappears into his house and returns with some ankle weights. Dropping them down on the deck, he descends the stairs again and comes over to stand by me as he reaches for one.

"A big part of hip and back stability is in the core and the glutes. With your broken hardware, working your core will be difficult, so we can focus on your glutes for now."

Great. My giant ass. The price of companionship officially sucks.

I watch in wonder as he drops to a knee and fastens a set of weights to my ankles. Trying to ignore how I look like my mother when she does her aerobic videos is made easy by how sexy Remy looks in the zone. I can see that he truly enjoys his work. The squirmy sensation of defeat I carried up his steps is replaced with pride in him for having the desire to help injured people. Not me, but *other* people. Helping me still feels like winning last place.

I opted for shorts today, as the weather's warmer than yesterday. San Antonio in the fall is still like summer to most places, so I wasn't about to take my chances by sweating in front of him. When his fingers brush against the bare skin above my feet, it's pitiful how good the innocent touch feels.

"If you pull that poison ivy on your fence off with your bare hands later, do me a favor and don't be touching my ankles in the near future," I deadpan, worried he'll somehow sense my reaction.

His head whips around in the direction of his fence. "That's poison ivy?"

Wow. I guess my deflection may have just saved a life. "Aren't you from Kansas or something?" I laugh.

"Yeah." He smiles, sounding surprised that I remembered. Rattling his head, he straps a set of weights to his own ankles. "But I lived in town, not out in the country, and my dad was pretty picky about the lawn."

Funny. Vince Mightener parked our riding mower for good and bought a push mower so I could work on my tackle strength. He was always coming up with shit like that; a modern-day Mr. Miyagi.

We knock out several repetitions of calf lifts and then go really wild, doing some backward leg lifts. Grudgingly, I feel the burn from the baby weights in my ass and hip flexors in less than two minutes. I don't want to think about how that means my senior citizen mother probably has more leg stamina than I do.

"Any pain?" Remy asks, his worried expression fixed on my grimace.

"No."

I spend the next few minutes trying not to let my brooding show on my face. The flash of new movement to my right snags my attention, though. I watch Remy bending his arms, doing push-ups against the railing while he does his leg lifts.

"Upper body combo now, huh?" I ask, joining in. My right elbow joint makes a cracking sound on the first iteration, which does nothing for my ego.

"Oh, you don't have to. I just don't do much upper body, so I thought I'd work on my arms a little."

"It's fine," I assure him, and it is, despite that first cracking sound. "I can't believe I haven't done a push-up in a decade, though."

"You can still probably do more than I can. Paver stones are pretty much weights."

That he remembers a single recently learned factoid about me or my house dances a comforting wisp of glee through me. I guess I technically wasn't lying when I said my landscaping was my workout. My arms are still in decent shape, unlike the rest of me.

Arching a brow at him, I cling to the rush of testosterone his off-handed compliment gives me. He groans when I quicken the succession of my push-ups, never taking my eyes off him.

"That wasn't a challenge. I have no doubt you'll kick my ass because I've probably only done about ten push-ups in the last ten years. I was just doing them to have something to do."

I laugh, but the humorous sound doesn't reach my heart as I stop, re-sorting to only the leg lifts. *Just something to do.* He's not injured. Right.

He said he goes jogging every morning. This isn't jogging. This is *'helping the broken guy try to learn how to touch his toes again.'* I'm slowing him down by being here. Slowing his life down. A hindrance.

"Alright, since you were okay with those, let's zone in on the hip flex-ors more while we've still got the weights on." He turns to face me, one hand resting on the deck railing like a ballerina hanging on for balance. I do the same when he looks at me hesitantly, like he's waiting to see if I follow his silent instruction. He lifts his left leg out to the side about a foot off the ground and then brings it back down. "Let me know if you have any hip joint or lower back pain. You want to work up to the pain but not through it. After this, we'll stretch everything out again so you don't have any cramping later."

I'm already working on an ass cramp, but I keep my mouth shut and follow along, staring at his stationary foot. With each pitiful swing of my foot, I become more and more aware of the disparity between Remy's treatment plan and my former exercise regimen. Sprints, lifts, squats, drills—I used to be wrecked afterward, not stopping until I was physical-ly drained. And yet I felt like a god, invincible, knowing that the next day I would be that much stronger. As my lower back tightens and begins to protest from the rise of the cramp into my spine, the sour taste of self-loathing threatens to taint the open-minded attitude I tried to don on my way over here.

He doesn't say anything to let on that he knows I've sadly already met my limit, but it sure feels like he knows because he stops and re-moves the weights. The enthusiastic praise he gives me as he does is the equivalent of congratulating a child on a finger painting.

We do a few more lunges to stretch out. I know it's meant to be a cool-down, but that only stokes the flames of my humility more. Cool down? It used to take a lot more to make my muscles scream and my heart rate accelerate.

"Can you lie down on the ground? I want to stretch your back well before you go so you're not sore later."

"Yeah, sure."

I'm torn between feeling like I'm being doted on and being useless. Part of me is impressed that he knows I'm limited in how I can stretch my back on my own, but another part of me isn't thrilled about him having to watch how rigidly I get to the ground. I look like the Tin Man before Dorothy came along with the oil can.

Kneeling at my side, he grips my ankle and the bottom of my foot, bending my knee close to my stomach. I feel the stretch immediately, running down my hamstring, across my ass, and into my lower back. Something snags, though, at my lower spine, and I wince.

"Shit. Are you okay?"

"Yeah," I grunt, lying like any proud man would in front of his former hookup.

"Can you bend your other leg at the knee? That will help keep your hips more aligned so we're not torquing your back."

I knew this already from countless times of trying to get up off the floor, but clearly, I don't think straight when he's around. Silently cursing myself, I bend my knee so my other foot is flat on the ground near my ass.

Remy's gaze is fixed on my face, concentrating with concern. I hate that it's an open book, and his attention is focused on signs of pain and not pleasure.

"Do you take anything for inflammation?"

"No," I mumble, fixing my focus on the cascade of poison ivy vines affixed to his fence.

"What do you do to manage your pain?"

"Heat. Ice. Stretching my back however I can."

"Are you…afraid to take anything for pain or swelling?"

I know what he's implying, and the answer is yes. Yes, I'm afraid of getting hooked on pills again. Mostly, I'm afraid of the way my parents would look at me—like I'm more of a shadow of their former son than they already do. Because guess what? Being doped up felt pretty damn good. I can't lie to myself about that. Detoxing, on the other hand, well, I think I'd rather be in another car accident.

"I've been clean for thirteen years. I don't think an aspirin here and there would hook me, but what's the point?"

He blinks at me, looking confused, moving around to my other side. "I don't understand."

"They don't even make a dent, and what little they do is just an illusion. As soon as they wear off, then it's like the pain is saying hello all over again. Better the devil you know, so to speak. You just…get used to it."

"Did your doctor say if you could take anything regularly without worrying about relapsing?"

I turn my head to stare at his deck, hoping he can't see me roll my eyes. He's got his hands on my body, and he wants to talk about this shit instead? That has to be the only reason I'm humoring the topic; he's loosened up my tongue with his touch. Apparently, I'll do anything for physical contact.

"Anti-inflammatories, yeah, but I don't want to screw up my kidneys on top of everything else. He said I should try that CDB shit, but…"—I shake my head, disgusted by the thought of giving my pain a victory—"it's fine. I made the bed, so I can sleep in it."

He sets my foot back down on the ground. I feel the loss of that non-sexual touch like a hand that just slipped out of mine in the darkness. Glancing at him for cues about my next bout of shame, I find him frowning down at me.

"What?"

"Chris…you know you don't have to make yourself suffer as much as you do. People make mistakes. It doesn't mean they need to punish themselves for them forever."

His words reach into my chest and squeeze something, twisting it in a painful grip. Only Remy could call stubbornness self-martyrdom. I'm not afraid of the pills. I'm afraid of still being nothing with them. The pain—at least I earned that.

"That's not why." I shake my head again. Leaning to the side, I roll onto my hands and knees to push myself up. "Besides," I clear my throat, dusting some grass off my shirt, "that's what I've got you for, right?"

He gets to his feet with a wry smile. Good. Maybe I've shifted the conversation.

"Yeah. I'll have you dragging tractor tires down the street in no time."

I'm sure he meant that as a joke or said it to lighten the mood, but visions of me staggering down the road, covered in sweat, gripping my side, and cringing in pain as he runs along behind me, shouting for me not to give up, assault me. He said we weren't going to fix me, but my own father should know good and well that he can't fix me. Yet, he still has ambitions I can't achieve. What exactly is Remy hoping for? Are his hopes higher than he's let on?

"I highly doubt that."

"Hey, you never know." He grins, gesturing to his deck railing. "You can do more push-ups than I can. You might be training *me* to haul tires."

I showed up here the other day, floating precariously on the idea that he wanted to get to know me, really know me, for the first time in our lives. I get the not crawling in through windows thing and the no sex thing. I honestly respect the hell out of him for that. It makes him a thousand percent more attractive than he already was. Right now, though, his playful forecast injects a shot of fear into my veins. The fall from having him in my orbit for however long is going to hurt more than any broken back once he discovers just how used up I am, and the light in his eyes dims.

Nodding like I concur with his aspirations, I head for the side of his house to make my exit. "Thanks for today."

"Chris?"

"Yeah?" I slow my steps, but don't look back, too afraid he'll see how disgruntled I feel.

"Is everything okay? Did I…say something?"

Fuck. I stop, sucking in a breath to try to calm my nerves. Except it doesn't work. All I can hear are my father's words, *You just need more confidence*. Confidence can't hide the truth. It's just smoke and mirrors.

Angling my head, I call over my shoulder. The least I can do is give him a warning. Let him know his protégé isn't going to go very far. Rip the bandage off, so I can swallow his disappointment now rather than later.

"That guy…the one you used to know—he isn't here. I'm not him anymore, and I'm never going to be. So if that's who you were hoping to get to know, I'm sorry to disappoint you."

The self-pitying sound of the words burns my skin. There's no way to polish them not to reek of victim mentality, even though they're the truth.

"I don't want that guy."

Well, that was quick. Spinning around, I wobble, acutely aware of how my spine makes me lean to the right.

"Then what the fuck *do* you want from me? Because in case you haven't noticed, I don't have much left to give."

He surprises me, answering as heatedly as I delivered, not missing a beat. "I want you to realize that you do."

I don't know what the hell he's talking about, but I'm too distracted by the instant regret on his face for raising his voice. I've never seen him look so adamant about something.

Grimacing, he smooths his hands over his T-shirt and clears his throat. "You're more than your physical abilities and appearance, Chris. It might not seem that way when you live in pain all day and were used to…feeling different, but I hope you know that."

That sounds a lot like the part in teen heartthrob movies where the preppy guy has to be told point-blank that he's shallow before he sees what everyone else does. I'm kind of getting tired of this mirror he keeps holding up in front of me. It looks worse than the one I have at home.

"And…I enjoy spending time with you."

"What? With a grumpy asshole?"

His mouth ticks up at the corner, and he shrugs. "How about a funny, intelligent man with big feelings?"

I snort, and his hesitant smirk turns into a smile of relief. That smile feels like I just defused a bomb created by my own hands, making me shake my head.

"You don't make any sense, Tanner."

"Can I translate that as *charmingly mysterious?*" he asks sheepishly.

A puff of laughter hits the back of my teeth. "Sure. Why not?"

We stand facing each other, he probably wondering if I'm going to bite his head off again, and I fully accepting that he is, in fact, charmingly mysterious. He *likes* spending time with me? It makes me want to dig way down deep inside until I find whatever it is he thinks I have left to give. I have a feeling I'll be searching for a long time, but knowing he might be here while I do, putting up with my shit, makes it seem less daunting.

"Mightener," he nods back, a flicker of a smile flashing at the corner of his mouth.

"I'll see you."

I smirk and head through his weeds, sore but somehow lighter knowing I'm off the hook for my latest outburst. How in the hell does he think *he's* a mess? He made it sound like he was hopeless and indecisive the other day—the qualities of a pushover—but he hasn't put up with anything I've dished out. Maybe having a history isn't working against us after all.

REMY

chapter 12

"Go-go dancers, huh?" Chris scrunches up his face into the morning sun, gripping onto my hands as I stand between his feet to provide tension for his lower back stretches.

"Yeah," I laugh. "I swear he went almost every weekend for months."

He shakes his head with an amused sound. I'm not sure how we got to talking about Jamie or his many quirky habits, but that's been our norm for the last two weeks. If we're not quizzing each other on random lists of favorites, we're jabbering about anything and everything from the news to childhood to awkward shopping encounters. Conversation has become as simplistic as breathing. It no longer matters that it's been fifteen years. Our time capsule has been opened, and we've picked up right where we should have started.

I release his hands reluctantly. I've got to get ready for work, and I'm sure he's likely had enough for one day.

"You good?"

"Yeah," he says as always, but I'm not sure I believe him.

He's been looking haggard for the last few days, with obvious bags under his eyes. I want to believe I'm helping him, but I don't know if that's just wishful thinking on my part. His flexibility is showing signs of improvement, but I can tell he's still in pain most of the time. I've spent years reading my patients, looking for cues that they're at their pain threshold. Maybe I'm hyperaware of Chris' facial expressions because of how many times I saw him basking in pleasure. A face can tell no lies to a former lover. The tick of his cheek, the clench of his jaw, a twitch near his eye—each micro-expression convinces me he powers through when there's no need to. I'm wary of grilling him too much, though, and sparking that pride he keeps strapped across his shoulders. I will never know how he feels or what he's had to endure, but I know a little of what it's like to lose faith in yourself. I experienced just a fraction of that in recent months, and it's certainly not a mood I'd want to live in for an extended period.

"Sounds like you guys made better use of your college experience than I did," he teases, getting to his feet, but there's a wistfulness there. "Hell, I've still never been to a go-go club."

"If you'd… been out back then do you think you would have gone?"

I can't decipher the emotion that crosses his face this time before he looks away. He shrugs, appearing to take a sudden interest in my lawn, his profile wearing a sad smile.

"Probably not. I'd have had no one to go with and would have just been some creepy guy, sitting by himself, ogling the dancers."

"Well, that worked for Jamie."

That's less loaded than saying *I'd* have gone with him. Plus, therapy has seemed to become my secondary goal to making him laugh. It is the best medicine, after all. Seeing him smile is a medicine of its own to my heart.

I watch him lumber to his feet, trying not to get caught staring. His weight sways momentarily before he almost rights himself, the curve in his spine preventing him from doing so. I hope he'll keep showing up every morning long enough for me to work through my knowledge to help him reduce the curve. It's also quite possible that I hope he'll keep showing up because it feels like I have a new friend. A new old friend.

"Do you regret anything? About the path you chose?" he asks curiously, just as I thought he was about to turn to leave. "I mean, would you have picked a different career? Lived somewhere else?"

The questions churn in my mind. Were they self-reflective, I wonder, but give up on dissecting them as I catch him waiting.

"I have plenty of regrets. I've beaten myself up over every single one of them, but I think we're supposed to a little. It's how we learn." I guess that wasn't an answer and partially TMI—typical me—so, I smile helplessly. "But no, I don't think so. I like helping people, and thought physical therapy was something I could be proud of. And San Antonio? Well, that just sort of happened. I figured there was as much for me here as anywhere else."

After saying all that, I realize the real answer is that all my choices were safe ones. Steady job. A city I was already familiar with. So, yeah. I guess I'm right where I should be—right in the middle of my comfort zone.

Spewing life reflections to Chris, however, doesn't feel safe when he looks at me like he is right now: haunted eyes sometimes clouded with troubled thoughts, searching for answers. I wish I could give him all the ones he's looking for. Pensive, he nods and gives me a smile.

"I'll see you tomorrow."

"See you, Chris."

Like each morning, I watch him disappear around the side of my house. At least, there are fewer weeds now that I've committed to doing some yard work. Hustling up the stairs to my deck, I snag my phone off the railing where I left it and find two messages from Jamie.

My, my. Someone's daily crisis started early.

Children should not get up before sunrise. I think there's something wrong with my family's genetics.

And no, it's not too early to commiserate with me. I know you're awake.

Snorting, I step inside and lock the patio door behind me before heading to my room to get dressed. Yes, I'm awake, but for all he knows, I'm just finishing up a jog. I may not have told him about my new morning workout routine.

Through my bedroom window, I catch sight of Chris hoisting himself into his truck at the curb. An ache blooms in my chest as I linger. Thank goodness he can't see my face. I've somehow avoided receiving any more accusations of giving him pity for the last two weeks. I don't want to break my record, so I move to my closet, but glance back to watch him pull away. The ache spreads, settling into my bones. It worsens the further away he gets.

It's not pity, my internal voice says calmly, the way you break something obvious to someone. A silent laugh gusts past my lips. The voice is right.

It's not pity at all. I think it's… longing.

Longing to go with him. To see how he spends the rest of his day, each minute he's not with me. Longing to hear his voice and those laughs of his that he gives up like a stiff coin wheel on an old gumball machine that requires a special touch.

It's a liberating realization, one not consumed by thoughts of passion. We haven't touched each other in the last two weeks, aside from my helping him stretch. And now that I think about it, I haven't had a single impure thought about him. My evenings have been spent reflecting on our conversations, quietly laughing to myself, and smiling.

"I have a crush," I laugh softly, oddly proud of myself.

My first real adult crush. It's calm and settles over me, wrapping around me like a warm hug. It's so unlike the overwhelming delirium I experienced back in college. Softer and far stronger than whatever I considered a crush after that.

I think…I'm falling for Chris Mightener. Again. Unlike then, however, I think there may be some place to land this time.

Dressing quickly, I know I don't need to rush since I've cut jogging out of my day lately. Switching to showering at night has given me more wiggle room in the morning, in case a certain man with *big feelings* decides to show up early or eke past my normal cut-off time. While I'm feeling inspired, I should use the extra few minutes to spread the good word…or at least part of it.

Jamie's phone rings once. A fumbling noise and a few curses follow, but then I'm treated to his breathy, whispered voice.

"I didn't mean you had to call. What's up?"

"Excuse me. I thought commiserating was best done vocally. Why? Did you go back to sleep or something?" There's an audible panting of labored breath while I talk. "Why do you sound like you're winded?"

"Nothing. You just scared me."

"You're…whispering. Why are you whispering?"

"Because I'm in the closet where little people can't invade my room at 5 a.m. asking for a bowl of Froot Loops."

Oh, boy. I don't know whether to laugh or to send a therapist over to help him. "You're sleeping in a closet?"

"No. Who the fuck can sleep in a closet? And there is no sleeping in this house. It's like one of those horror films with the creepy little insomniac children. No matter where you go or what you do, whenever you turn around, one is staring at you, asking for things—your soul, your wallet, oat milk for an alley cat, the answer to fourteen to the third power. It never ends."

"Uh…and the closet is a safe zone from pesky zombie children who need regular, natural nurturing?"

"It is *not* natural, Jeremy! Don't give me that until you've waded through the hellscape that is currently a day in my life. Do you know how long it's been since I've gotten laid? I can't even jerk off in my own house. My hand thinks I don't love it anymore, and this closet smells like mothballs. Gran must have had a fear of moths, because the stench is so potent it's sure to kill any of them well beyond *my* dying years. You try having some happy time while inhaling pesticides with limited elbow room, and then tell me how much patience you have."

"Wait…are you…jerking off in the closet?"

"Well, not anymore! *You* called."

Rubbing my eyes, I wish I could go back and rethink the use of my free time. I shove my shoes on and grab my keys off the hook on the hall tree.

"I'm *sorry*. You sounded like you needed to talk, but I think I have a pretty good picture now as to why."

Locking my door behind me, I hear a sigh over the line. "I'm fine. Everything's fine."

Snickering, I tuck my keys into my pocket and bound down my steps, happy he's come back to the land of sanity. "You sure about that?"

"Ha. Ha. *I'm* the snarky, dramatic friend. Not you. At least let me keep that. It's all I have left."

"I'd never dream of stealing your title. Everything else okay though?"

"Yeah. Fabulous, but now that I've got you on the phone, there's something I want to ask you. What would you think about a fun getaway for Thanksgiving?"

"To where?"

He delays answering for a beat, setting my suspicion meter on red alert. "California," he finally says innocently.

"To *your* house?"

"Yeah. It'll be fun." His false bravado tells me it will be anything but fun, especially when he tries to sweeten the deal with, "You can come watch the chaos first-hand. It'll be like having front row seats to a mud wrestling competition. Biting is allowed at those things, by the way."

Starting my car, I wait for my phone to broadcast him over my speakers. As much as I'd love to experience a California Thanksgiving with Jamie, I think I'd have to pass on watching him lose his mind. "I can't. I was going to go home to see my parents."

"Oh, come on. I'll call them. They'll understand."

"Jamie, I haven't been home since last Christmas. I already told them I'm coming."

He mutters something that sounds like *'fucking coward.'*

"Fine." That four-letter word has never been uttered with such exasperation. "What's new with you? Still happily single and saving one sciatica at a time, I hope?"

"Yes," I snort, but a niggle of guilt has me tugging at my collar. "I've been giving someone personal therapy in the mornings before work."

"Oooh, now we're talking. Give me all the dirt. Is it a pulled hammy? Do you have to get way up in there?"

"Oh, God. You'd better not be jerking off while I'm talking to you."

"I don't think I can. I think the chemicals have caused permanent damage."

I'll say.

"So, what's the scoop?"

Here goes nothing. And I thought he was wound up when I first called.

"It's…Chris. I ran into him again after you left."

Three thumps resound, the sound of something solid rapping against something else solid. It's followed by a low groan.

"Are you…banging your head?"

"*Yes!* I'm trying to activate my mind control powers so you'll do the same and knock some sense into yours. Tell me, does this *'therapy'* involve lube and lots of filthy sex followed by not a single solitary thought about building a house with a white picket fence? Because *that* is the only acceptable kind of therapy for a scenario that includes you and the football king."

"*No.* And there are *other* possible scenarios, believe it or not." I ignore his sputter of disbelief. "It's…we're friends. He's got…a lot of problems and I'm helping him."

"Because that's what you *do*, Remy! Ugh. Please do not let him take advantage of you."

"Jay, it's not like that. Not this time. I swear. He's…different. Not like he was at the bar that night. I think he was just…desperate for comfort and hurting. We talk." I'm quick to add, "*Without* any sex, and…it's nice. Really nice." He's unusually quiet for once. The campus comes into view, so I wrap it up, hoping that will signal that I'm putting a pin in this before he can analyze things too much. "Anyway. That's what's new, and I'm fine. I promise."

"If *'fine'* means you're lying to me and getting dicked down twice a day, I swear I will fly my blue-balled ass out there, drag you back here, and feed you to the zombie children if you end up a crying mess after it ends."

I'm about to blurt out that it's not going to end but catch myself. There's nothing to end. Whether Chris and I ever part as friends, something more, or something less, I know it would hurt, but it would hurt in a way that would be acceptable now that I know where I stand. Unlike months ago, I don't think I'd have a sense of being less or missing out on something if I were single after that. Because I can see that I was right about one thing all those years ago. I just had no proof to understand why I was right. *Chris is it for me.* If it never happens, I'll be okay with that because I got to know him at least. I don't know if I'll want to tell him he's *it*, but I trust how I feel. Trusting how I feel for the first time in my life is really fucking freeing.

I guess my fairy tale happened after all. It just looks a little different than I thought it would.

CHRIS

chapter 13

They say it takes two weeks to form a new habit. That means only three more days until the extra workout I've added after my morning routine with Remy will stop kicking my ass. Putting my leftovers away in the fridge, I spot a lone beer in the back when I move some things around to make room.

Glancing out the kitchen window at the way the wind is picking up, I don't have to watch the weather to know it's going to rain. The familiar pin needles splintering themselves down my hips and legs tell me a downpour is coming. The twelve ounces of beer sitting in my fridge are tempting, but I've managed to stay away from Mahoney's every evening since seeing Remy there. Grabbing it, I pull it out and toss it into my trash can. What's the point of eating broiled fish and steamed vegetables if you pack the love back on your handles with hops?

Gale comes in, the clip of her nails on the tile floor announcing her entrance. "We don't need that," I inform her, although I know she's probably more interested in the leftovers.

Moving to the sink, I wash and dry the pan I used to cook my dinner. Gale follows, still looking hopeful. Such a beggar.

Ambling across the kitchen, I open the top cabinet to grab a treat for when she does her business later, covertly trying to slip it into my pocket. There is nothing covert when a dog knows where the good stuff is, though. I can practically feel her ears perk to attention behind me.

Surveying the cabinet contents, I look longingly at a peanut butter cracker sandwich snack packet. I guess I've made enough progress that I can indulge a little. When I grab it, the familiar foil blue wrapper of a more enticing treat behind it comes into view. Damn. I thought I'd thrown all of those out.

Grabbing the Rice Krispies Treat, I head back to the trash can, where Gale skitters over, tongue hanging out. "No. We don't need these either."

I toss it in. She gives an annoyed huff, looking at me like her human has been replaced by an alien. I wonder how long it takes dogs to adapt to new habits. I feel her pain because I kind of want to dumpster dive for that little marshmallow snack.

Smoothing my hand over my midsection, I'm pleased by the decrease in the squish there. It's not a vast difference, but hopefully it means I'm working toward better spine stability like Remy talks about. My trips down to the basement to reunite with my old exercise equipment have taken motivation that I didn't know I had left. I've certainly not hit my crunch bar the way I used to, but it's enough that I've made a dent in my Rice Krispies band. My back, while still completely fucked, actually feels a bit stronger. At the games, whether I'm sitting in the press box or the bleachers, I'm also mindful about catching myself hunching over. Baby steps.

We can't fix me, like Remy says, but once I'm over this hurdle, hopefully I'll have reclaimed a fragment of my former posture.

Heading into my living room, I sit down at my computer, muscles stiff and tight from overdoing it earlier. I should probably stretch some more, but I know Old Man Weather is playing into the discomfort. For now, a distraction will do me better than thinking about how fun it's going to be trying to fall asleep later without liquid medication.

Overall, I feel…good. Lighter, but not necessarily because of my weight. It's the first time since my accident that I feel like I have at least as equal an amount of control over my body as it does over me.

I don't need to hit the two-week mark to know that Remy is the cause of that. He's a welcome habit. He's… changed in new and surprising ways from the guy I thought I knew, and yet, he's somehow still the same in the best ways. I can't believe I scoffed at him for suggesting we get to know each other better, when it's been the best thing that's happened to me in forever.

Blurting out random questions while we work out is still taking me some getting used to, but he never seems to bat an eye, always open and honest. He's so easy to talk to, I don't know why it's so difficult for me. And…he does this thing when he thinks he's rambling…

His cheeks go pink, and he'll laugh softly at himself, while all I can think is that I don't want him to stop. I could listen to a twenty-four-hour marathon of the Jeremy Tanner documentary and not get bored. It's becoming difficult to remember that I go over there for physical therapy and not just for a chance to listen to and sneak glances at him.

When he first suggested physical therapy, I thought I was in for some brutal physical torture that would leave me frustrated from day one, with no hope of having the stomach to show up for day two. Except I *do* feel better. My muscles are more limber, and I swear my gait is a little smoother. We started walking around the block a few days ago, and the soles of my feet haven't even cramped up once. It's invigorating. My body is less of a prison already.

Digging my fingers into the tight muscles at the base of my neck, I groan. At least, it was invigorating until I started doubling down on my abs at home last week. Doing suspended crunches in my early twenties never felt like I was pulling an anchor up from the bottom of the ocean.

God, I really let myself go. I know, to some extent, I had no choice, but I can see now how I gave up and let my injuries win. They don't need to win every day.

Reviewing my last article, I pop a peanut butter cracker into my mouth. I wonder what Remy's having for dinner. This morning, he was talking about a baked squash and roasted red pepper soup he made last night, his eyes lighting up over his culinary victory. I've never seen someone so exuberant about conquering their kitchen. Did he just bow down and let all his exes decide on dinner?

I'm kind of kicking myself for taking him up on mornings for our workouts. If we switched them to the afternoons, he wouldn't have to rush off to work, and we'd have more time. *I'd* have more time…to spend with *him*.

And that's not even me thinking with my dick, although I've caught myself thinking about the state of my dick more than ever lately. Scrubbing my face won't alleviate the burning sensation over the memory of taking my doctor up on his offer of a little blue pill when I brought up my issue again the other day. God knows I probably won't even have the chance to use them with Remy after the way I came on that night at the bar. I couldn't care less, honestly. It's not even a priority. I just want to be prepared. If Remy ever…*wanted* me again, I don't want to let him down.

He's…something. Really something. So full of life and optimism that any traces of self-pity I haven't kicked to the curb yet die a quick death whenever I'm around him. He's a new drug that I don't mind being addicted to. I think I actually have a friend.

A friend that you still think about kissing sometimes, I remind myself.

Blowing out a breath, I dust the crumbs off my fingers onto my jeans. My article looks up to snuff, so I call out to Gale. We could both use some cool fresh air, her for her bladder and me for the warmth in my skin.

That *was* some kiss, though. I can't help thinking about it now and then. In my defense, when I'm trying to get comfortable enough to go to sleep at night, I only have two choices to distract me from my pain—TV or fantasies. I honestly don't think you could call them fantasies anymore. My stomach flab isn't the only thing that's looking different.

Last night, I dreamt we were back in Remy's old room at college. He was still twenty-something Remy, but I wasn't. I was me now.

I knocked on his front door and told him to ignore the noise at his bedroom window, to not let *that* guy in. He said okay, trusting and compliant as always, and invited me in to sit on the couch. And then… we just talked. Just like we do now.

I asked him about all his hopes and dreams. He told me he was scared of the future and that he liked this guy who didn't know he existed. I told him not to be scared, that he'd be great at whatever he did. And on the other matter, I said it was because the guy didn't deserve him yet, but to be patient, that maybe he would someday.

I held him, and he fell asleep in my arms, at peace, his innocence protected from the darkness. And I felt no pain. None in my body nor in my heart.

I woke up sobbing. For a while, I didn't think I'd be able to get it together enough to go over to his house, but seeing him, honestly, felt like the only cure.

Standing in the doorway of my sunporch, watching Gale find the perfect spot, I have no idea what that dream was supposed to mean. Maybe it was a punishment from my subconscious for all the times I conjured self-serving fantasies of Remy and faceless men. Because if I think about it, I'm not even that older version of me who walked into his room in my dream. When have I ever been that wise and compassionate?

Moving to my worktable, I pull away a sheet of kraft paper that I placed to keep dust and bugs off the latest paver stone I've been working on. It's good, but I don't know if it's good enough. I could break it up and start all over again, but it took me days to decide how I wanted the pieces laid out before I set the mold. Grabbing a piece of sandpaper, I set to smoothing out the rough bits of the *Sakrete* one more time. This was always busywork for me, a project to keep boredom at bay. Remembering how Remy fawned over my stones, however, I'm sickened by how I've taken for granted small achievements. I'm not DaVinci or anything, but I've spent years essentially pouting over what I'm not and what I haven't done, never stopping to appreciate what I can do. What I am. Who I am. I can't say I'm thrilled with who I am, but I'd rather buy a beer for today-Chris than last-year-Chris. Well, a soda rather. I mean… maybe just living is enough. Because it's not always easy. Is it? I think I'm proof of that if nothing else.

Speaking of new ambitions… I pull my phone out of my pocket and call Gale to come back inside so I can close out some of the horrid pressure building outside. Pulling up my email, my steps falter just as I reach the door to the living room.

Oh, shit. They answered.

My pulse flickers in anticipation, opening the email from the communications director of the college. I'm going to owe the editor of the Gazette dinner for telling me about this opportunity if they select me. I still don't know how I'll manage speaking in front of a classroom about sports writing, but pushing my boundaries has apparently become my new thing.

I only make it halfway to my recliner. That lightness that so happily made a home in my chest of late dims like no one left in the world believes in fairies. It's not because they didn't select me for their sports writing seminar—which has been delayed until next semester—that has me at a standstill. It's what comes after: a big, fat bargaining chip. At least, that's how I see it. The words feel like a cruel joke.

> *Given your alumnus status and NFL career experience, we would be honored if you would consider speaking at this year's upcoming pre-winter break safety briefing. Many of our students will be faced with situations and decisions during the holidays that could put them and others in harm's way. As a former Panther, we feel that our students will find you relatable and inspiring. Our safety briefing will include the topics of alcohol and substance abuse, driving under the influence, situational awareness, and taking proactive safety measures. If you would be comfortable sharing some of your experiences and the trials you faced on any of these topics that may benefit the students as they continue on their college journey, we would be greatly appreciative to have you as our host.*

Well…

How about that?

I saw a western movie once where a parched prisoner was about to be given a drink of water, only to have it spilled on the ground in front of him, just out of reach. The semblance of accomplishment I've felt I've achieved lately threatens to topple off a high shelf and crash to the floor as I stare at the invitation. My sins will never leave me, will they?

I quit giving in to drinking, quit moping on my ass, quit trying to punish Remy for my bitterness, but none of it matters. Not when you take away every brick I manage to lay, because behind the façade, my crimes will always be there. *Me*…barreling off the road, smashing into a guardrail, pinned inside a car, blasted all over the news, and crushing the adoration of fans.

Fuck. I wish their invitation were on a piece of paper so I could wad it up, pitch it across the room, and watch Gale maul it into a sloppy mess of sogginess.

I move to my chair, suddenly heavier than I've felt in months. I'm so fucking tired of being mad. I don't want to be angry anymore. I don't want to hate myself. Hate life. Hate the dark days when I have to plaster myself to a heating pad or an ice pack. I just want…some sunshine.

Clicking the power button on my heating pad, I close my eyes and brace for the storm, trying not to grind my teeth when the rogue spikes of pain protest against the warmth like kernels of corn popping in an oil pan. I don't even like my dentist enough for how much I've had to shell out to him.

Something damp saturates the side of my leg, applying pressure. I don't have to crack an eye to know it's my trusty companion. I reach out, giving her ears a scratch, then petting her softly to ease her protector instincts. I'm sure she could use a night off.

I try to picture joyful things: warmth and light. Food for the soul, to feed the mind, to overpower my agony, both physical and emotional. *Big feelings*, I muse, grateful for something to make me smile. My mind latches onto that radiant luminosity, taking me across town to its source. It soothes my agitation over my failed mission of getting the world to forget all about me and my *'trials.'*

He didn't forget me.

But he doesn't see football, or an entitled drunk driver. He just sees *me*.

If the sun can peek through a storm cloud, does that mean they can co-exist? Does the cloud become less of a cloud, evaporating until finally the darkness is gone? If so, what the heck is in it for the sun? A sweet-as-hell, witty, sexy, kind-hearted sun.

I let out a huff to rival Gale's when Mom visits and tries to put one of those stupid doggy bandanas on her. What does it matter? Even if the sun ended up wanting the *'grumpy asshole'* cloud, the cloud doesn't even know how to date.

REMY

chapter 14

What was I expecting? That he'd be sitting on my front porch, waiting for me? Turning off the ignition, I lean against the steering wheel of my car, still unable to tear my gaze away from my front steps as though doing so will manifest Chris.

He said he'd be here this morning, but never showed. He could have forgotten. Something could have come up that prevented him from making it. Maybe he just slept in. The possibilities have crossed my mind all day.

It's the bleaker possibilities that have my stomach queasy. What if something happened to him? When he showed up at the center that day for therapy, he said it was because he'd fallen off his porch. He could be hurt. He seemed melancholy when he was leaving yesterday. I hadn't stopped to consider that seeing an old college classmate, who went on to have a successful career, might make the sting of his collapsed dreams more pronounced. What if he drove to a bar for what he calls '*liquid medication*' and broke his rule about not driving?

"Shit," I whisper, gripping the steering wheel tighter.

On the drive over to his house, I tell myself that it's probably nothing and that I'll end up looking like a fool for just showing up again. It would be worth it for the peace of mind it will bring me. He said no one called after he got in his accident. I can see now that it's not always safe to assume a person has plenty of people to check on them.

His truck is in his driveway in one piece. That rules out one theory, thank goodness. I don't think he'd survive another car wreck. Hurrying to the door, I don't bother checking his backyard. The gate is closed, and everything is still wet from the rain we had yesterday.

My knock is answered by a beat of silence and then a low *woof*. Good old Gale, his protector. I won't be appeased, however, until I know it's not a bark of distress. I've never had a dog, so I don't know how to distinguish signs of distress from an excited bark that someone is at the door. She keeps barking, though, and now I'm worried that I'm learning what a K-9 cry for help sounds like.

Trying the knob, the door is unlocked and opens for me. She stops as soon as I peek my head inside, licking her lips and wagging her tail.

"Gale," Chris's voice calls from deeper in the house, sounding groggy. "Knock it off."

Closing the door behind me, I spot him down the hall through the open door of his bedroom. One arm slung over his eyes, bare-chested in nothing but a pair of blue jeans, there's an open book lying at his side. A blue ice pack peeks out from underneath his back.

"Chris?" I call back. "Are you all right?"

Jerking, his arm comes down, and he glances over at me in surprise. "Remy?"

"Hey." I give him an awkward wave as I slowly close the distance, feeling like an intruder now that I know he's alive and well. "I got worried when you didn't show up this morning and…well, it looks like maybe I was right to do so. Wild night on the town?" I joke, hoping to take some of the spotlight off the fact that I just barged into his house uninvited.

He presses a hand on the mattress and starts to sit up. It's a short-lived effort. He makes a hissing noise and grimaces, clutching his back with his other hand.

"Hey, just stay there. You're clearly in bed for a reason." I rush over, no longer giving a damn about an invitation. Stopping by the bed, I give him a quick survey but don't see any signs of new injuries. Gale hops up on the bed like she thinks a party is starting, her weight shifting the mattress and making him wince. "What did you do?

When his flash of pain passes, he lets out a haggard breath of relief, gripping her leg like he's silently begging her to hold still. Flicking his gaze up to mine, his expression has a chastened appearance. He sighs, lowers himself back onto his pillow, and scrubs a hand down his face.

"I've been working on my abs on my crunch bar after our workouts every day. I guess I overdid it a little. Add in the spillover from the hurricane going on in the Gulf, and it didn't make for a very wise combo. I'm done with the other kind of wild nights, though. I haven't had a drop since that night at the bar. Getting to sleep isn't worth becoming an alcoholic in the process."

I hadn't even considered that the weather might be impacting him today. Jumping to conclusions about him has probably made me look like I suck at my job. Still, I'm glad to hear it was only Mother Nature and ambition that laid him up. I thought he was looking a little slimmer.

"You've been cheating on me, huh?" I tease, hoping some humor will alleviate his frustration.

Peering out from behind his hand, he snorts. "With myself."

Lying in his bed like this, hair askew, dark circles under his eyes, and a book by his side, he looks like a big kid who's mournful that he can't go outside to play. I don't want to stick a feather in my cap, but it's kind of cool if I motivated him, even though he's a damn fool for going about it all wrong.

It smells of Mentholatum in his room. The piquant odor overpowers his wonderful Chris scent. The tube of muscle ache rub and a handheld massager on his nightstand topple any reservations I had about violating his space, especially when he adds remorsefully, "I'm sorry I stood you up."

Stepping forward, I wave my hands and ease my hip onto his mattress. "Roll over."

Gale flops down onto the mattress, causing Chris to let out a grunt. Her body twists, all four of her legs extending into the air as she looks over at me with what can only be described as a hopeful doggy smile.

"Are you talking to me or Gale?" Chris deadpans.

I hiccup a laugh at both of them and motion again. "Now you." His expression turns reluctant, so I add, "Can you handle being on your stomach for a few minutes? I can try to make you feel better."

Judging by the way he cocks a brow, that seemed to pique his interest. "You can actually scratch my belly just like this."

The bit of adorable flirting has me fighting a smile, considering how his face looks like he thinks he's pushing his luck. It's sweet and humble, not a rushing waterfall that will drown me.

"Yeah, but you can't get a free massage that way."

"You want to massage me?"

"No, I want you to listen and stop being a grumpy asshole."

He lets out an amused sound, but a veil of wariness shutters his face again. Pursing his lips, he gestures to where his back is pressed against his mattress. "It's not pretty," he warns.

"You've never been pretty."

The little bark of laughter he lets out is a beautiful sound. When he realizes my deadpan expression means I'm serious, he sighs. Shaking his head, he digs his elbow into the mattress and turns onto his side. I hear something in his back make an unnatural popping sound, almost like a dull *clanking* noise if someone were to drop a bolt on a hardwood floor a room away. He gives no comment or reaction other than a stifled huff. Jesus, it must be his broken hardware. I can't stand the thought that any wrong turn could potentially paralyze him.

"On your side is fine, if that's better for you," I insist, dreading the thought of him having to twist everything back around when we're done.

"Yeah, the side is good."

I wait until he gets comfortable, hugging his pillow with one arm underneath his head. There's a bottle of lotion among the remedies on his nightstand, but oil would be better so my fingers don't skid against his flesh and cause him any more pain than he's already in. Eyeing his nightstand drawer, I hope to the gods of men that he'll have the alternative I'm hoping for. Tugging it open, I suppress a sad laugh at the sight of more ointments, a gay men's magazine that I know Jamie has had articles featured in, several individually wrapped Rice Krispies Treats, and one very small bottle of lube that's nearly empty. That will do.

"Are you…in my drawer?" He tenses.

And now I want to laugh because mine is much more incriminating than his. "Just looking for something."

Flipping the cap, I dribble some of the liquid onto his skin and use my hand to stop it from flowing down onto his sheets. He stiffens again under my touch.

"Sorry. Is it cold?"

"Is that…lube?"

"How about we think of it as a massage oil alternative?"

The choked sound he lets out is cut off by a low groan when I apply pressure to the tight muscles on each side of his spine. I wish I had a magic eraser to remove the red and white scarring on his back and the event that caused them, but I'll settle for that sound. Circling over the cords in his back, I make slow sweeps toward his sides, drawing away the tension. His breathing deepens, his body relaxing a fraction like he's no longer fighting the idea of letting me pamper him.

"That feels good," he whispers, his voice tight.

"See? Lube for the win. You'll be '*Mighty*' again in no time." The grunt he makes doesn't sound like it's from relief. Eyes closed, lines form around the corner of his mouth. I think I hit a nerve, and not one in his back. "I guess no one probably calls you that anymore."

"If they did, I'd ask them not to. It was a stupid fucking name."

"You didn't like it? I thought you used to have a keychain with—" I'm quick to cut myself off when he glances back at me in surprise. Face burning, I shift my attention to his back, grateful for the dim lighting in here. "It was just something I noticed," I add to cover my tracks, but now I'm curious. "So…when all your fans were chanting your nickname, that's why you were out there scowling? And here I thought it was just your game face."

I think one of my favorite things about older Chris is that he likes my stupid jokes and never makes me feel awkward for blurting out something embarrassing, like I just did. I still don't see how it wasn't obvious that I was a sucker for him back then, but I plan to ease into this crush with better compliments than that one.

He makes no comment, so I focus on working systematically up his spine to the brick wall that is his overworked shoulders. Damn, how many crunches did he do? There are enough knots here to open a Shibari exhibit.

"After the accident…there was an article…"

My hands slow. His voice comes out so quiet and forlorn that I barely catch what he's saying.

"Well, there were a lot of articles, but there was this one sports journal, *Football Today*. I'd never even read *Football Today* before. I'll never forget the headline: *Mighty The Fallen*. I remember staring at it through a swollen eyelid from where my face hit the dashboard and thinking, yeah, that about sums it up."

I don't realize my hands have gone still until his back rises and falls on a sigh. My heart twists inside my chest.

"It was a good article," he remarks casually. "The guy was a hell of a writer. A year later, I was sitting at Austin Limits High School, my cane propped against the bleachers, watching a game just as a reason to get away from my parents for a few hours, and then it hit me. *I could be that guy, maybe…* I mean, my fingers still worked. I could cover athletics—without the poetic doom and gloom that he did, of course. That was my one condition. Anyhow." He shrugs against my hands. "So, what do I know? Maybe it *was* the perfect name."

The pain in the center of my chest radiates to my throat, making it difficult to form words. He'd just realized his ambitions were ruined, only to have someone come along and trample all over the rubble. He was twenty-three. *Only* twenty-three, and a news headline essentially told him he was nothing and never would be again. I don't condone the poor decision he made, but that doesn't seem fair.

Clearing his throat, he shifts in place. "Sorry. You were expecting a workout partner and instead got sucked into having to put your hands on an ex-hookup while he tells you uplifting stories." He leans back like he's intent on rolling back onto the mattress, but my knee prevents him from going further. Craning his head, he flashes me a stoic look. "You don't have to doctor me. I've lived with this for years."

"It's fine," I practically choke, rattling my head back and forth. I ease my hands off him, though. "Did I hurt you?"

"No, thank you. Don't get me wrong. It felt good, but…I'd rather be in pain than see you feeling sorry for me."

He lets out a self-deprecating puff, a meek smile playing on his lips. However, there's nothing humorous about the moment. He just shared a piece of his trauma with me, and I can tell it cost him something. I want to trade him a hell of a lot more than a massage for that in return.

I think now is a good time to quit holding back the sentimental thoughts I've had about him. This isn't a crush. It's an attachment that's rooted so deep in my heart that whatever home I build on it will withstand a lifetime of storms with a foundation that strong.

"I *feel sorry*… for *not being there* when you needed someone, because I would have been. And I put my hands on you because… Well, I'm kind of addicted to making you feel better."

You'd think I spoke in tongues the way he's gaping at me. I see the moment when my spilled secrets really register. A flush creeps up his cheeks, and he redirects his gaze to the mattress. Okay. Not awkward.

He clears his throat as his fingers play with a ripple in the duvet. "As a Narcotics Anonymous graduate, I feel like I should probably tell you to seek some kind of treatment program for that, but,"—he pauses, darting a peek at me, his tongue slipping out to wet his lips—"if you're looking for an enabler, I won't complain if you don't stop."

Well…that settles that. Now *my* face is probably red too. I cover my chuckle with a cough and pick up where I left off. The soft grunt he makes as I knead his shoulders has me wanting to bend down and press a kiss to the offended area.

"I doubt there's a cure," I murmur, half-intending that to have only been for my ears. But heck, I'm on a roll. I still have the need to heal young Chris as much as older Chris, so I set another confession free. "I, um, had a really hard time seeing you go, actually. That's why Jamie was so standoffish with you. I kind of sulked about it for…" Okay, maybe specifics would be too much of a confession. "For a while."

This time, I don't get a flirty, encouraging reply. I get silence. He's gone tense again under my touch. The longer I continue to work on his muscles, the more self-conscious I feel. Side note: Some secrets are apparently better left unspoken. I open my mouth to try to get my foot out of it, but a stupefied whisper beats me to it.

"You never said anything."

"You…had plans. It would have been wrong of me to say anything, and… and I didn't think you'd want me to. Which is fine," I'm quick to add, pulling my hands back because, shit, this is a whole new level of awkward. "You told me from the start that we were nothing."

He reaches over his hip and places a hand on my forearm. "It *wasn't* nothing. I didn't think I was allowed to have anything else besides the future I'd been training for, so I…" And like that, his hand is gone. He grips his hair above his forehead and mutters a curse.

I want to crawl in on myself until I disappear. Curling my toes inside my shoes, I force myself to stay put.

I think I'm the one being turned down now. It's fine. It isn't, but it is. I told myself I would be okay with whatever happens between us, and I meant it. Honestly, I'm glad I got that off my chest. Fifteen years was a long time to hold it in, and someone needed to restore whatever that reporter's words took from him.

"I knew."

The soft words have me blinking at his shadowed profile. Eyes closed, he lets out a long stream of air. "I think I knew sometimes—the way you looked at me… It made my heart feel like it was going to beat out of my chest. It scared the shit out of me, because the only other thing that made me feel anywhere close to that good was when I was on the field winning. *That*, I knew how to do."

My obsession was too much. Imagine that? I chuckle despite the fresh loss of both my old and new hopes, plucking at the comforter.

"Well, I'm flattered to know I was as good as football. Coming from you, that's huge."

He reaches out and grips my arm again, giving it a squeeze. "You are so much more than that, Remy. But that probably doesn't do the sentiment any justice, considering I don't have football now." Shifting, he turns over and leans up on an elbow. I wait, suspended, snared by the pleading in his eyes. "I never imagined anyone could look at me the way you do—like they see something and they mean it. Seeing myself in your eyes and wondering if it's a dream…" His head shakes. "All the pain, the accident, the years in between then and now, I'd go through it all over again if I knew that getting to know you was the reward on the other side."

Don't kiss him. Don't. *Kiss. Him.*

Yes, that's the sweetest thing I've ever heard, but maybe he's just having a moment of gratitude over pulling himself out of the rut he was in. He did that, not me. He didn't have to show up at my house every morning for the last two weeks and force himself to socialize out of his comfort zone.

Swallowing, my nervous laughter is as weak as I feel. "You don't have to sweet-talk me for a massage."

He smiles and rubs his thumb over the soft skin at the hinge of my elbow, spreading gooseflesh up my arm. His lips part and then…my stomach produces a ferocious growl that has Gale popping up on all fours at attention. Can you say bad timing?

"Shit. Have you eaten?"

"Yes. I had a kraken for lunch. He's still digesting." He snickers at that, but still looks endearingly concerned over the state of my noisy stomach. "I was too busy to take my lunch break today, but I'm fine. I'll grab something when I get home."

Pressing his other hand to the mattress, he hefts himself up and nods for me to move, swinging his legs off the edge of the bed when I get up. "Let me make you dinner."

"Oh, no. Chris, you don't have to feed me."

Swiping a shirt off the end of his bed, he wrestles it over his shoulders and stands, concealing the patterns on his skin. I can tell he's still stiff, his spine forcing him to lean forward slightly. That puts his gaze nearly level with mine when he turns around. And, holy shit, I could swim in it, the tender set of his brow doing all sorts of things to my heart.

"Let me make you dinner," he repeats, softer this time, tilting one brow higher, but there's nothing intimidating about it. Gale hops off the bed with a half-sneeze, half-snort, wagging her tail excitedly as though she knows what the word *'dinner'* means. God, they're a pair.

"*Only* if I can help."

If victory had a name, it would be the smile that stretches across his face. He leans in and gives the side of my hip a swat.

"Fucking-A right you're gonna help. We don't take no freeloaders here, do we, Gale?"

Patting his leg, he hobbles out of the room, his uneven footsteps echoing a cadence similar to my pulse, Gale eagerly trotting at his side. Yeah. He's it for me. Sighing, I follow the big man with big feelings and his big dog down the hallway.

CHRIS
chapter 15

The steamroller I feel like I got hit with is still idling like it wants another go at me, but laughing, cooking, and eating dinner with Remy have put a wheel chock under its rollers for the past hour and a half. The massage also helped. The man has magic hands. Why am I even surprised?

He looks good in my house. Good in my kitchen. Good standing next to me at the sink while I pass him dishes to dry. The glow of the overhead light is highlighting all his features, giving him an angelic aura that he completely embodies.

He had *a hard time seeing me go...*

I want to go back in time and kick my own ass. Fifteen years wasted.

All right, I shouldn't say they were wasted, considering that would mean he would have had to see me all messed up in those early days. However, I might not have made the same stupid mistake if he'd been waiting for me to come home to after that party. If I'd known his worth back then.

I know the value of what's standing next to me now, though. Do I ever.

I can't take back how I hurt him, but at least I seem to make him smile. That's something.

He's humming softly with a contented little smile on his face, wiping down a wet plate with the same care he took on my back earlier. Gale is standing to his right, periodically snorting at him. She wants couch snuggles, I can tell, but Remy doesn't know that. He pauses for the dozenth time, cooing in a sweet voice, asking her what's the matter.

He asked me when and how I got her. During dinner, when she rested her chin on his thigh and gave him mooch eyes, no matter how many times I scolded her, he just kept laughing and petting her, not bothered in the slightest. I'm in danger of drowning in his cuteness.

It's going to be too many days that he's gone—the rest of this week and the weekend for his trip back home to see his family for Thanksgiving. Monday can't come soon enough.

"What?" He laughs, catching me staring.

Shaking my head, I make a show of wiping down the sink. "Nothing."

"It didn't look like nothing."

I watch him fold the hand towel and rest it over the dish rack. When he turns to face me, that glowing, unassuming Remy smile is still lighting up his face. The wishes bursting at the seams inside my chest are fighting to get lost in the well of his blue eyes. Could I ever have a chance with him? I want to be greedy and ask if I can graduate from friend and workout partner to…something more.

"I was thinking about how much I want to kiss you."

"You…want to kiss me?"

Splotches of color pop up on his cheeks and neck. How can he not know when it feels like it's tattooed on every inch of my skin? I know I'm still not enough for him, but I'm sick of hiding. I hid feelings the first time around, and look at the damage that did.

"I always want to kiss you."

"Oh." His puff of nervous laughter dances between us. Glancing down at the sink, his fingertip rubs anxiously through a droplet of water on the counter ledge. "It never seemed like that back in the day."

The damage I've done. The fucking damage.

"I was worried I wouldn't be able to stop if I did."

Quivers rack through me until he glances up, the doubt in his eyes replaced by something that looks a lot like surprise. Stepping forward, his tongue peeks out, wetting his lips. I follow his hand, watching it reach up, and don't exhale until it settles on the side of my neck. I didn't think my honesty would actually pay off.

When my nephews were young, they used to crack up while watching the cartoon movie *Ferdinand* when the oversized bull was tiptoeing his way through a china shop. I never laughed. I could relate too much.

Time comes to a standstill as I lean in. I don't care if it's taking me too long. I'm determined to stretch out each second. I refuse to be Ferdinand right now.

The heat of his breath warms my lips. I cradle his forearm and close my eyes, my nose brushing against his. When the plush feel of his lips connects with mine, it's so soft I wouldn't know he's even there if it weren't for the way I feel like I've come home. The sensation flows through me, a celebration of invisible shooting stars coiling around us in figure eights. It's sweet and soft like a first kiss—or the one we should have had. It's our do-over.

When I draw back, I rest my forehead against his, bringing my hand up to touch his cheek. His jaw shifts under my trembling touch, and I hear him swallow. Getting to know him again has been more of a twelve-step program than my opioid counseling ever was. Admitting my careless addiction to him to myself, taking a moral inventory, and making amends. It's all there, just not quite in the same order.

Step 2—We came to believe that a Power greater than ourselves could restore us to sanity.

Remy is my restoration. My return to sanity.

I continue to make amends, gently feathering his lips with mine. His fingers fist a handful of my T-shirt, pulling it tight against my stomach. A beautiful sound tumbles out of his throat, and he parts his lips, capturing one of mine. I feel his tongue sweep against the seam of my mouth and sigh as his fingers delve into my hair at the back of my head. And then he's tasting me, his tongue slipping against mine as I taste him, melting into each other.

His feet stagger forward, one slipping between mine until our chests are flush. The moan he lets out vibrates through me down to my toes. His cock brushes against my thigh, sending tingles down to mine, seeing if it will wake up. I don't even need it to. I could lie him down on the floor right here and happily spend hours putting my mouth all over him. But that's not what this is about. It's not what I want it to be about. I want to be more than that for him. He needs more than that, deserves more than that.

Squeezing his arm, I ease back, suppressing a groan at his half-lidded eyes and reddened lips. "You'd better go home," I caution softly, trying to get my breathing under control.

The haze in his eyes clears, and his hands fall away from me. Taking a step back, his hands go immediately into the pockets of his jeans. "I guess it's still not difficult for you to stop."

It takes me a second to decipher his words as I stare at the new red splotches on his face. Oh, hell.

Reaching out, I snag his arm before he can inch further away. "You'd better go home," I repeat tenderly, "so I can dream about kissing you when you get back."

The tension in his shoulders and expression drains, traded for a radiant smile that has me rethinking the romantic, gentlemanly shit I just said. Monday is *way* too far away.

"Do you have a game to cover Monday night?" he asks.

"No."

"How about we meet after I get off work instead of in the morning? I can return the dinner favor."

Dinner wasn't a favor. He came to my house to check on me and gave me a rubdown. He's killing me. But dinner with Remy sounds like longer than an hour in the morning. I'm down for any arrangement that gives me more time with him.

"Sure."

"Great," he enthuses as I walk him to the door.

Gale prances along beside us and stops at the door like she wants to go with him. I know exactly how she feels. He gives her a scratch behind her ears and then glances around like he isn't sure what to say either.

"Um, do you want me to come over here or…"

What he said that night outside the Westin might have been meta-phorical, but I want to give him what he asked for. "No. I'll be at your front door."

The way his lips part and his eyes go glassy ignites a flame of hope in my chest. Maybe I won't fuck this up. Maybe it's actually really happening.

I open the door before my luck runs out, and then I plant a quick peck on his cheek because I can't help myself. Is that something almost forty-year-old men do?

"Goodnight," he murmurs.

Holding Gale's collar so she won't cause any chaos, I watch him make his way down my steps. I hate that he'll be out of our zip code for five whole days. Anything could happen. A kid like I was could be on the road, thinking they're coherent and invincible. He could meet a charm-ing man who's ten times more worthy of him than I am. The possibilities are terrifying. I just found him. I don't want to lose him again. Does he know how important it is that he comes back?

I need the universe to return him to me so I have more time to get things right. More time to let him know that—

"Remy?"

Already halfway down the path from my door, he stops, turning back. "Yeah?"

I smile sadly, wondering if he can see my heart on my sleeve from there. "Lock your windows."

The look he gives me isn't the one he used to give me in college. It's a thousand times better. He'll come home. *To me.*

CHRIS

chapter 16

Goldilocks must have had as much spinal stenosis and arthritis as I do. That's the most logical explanation of why she tried out all those beds. Sitting around on my parents' couch for most of the weekend without my heating pad, stuffing my face, and skipping my new stretching regimen were just the tip of the iceberg for today's flare-up. It took sheer will fueled by visions of Remy's excited face to power through the surprise I worked on at his house today while he was at work, but it was worth it. At least, I hope it was. If I could get my ass moving a little faster and get over there, I'll find out.

I've stood under the hot spray of my shower for as long as my water heater allows. Getting out, I grunt while I towel myself off and slip on a change of clothes. I feel like I survived a paintball match, but instead of paintballs, my opponent used shot put balls. Hurricane Fuck My Life is still lingering in the Gulf, not helping matters.

Leaning against my bathroom counter, I tilt my head down and stretch, remembering how Remy said to breathe. *Move, Chris*, I shout at myself, eager to see his face again.

Tapping the screen of my phone to check the time, I cringe. He's probably been home from work for almost an hour now. I am not missing dinner with Remy because I'm an idiot who can't manage his pain.

My notifications show a text from an unknown number. It's probably one of the usual Medicare supplier advertisements that don't know what STOP means.

Is this Chris?

Ominous. It's a San Antonio area code.

Who is this?

Typing bubbles appear, giving me a start, knowing I'm suddenly communicating with a stranger on the other end in real time. Turning off the bathroom light, I lumber over to the back of my couch, where I left a clean pair of socks, and wait.

It's Remy. We didn't trade numbers, but then I realized I still had yours saved from years ago and took a chance.

The smile I get probably takes up my entire face. He still had my number after all these years? I've had half a dozen new phones since then and deleted nearly every contact from my old life in my bitterness at one point, a few months after my second surgery. I wasn't lying when I told him no one called.

Maybe he really did call back then. A vague memory of Dad looking guilty, returning my phone when I was out of the woods, crosses my mind. I'd seen him on it a few times, answering calls from the League on my behalf. I remember wondering if he'd seen any of my old messages from Remy. He'd acted kind of strange this weekend when I mentioned I'd started working out with an '*old friend*' from college. Remy's more than an old friend—hopefully—and I don't care what Vince Mightener will think about that.

Yeah, sorry. Hurting a bit today, running late. Wonderful weather.

I hope that's not too self-pitying. It's just the facts, and he hasn't shied away yet.

REMY: How about you stay put and I come to you? Dinner's almost ready. I can bring it with me. We can take the evening off.

That sounds like hanging out without using exercise as an excuse. I find myself grinning over more than not having to torture my body tonight.

As long as you're prepared for a very boring evening in.

REMY: Boring is my favorite.

Half an hour later, I'm in the kitchen, leaning on my counter with my eyes closed, begging my misery to subside a little so I can be good company for Remy. I don't want to wait in my recliner and have to crawl out of it to get to the door. Gale alerts me to his arrival a few seconds before I hear him knock on the door.

"Hi." He says it so adorably, but it's the warmth in his eyes that does me in.

"Hi."

"So, someone saved me from being the laughingstock of the neighborhood and installed a beautiful walking path to my door while I was at work. Any ideas on who that could have been?"

"I might know a guy."

Beaming, he shifts in place, the foil on the pan he's holding crinkling. "I love the sun mosaic."

"Well, I owed you a coffee mug." I shrug, slightly uncomfortable under the praise, like he'll know I went with that design because he reminds me of sunshine.

"Thank you. It's incredible, but I hope that's not why you're hurting today."

No comment. It was totally worth it. Stepping aside to let him in, I shoo Gale to keep her from prancing around his feet, which proves difficult since he has food. I offer to take the warm pan from his hands. When I do, he leans up and plants a quick peck on my cheek.

I can't believe he's really here again, and not for therapy. That little kiss means more to me than he knows. It's difficult to believe that I may actually have a chance. He must notice me blinking in disbelief, because his cheeks go pink and he shrugs.

"I was thinking about how much I wanted to kiss you."

After stealing my line from last week, he turns to head into the kitchen, but I reach out and snag the back of his jacket, the droplets of rain on it wetting my fingers. Half-tugging him back, half-stepping forward, I bend and press a soft kiss to his lips.

"Me too."

The smile he gives me makes me less anxious about leaving it chaste. I'm in no condition for heated kisses tonight. Even if I took one of those little wonder pills that the doctor gave me, I don't think my face would be able to hide my pain. The worried glances he shoots at me as we set the table and eat the roasted chicken and potatoes he made are proof of that. I do my best to swallow grunts of pain behind bites of his delicious cooking, hoping they sound like moans of appreciation.

I listen to him talk about his visit with his family. He doesn't mention meeting any charismatic men with full-body function on his trip, which makes me gloat even more over that kiss. I tell him about how my energetic nephews played football in the backyard, and about the camper my sister Alice and her husband just bought.

We clear the dishes, and he grabs a towel like he's intent on drying them again. I'm not in the mood to stand at the sink and wash them, but I don't have the heart to tell him that. Plus, he's still here, so I power through, shifting my weight when I think he's not looking.

"You look like you could use another rubdown," he says casually at one point.

I would cry in gratitude if he gave me another one, but hate that it means I'm not concealing shit. I really wanted him to see me as a whole man tonight after our time apart, but apparently that's not going to happen.

"Thank you, but it's all right. I can handle it."

Drying his hands, he walks back to the table where his jacket is slung over the back of it. My heart sinks. It's barely been an hour. I thought I'd get more time with him.

He doesn't put it on, though. I hear a rustling sound as he digs into the inside pocket and glances back at me sheepishly.

"Well…I brought you a present."

He went from offering a rubdown to announcing a gift. There must still be some sexually repressed jock hormones in me because I'm instantly intrigued about this present. Wetting my lips, I raise one of my eyebrows in question.

"Get your mind out of the gutter." He snickers.

"What?" I laugh when I know I don't look innocent at all. "I didn't say anything."

"No, but you were thinking something. What was it?"

"Flavored massage oil?"

Laughing, he reveals a flat brown lunch sack type of bag and walks toward me, wriggling his eyebrows. "Maybe better than that."

"What could be better than that?" I mumble under my breath, kind of lost in the idea of him massaging my body with his mouth now.

Smiling, he reaches inside the sack and pulls out a tiny cellophane baggie. Four different colored gummy bears pressed against the plastic stare back at me with their eyeless faces. I'm confused about this present for a second until I see the label on it. *CBD*.

"So, I know opioids are a big no for you, and you don't want anti-inflammatories. But since you said your doctor told you that it would be okay for you to try CBD, I thought…" He frowns, looking at me warily. "Shit. I don't want to enable you. Maybe I shouldn't have brought them. When Jamie came to stay, he left these," he says, starting to do his anxious rambling thing, "probably on purpose, since he's always saying I need to loosen up. I did some research on them at work and asked the sports medicine doctor about using them for pain management if someone had…." I can tell he's trying to avoid the word *'addiction,'* and I take pity on him.

"It's fine. I honestly don't have the urge anymore. I've learned my lesson. I just go to Mahoney's now and then when I've gone without sleep after a long flare-up, but I haven't been there since that night I saw you and Jamie."

"You haven't?" he asks, sounding proud.

"Somebody showed me a better way to manage my pain."

He smiles, looking humbled, and then glances at the baggie in his hand. "Um…I am sorry, though. I just wanted to offer you another option to try since you said you were having extra pain today, and I don't think the rain is going to let up anytime soon. I…hate the idea of you hurting so much."

Being a recovering addict makes you put up barriers and just say *no* to everything for so long that sometimes you don't stop to question if saying no always makes sense. I read a book about Johnny Cash once where he was quoted as saying, *'One was too many, and a thousand was never enough.'* That mantra has kept me away from hard painkillers for over a decade, but if I could manage to control my liquid medicating for as long as I had, maybe a gummy bear won't kick my ass. They were doctor-approved by a physician who knows my history, so, worst-case scenario, I can tell him he was wrong. Also, it would be nice not to grimace my way through the evening while Remy is here after his first day back from his trip.

Reaching out, I snatch the baggie from his fingers and open it up. The confusion on his face is laughable, as though he's worried he just gave me a ticking bomb.

"How about half of one?" I suggest, starting toward my living room. Not standing while possibly falling down a rabbit hole sounds like a wise plan, even though I don't think these things are supposed to be like smoking marijuana. "But only if you stay with me and take the other half," I amend when I hear Remy following behind me.

"But…I don't have any pain."

Smirking, I'm glad he can't see my face. He's not the first person to offer me gummies. Alice and her husband told me about how they do them once a year when the boys go see his parents during the summer. The stories they've told me had me cracking up. I'm pretty sure I'm the enabler here, because I turn around and dig one of my knuckles in between two of Remy's ribs at his side. He yelps, jumping back in surprise.

"Hm," I hum. "That sounded like it hurt."

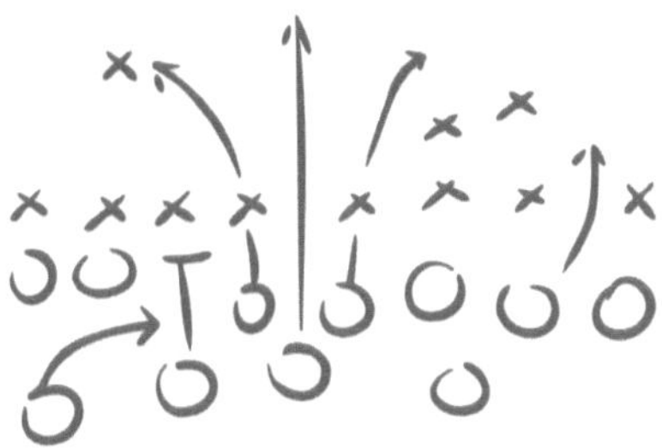

Two hours later

Moving my heating pad to the couch so I could be closer to Remy was a smart idea. The addition of his body heat being so close by adds another level of serenity to the effects of the gummy bear. Sagging, he ended up with his head on my shoulder at some point. I can feel every vibration from him munching on his snack, connecting us at the moment as we stare mindlessly at my television.

"Would it be wrong if we DoorDash more Rice Krispies Treats?" he asks around a mouthful, still holding the box in his lap that we had delivered earlier. There's a pile of wrappers on the couch between our thighs like a giant heap of blue confetti. My gaze flicks to his chip-munked cheeks as he chews, eyelids half-drooped. "Asking for Gale?" he adds lazily.

Gale is sound asleep on the other side of him with her head on his leg. Whatever he just said, I'm sure it made sense, so I grab my phone off the end table, but decide I'm too tired to deal with it.

"No, but you do it. I can't type right now." I hold my phone out to him, and he finally grabs it after missing my hand a few times. Reaching into the box, I find one remaining treat.

Damn. We ploughed through these things.

On my TV, I watch a man who's been possessed by his psychotic abuelo's dead spirit. I can't tear my eyes away.

"How have I never watched this?"

"It's fucking bananas," Remy mumbles around a mouthful, pointing at the TV. "And then as soon as there are bananas, there are even more bananas."

I really want to know what happens next, but while that little bear didn't knock out all my pain, it sure as hell mellowed me out enough that it made it easier not to think about it. I let out a yawn and fight to keep my eyes open.

"You can fall asleep. It's okay," Remy assures me, like this isn't my house. He's really fucking cute when he's *stoned*. "I have the box set, and I have it saved on my stream list."

There is no way I want him to go home like this. Those things can take between three and five hours to wear off. Considering I'm almost twice his size in mass, I don't see him coming back to the land of blushing when he says silly shit any time soon. Not that I mind.

"I have a TV in my room," I suggest.

"I know. I *love* TV."

I snort, watching his thousand-yard stare as he shoves another bite of marshmallow-y goodness into his mouth. Yeah. Gummies were definitely a good idea. For Remy, at least. I don't know that they did much for me, but that's probably a good thing. They took the edge off a bit and certainly provided me with some interesting entertainment.

"You should come to my room," I clarify, feeling the slow scrape of my eyelids over my eyes.

His jaw stops moving, and his hand freezes in mid-air. Funny how *that* registered quickly. He turns his head, and I swear he's looking right at my mouth.

"Okay."

With that, he hops up, wrappers toppling to the floor, and does a one-eighty. I gape, watching him round the couch and then tromp straight to my room. Well, not exactly straight—his movements are more animated than usual, taking him on a bit of a zigzag route.

Oh, my gosh. No more gummies for Remy, ever.

Chuckling, I peel myself off the couch and yawn again, suddenly aware of how exhausted each of my appendages feels. Holy shit. Maybe I *was* taken down by a tiny little gummy bear.

I turn off the living room TV and head to my room. Remy drops his pants, kicks them off like an angry toddler, and then pulls back my comforter. I'm not even sure if he knows I'm standing in the doorway trying not to laugh. For all the times I thought about having sex with him, I can't believe I'm thinking this right now—I hope to hell gummy bears don't make people horny, because I'm way too damn tired.

Gale hops up on the bed and looks at him like she's asking for approval. He pats the top of the comforter next to him. "Come here, girl."

I watch in awe. She finds a spot, plopping down right next to him. What a traitor.

Flipping on my TV, I manage to bring up the Vampire Diaries where we left off and slide in under the covers next to him. I situate one of my many pillows under my knees just the way I like it while Remy stares at the TV in a trance, idly petting Gale. I can't believe we're in a bed, not having sex, and how natural that feels. I really like it.

Reaching over, I find his hand and rub my thumb over it, just wanting to be connected somehow. I want to thank him for being him and being here, doing nothing. Doing nothing with him turned out to not be boring at all.

His hand slips out from under mine, though. I wonder if I've made a misstep, but he rolls, and the next thing I know, he flings his arm across my chest. Nestled close to my side, he rests his head on my shoulder and makes a contented noise.

Some of his non-gummy-bear brain cells must catch up as I lie here stunned, because he asks, "This okay?"

It's muffled, his mouth squished against the front of my shoulder. The irony of how we've somehow gone from pawing at each other with very few words back in the day to asking permission for the slightest of touches is not lost on me. I don't know if it was the gummy, but despite the dull ache in my bones, I feel more at peace than I have been in a long time. Maybe we both just needed to grow up a little.

Sliding my arm underneath him, I wrap it around the back of his shoulders and pull him closer. "Yeah. Very okay."

I'm in a bed. With Chris. And he's sleeping.

I'm in *Chris'* bed, and we didn't have sex. I love how good that feels.

He's on his side, facing me, a slow, even stream of breath hitting his pillow. I got back from Kansas Sunday night and could barely get to sleep, knowing I'd get to see him in less than twenty-four hours. Coming home from work to find the old, cracked pavers removed from my front yard and replaced by a meticulously pea-gravel-lined path of his mosaic stones made me want to sprint across town the second I saw it. How is this my life?

Hair mussed, a flake of baked rice stuck to the bottom of his lower lip for some reason, he couldn't look more endearing at the moment. Reaching out, I brush it off his face, and he stirs.

Blinking, his blown pupils locate me. He jerks his head up.

"Huh? Remy?" he grunts groggily. Gaze darting around the room as though he's checking for threats, he exhales and drops his head back to his pillow with a smile. "What time is it?"

"Like…four in the morning."

"Oh, my God," he groans, scrubbing a hand down his face. "I've never slept that long."

"Yeah, I think that's the last gummy bear I'll ever eat."

Reaching over, he runs the backs of his knuckles across my jaw. "You okay?"

"Yeah." I chuckle, flattered that he's concerned about my first time doing something so foolish. "Are you? Is the pain any better? I think it finally stopped raining."

"Yeah, a little bit."

He canvases the lump that I am under his covers, his smile growing. "This is a change."

"What?"

"*You* in *my* bed."

"I think Gale is mad at me. She snorted and walked out."

"She's a diva about her beauty sleep. She'll get used to it."

His mouth drops open while a flutter tickles my chest over the permanence he insinuated. He has nothing to be embarrassed about, though. I'm ready for permanence.

Being here and how our time together has progressed to shy kisses feels…natural. For once, I don't have the nagging worry that I'm jumping into something because it seems comfortable or expected. Leaning half over him, I cup his cheek and press my lips to his.

His stubble is soft against my palm, his body going pliant beneath me where our chests are touching. I don't understand how anyone ever could have seen him as an emotionless, iron bulldozer, even when he was playing ball. The way his hand slips onto my waist, kneading my skin, is hungry but gentle.

I taste and taste, rediscovering his mouth. His tongue tangles gently with mine, saturating my taste buds with his flavor. His gasps and the needy vocals he lets out pull me under with each drag of his lips over mine. I feel like I've come home even though I just left there. The pads of his fingertips graze my side where my shirt has ridden up, and just that skin-to-skin touch washes my body in gooseflesh. I need air, but that would require me to stop kissing him. Air is overrated right now.

"I missed you," I confess, sliding my hand under his shirt, smoothing my palm over his warm skin.

"You have no idea," he rasps, moving his mouth to my neck.

His lips drag kisses over the base of my throat, stopping to suck on the spot just below my Adam's apple. A wisp of static zings down to my toes, and I moan. Whatever he just did, I can't get close enough to him now, or maybe it's from knowing how much he missed me, too.

I drag the inside of my knee up to his hip, not caring what an invitation that must look like. I think we've both signed up for the same party, judging by the way his hand grips my ass and squeezes. Sliding my hand up his back, I can feel the puckered lines of his scars. I should have asked him if he was okay. I pull back to do so, but stop myself, seeing the hunger in his eyes. He lives with this every single day. While it's kind to be thoughtful, I don't think anyone would want to be reminded of that in the throes of passion. So, instead, I tug his shirt up, silently letting him know I like looking at him, no matter how his body has changed.

He raises his arms and takes over, so I wrestle my shirt off. When we embrace again, our appreciative sounds collide just before our mouths crash into each other's.

Nothing is enough, and yet every touch is more profound than any other I've ever felt. The path his fingertips make across my skin, his hot breath against my face, next to my ear, and the rise and fall of his stomach against mine. When I reach for the button of his jeans, I remember I'm at a disadvantage. Dear Lord, did I really crawl into his bed last night in just my underwear?

Those calloused hands that made the most breathtaking sun mosaic as the centerpiece of my new walk-up slip under the elastic waistband. A fingertip traces the vein on the underside of my cock all the way up to the tip. My hand forgets how to unfasten a button, and my lungs forget how to work when that fingertip draws the glossy fluid I'm leaking over the dome of my cockhead. You'd think I've never been touched before by the high-pitched sound I make, my eyes pinching shut. I'm starting to think I haven't. It's not really a touch unless it's by Chris. My body still lives only for this man.

"Remy," he rumbles reverently, rubbing his thigh against my balls and wrapping his hand around me.

I bury my next noise against his lips and fumble between us, finally getting the snap on his jeans undone. Before I can capture his zipper, he rolls us. And then he's gone, out of reach for me to reciprocate, kissing a trail of hot, wet kisses down my torso and kneading my thigh. I work the muscles in his shoulders, wanting to give back something pleasing in return as his stubble tickles the sensitive skin just above my underwear. Glancing down past my heaving chest, the look of focus on his face has my cock jerking under the damp fabric of my underwear. He hooks his fingers under the elastic again and tugs them down, not even bothering to slide them all the way off. I have the foresight to blurt out that I'm on PrEP, to which he smiles and informs me that he's clear, making me know this really is probably about to happen. His mouth is back on me a second later, meticulously lavishing every inch of skin on the insides of my thighs.

"Chris," I rasp, my stomach muscles quivering.

His hot breath moves to my cock. I'm stone-still, remembering how very few times I saw his face down there in college. He'd give me a few teasing licks or capture my tip with curiosity and wonder in his expressions that told me it was foreign to him. I think he wasn't just not out, but even less experienced than I was. We were each other's education in some ways, and usually in too much of a hurry for more foreplay than grasping me in his fist or my teasing him with *my* mouth.

So, when his tongue traces a slow path up my length and he presses a kiss to the tip of my cock, I nearly choke seeing him engulf me in his mouth next. His eyes slip closed, and he groans. The vibrations hum through my groin. The drag of the undersides of his lips up my sensitive skin sends a shudder through me. He stops to lap and kiss my glans. It's the torturous edging he used to do with words, but this time with actions. Mature, humble, more patient Chris is going to make me lose my mind.

When I slide my fingers into his hair, he moans and shifts his head into the touch, taking me back in. All the while, his fingertips lightly trace the V of my hip juncture, down to the inside of my thigh, and back. I'm being adored, and I don't know how much more of it I can take. Widening my legs, I fist the comforter with my toes, trying to fight the urge to thrust my hips.

"Chris…please."

I don't even know what I'm begging for. For him to finish? For him to stop so I can get my mouth on him that much sooner?

He doesn't take much pity on me. While his mouth tightens and his tongue continues to dance around me on every upstroke, his pace stays the same, as if to say, *'Enjoy it. We have all the time in the world.'*

But we don't. We've already missed fifteen years, and I suddenly want to catch up immediately. I want to touch him, too, like it will subliminally transfer the new feelings I have as well as reinforce the old ones.

His hand fists the base of my cock, tightening the pressure that's built inside of me. Lips stretched and shiny with his slobber, he makes another tight draw with his mouth in time with the movement of his hand. I'm done for, and I try to warn him by tugging on his hair. He stays put, picking up the pace with determination. That alone is so fucking sexy, I have to fight to keep my eyes open to watch as I come. He makes little moans and half-growls, feeding on all the pent-up tension that drains from my body down his throat. It's nothing short of devouring.

He pulls off and presses a few kisses to my waning cock while I twitch and reach for him mindlessly, willing my pulse to get under control.

"Come here," I beg.

His puffy mouth is a hundred percent more kissable than before, but I manage to roll into him enough that he flops onto his back beside me. Moving to his neck, I press a quick kiss there, too eager to hear him moaning from my mouth around him for the first time in years to linger any longer.

"That was definitely one way to make me feel not awkward about falling asleep in your bed."

He chuckles and rubs my shoulders. My waistband is still down around my knees, so I tug it up to let me move and then proceed to scoot further down the bed. I reach for his fly, eager to pick up where I left off. My fingers graze over the denim. Feeling the outline of his cock, I can tell he's not even half hard. Did he not enjoy giving? Because it really seemed like he did.

His hand clasps around my wrist, gently drawing it away. I look up at him, confusion probably written all over my face. He tugs me back up to him and kisses me, soft and slow, spreading more of that satiated warmth I'm still living on through me. When he draws back, still holding my wrist like he's afraid to release it, though, he must see the uncertainty in my eyes. I don't understand the guilt on his face.

"It, uh, doesn't always work, especially when I'm in pain." He releases my wrist and rubs my arm soothingly. "Sorry."

Oh, shit. Shit. I hadn't even considered that. I deal with nerve damage all day at work, and yet I let the heat of the moment lead me off a cliff of anticipation. Shifting, I lie down next to him, wishing the stroke of my hand against his cheek could wipe away the shame he's trying to hold back.

"Why are you sorry?"

"Yeah, I guess you got out of a blow job. So, nothing to be sorry for," he jokes.

"I wasn't going to just to reciprocate. I was looking forward to it, but don't think I mind. And just for the record, please don't think you need to do that if you don't like it."

"Hey, my mouth has lots of plans for that cock," he assures me, cupping my face and giving me a kiss. "It still turns me on to touch you, even if my dick doesn't show it all the time."

"Well, you certainly showed it."

"I am sorry, though." His thumb traces the edge of my chin where he fixes his gaze. "I should have warned you. About my problem."

I hate that he might be avoiding looking at me, so I dip my head. "Chris, I just forgot my own name. Please stop apologizing."

He searches my eyes, looking so vulnerable it breaks something in my heart, but then he smirks. "Well, you seemed to remember mine, so I guess I can live with that."

And there's the other side of Chris that's had my soul signing itself over to him recently. I press my lips to his, holding them there. It's a thank you to life and to him for giving us this second chance. He smiles at me so tenderly that I want to call off work and lie here with him all day. However, I imagine bringing over a controlled substance, stripping down to my underwear, and falling asleep in his bed were enough for one day.

Sighing, I lay my head on his chest, wanting to laugh at myself. He watched The Vampire Diaries with me. I may have missed a few things in the past twelve hours, but not that. My soul seals the envelope and silently delivers it to him in companionable silence. Smiling, I trace circles above his nipple.

"So, I noticed I lost my pants… Fucking gummy bears, huh?"

The laugh that rumbles underneath my ear tells me that I've recalled all I really need to know about the evening. Chris is happy. I'm happy, and we're happy together.

CHRIS
chapter 18

The sky is clear, and the temperature has cooled to a comfortable sixty degrees as we stretch in Remy's front yard. It's been nearly a week since Thanksgiving break ended, and it's hands down the best week I've had in years. Remy and I spent each afternoon exercising, cooking dinner, and then either making out or cuddling on each other's couches, talking and laughing late into the evening.

Today, we graduated from his backyard because he says he enjoys looking at his new walk up. Me, I just enjoy looking at him. And listening. Each day he talks about his time at the center, I'm left with a sense of solidarity with his patients. I've learned plenty about experiencing setbacks and having to accept a new normal. A billow of empathy rolls through me when he laments about their frustrations. Yet, I'm likewise filled with gratitude knowing that Remy is the one there to help them. I've noticed he often downplays himself. It makes me think he has no clue how compassionate he is. You can see it in his expression when he talks about what the patients are going through and his genuine hope to get them back to full functionality. He's an inspiration, even if he doesn't see it. When you're around someone inspiring, it must make you want to try harder.

"So…there's this thing the college asked me to come speak at before Christmas break," I hedge when it looks like he doesn't have more to say.

"What kind of thing?"

"Do you remember those safety briefings they used to do before we all went on Spring or Christmas break?"

"Yeah." He laughs. "Jamie always complained that I made him come with me when I had a professor who was giving extra credit points for attendance at them."

"Well, I only went to one during freshman year, which means it was probably stupid of me to agree to do it." His nose scrunches up adorably as he shields his eyes from the sun. "They asked me to talk about my *'struggles.'* Basically, I got the impression they were hoping I'd be an example of why driving while intoxicated is a bad idea."

"Oh." He straightens up, his face full of apprehension. "And…you said you'd do it?"

When I nod, his expression goes even more grim. "Are you… How do you feel about that? Have you ever talked about it before?"

He snaps his mouth shut and chews on the inside of his lip, making me want to chuckle. It's another *Remy*-ism I'm fond of, something he does when he catches himself shooting off questions or information rapid fire.

"How do I *feel?*" Blowing out a breath, I stuff my hands into the pockets of my hoodie and give it some thought. "Scared shitless? Mortified? On a scale of one to ten, one being showing up with bells on and ten being to unsend my email response, mostly I've been at an eleven."

Cringing, he adds delicately, "What's an eleven?"

"Throwing my phone in a dumpster, blowing it up so it's not traceable, and joining the Witness Protection Program to get a new identity."

"Hey, I wouldn't be able to call you!" He chuckles.

I groan, scrubbing my face with my hands even as I join in, albeit morosely. "Don't worry. I'd send you smoke signals or a picture of me with my new fake mustache so you could find me."

I feel hands on my wrists, tugging them down from my face.

"Hey," he says softly, releasing my hands to tug on the front of my sweatshirt. "You don't have to do anything you're not comfortable doing. You know that, right?"

I do. The thing is…I want to. I've spent years doing nothing. I want to do one damn thing in my life that's good. I just don't know if I can.

Shaking my head, I press a kiss to his forehead and wrap my arms around him. "No. I need to. Maybe I can say something that will make at least one student stop and think about making a bad decision. Even if it's only one kid, it'd be worth it. Just…if you're free that day…I was wondering if you wouldn't mind coming."

"I'll be free."

I squeeze him tighter for the solemnity. It might make it difficult having him there, seeing me so raw, but that's the thing I'm starting to realize about my attraction to Remy. As much as I have a desire to protect and be strong for him, it's also comforting to know I can be vulnerable with him. I bury my face in his hair, breathing in his scent.

"Thank you."

"I've got you, Chris."

That's enough vulnerability for one day. I bend my head, loving how he seems to anticipate my need to have his lips against mine. It's sweet and slow at first, but when his mouth parts and I get a taste of him, I'm helpless for more. He's more addictive than Rice Krispies Treats. He lets out a soft moan, gripping my back and leaning into me. Holding and kissing Remy is like falling into a bed of down pillows, pulling me down into weightlessness. I slip my hand under his shirt. His warm skin under my palm grounds me and sends delightful tingles to my cock. He pulls back, panting, looking pleasantly loved up.

"Come on. Let's go for our walk before I get other ideas."

Groaning for effect, I bury my face in the side of his neck and press another kiss there. It occurs to me we're making out on his front lawn for all the neighborhood to see. That's a first for me. I really like hoping someone will see, so they know it means he's taken. That's a valid enough excuse to stay buried in his neck a little longer, right?

"Hey," he laughs, pulling back. "You *told me* to make you walk today."

I did tell him that. Since I've stopped doubling down, I've been feeling much better. Slow and steady wins the race, I guess. Judging by the mirth in his eyes, I think he knows the put-out expression on my face means I value kissing him more than exercising.

"Go on. You start and set the pace."

Walking needs a pace? That's comical. Stepping backward, I give him a taunt for having his priorities all screwed up. "Admit it. You just want to see how my big ass jiggles now."

"It jiggles?"

I think all asses are meant to jiggle, even though I suspect mine has firmed up a bit. Turning around, I exaggerate my steps, however, to reward the intrigue in his eyes.

"Yup, get a good look," I call over my shoulder. "This is what thirty-seven looks like—having a boyfriend with a fat, jiggly ass."

I shift my hips and tromp a few more steps until I realize what just came out of my mouth. Shit. Oh, shit.

First, I asked him to be my emotional support person at an event I willingly signed up for, and now I just dropped the *B-word*. If he hasn't taken up jogging again—in the opposite direction—I don't know what else would do it.

Peering back, it's not the verdict I expected. The way he's beaming at me and the wistful look in his eyes have just become the greatest gift I've ever received in my life. He walks toward me, schooling his features, gaze fixed on the sidewalk. The next thing I know, his hand slips into mine.

"I can't wait to see what thirty-eight looks like," he murmurs, starting us down the sidewalk, hand in hand.

That's a pace I can get fully on board with. I think I have my first boyfriend. Thirty-seven is starting to look pretty good.

REMY

chapter 19

I picture Jamie trying to peel a homemade face mask off his face, listening to him curse as it plucks out stubble and eyebrow hairs. I guess he won't be leaving glue lying around his house after this. How cute would Chris look with green paste smeared all over his face and cucumber slices on his eyes, though? Honestly, we should do a facial night sometime. I'll try anything that helps him relax better and keep his mind off his pain.

"Are you even listening to me?" Jamie's impatient tone comes over the line.

Crawling into bed alone, I turn out my bedside lamp. It's Monday. That means an entire week of falling asleep alone, I gather, since Chris and I just did the sleepover thing on the weekend again. I don't want to look too clingy, being that he only mentioned '*boyfriend*' the other day.

"Hello?" Jamie calls.

Shit. What was he saying? I don't think I can listen to him grumbling about his nephews' latest shenanigans for much longer. I can think of one thing that might distract him long enough to put him out of his misery.

"Chris and I are dating," I throw out casually.

"Oh my God. You *did* have sex with him. I knew it!"

"Not that it's any of your business, but no, I didn't."

"I smell lies."

"You smell glue, and it's gone to your head."

He snorts and makes another wincing sound. "Probably. Well, that's…weird, and don't even get me started on dating, but at least I'm not the only one not getting any."

Before he can go any more '*Jamie*' on me, I think another change in subject is in order. "Why don't you come visit for Christmas, unless you have a mani-pedi day planned with your nephews?"

"Ha-fucking-ha."

Snickering, I nestle deeper under my covers. "My parents are going to a ski resort, but I've grown so acclimated to snowless winters, I think I'm going to pass on joining them. You could come hang with me and,"—plucking at my blanket, a smile creeps over my face even as it feels strange to imagine—"we could have dinner here with Chris one night while you're in town."

"Well, as much as I'd love to be the third wheel to you and the mountain with a penis, I can't. I have a girlfriend, and she wants me all to herself for the holidays."

"What?" I laugh because there has to be some dry Jamie joke in there somewhere. I'd sooner believe he fell in love with cats than that he was suddenly bisexual.

"Yup. Your bachelor bestie is officially taken. Janessa is now the proud, happy owner of all this sex appeal."

And there's the joke. I snort, wondering why he wasted thirty seconds of my life on that BS story. But hey, at least he's not bitching about Chris.

"Uh, I've met Janessa. She can absolutely live without you, and so can all the heterosexual men she dates."

He proceeds to tell me about how he's going to pretend to be her boyfriend for her family's Christmas up in Montana. Ironically, he sounds excited about the prospect because it will mean he won't have to watch his house get destroyed by his nephews while they're on their holiday break from school.

"Let me get this straight…"

"Exactly," he quips.

"*You* can have a *fake* girlfriend that you don't have sex with, but I can't have a real boyfriend I don't have sex with?"

"I didn't say can't. You are a free agent to tangle whatever intricate web you want to weave. I'm not saying a word this time. I'm prepping for vacation mode to recharge and leaving all bad juju behind me. Cowboy country and peace of mind, here I come."

Wow, that's a first. "Well, good luck with that."

He knows it gets really cold there, right? A hundred bucks says Janessa finds him frozen like a popsicle on day one.

"Thank you for the enthusiasm. Good luck to you, too."

I don't know why I'm frowning. Given that he knows the entire history of my love life, he probably isn't taking me seriously or assumes we're doomed to fail.

"I'm in love with him, Jay," I blurt even as a rush of anxiety and joy closes up my windpipe. It feels good to say out loud. "Really in love with him. Like, I mean, I finally feel like I know what love is. It's... I can't even explain it."

Silence follows. I don't even hear signs of movement or the hiss of pain on his end, as though he's stopped messing with his glue mask.

"Ugh...I'm going to have to be nice to him now, aren't I?"

That sounds so much like acceptance from my biggest protector and anti-Chris advocate that I beam uncontrollably. "No," I offer gently, "He doesn't believe in miracles."

"Hallelujah."

"Well, I'm going to sleep. Call or text me before you cowboy up, okay?"

"Yeehaw, Romeo."

Staring at my phone when the screen goes dark, I let my declaration swaddle me, basking in the truth of it. My vigilance taunts me with quiet questions, though. Is it too soon? Is it too late, considering the years that have passed? They all seem laughable, and I discard them as quickly as they pop up. I'm in love, plain and simple. It's apparently the exact right time to be because I have no concerns.

Setting my phone on my nightstand, I stare at it, knowing that's not entirely true. The concern I have is for Chris. I spent an hour researching erectile dysfunction before Jamie called, cursing his face mask off. My concern isn't that Chris has it. What worries me is that he might think it bothers me. I'm not complaining about the number of blowjobs he's given me in the past week and a half, but I think I'd prefer to get him over his fear of letting me anywhere near his dick. I don't care what state it's in. I mean, sometimes, you'd like to graze your fingers lovingly over your man's upper thigh, but so far, it's been a caution zone for him. He, however, seems determined to give me as many orgasms as he can. He went from being a slightly selfish lover when we were in college to being an overzealous man on a mission.

From what I read, the all-knowing internet said to focus on non-sexual intimacy to make your partner feel wanted. I can totally get on board with that and think it's what I've been doing. I don't need sex to feel desired and appreciated. I can see it each time he looks at me. Holding hands, hugging, and kissing do it for me now more than they ever have in my life. I just wish Chris would realize I don't need my eyes to roll back in my head multiple times a week to enjoy his company.

Ugh. Why does it always come back to sex with me and Chris? Rolling over, I pull my blanket tighter around me and close my eyes. Maybe it's because this time everything matters.

CHRIS

chapter 20

Kinnion's arm snaps forward, letting the ball fly a second before the Cougars' center lineman breaks through and takes him down. Clenching my fists, I suck in a breath and rise to my feet, loving the vantage point in our seats at the fifty-yard line. Fifteen, eighteen, twenty!

"Fuck yeah!" I punch the air. "Twenty yards," I exclaim, easing back down and beaming at Remy.

He gives me an adoring grin like he cares more about seeing me looking pumped than that we're at a game with great seats. I don't regret my decision to skip the press box this time after Remy asked if he could see a game with me.

Reaching over, I give his knee a squeeze, feeling compelled to explain my zeal. "He's been out with a knee injury for a few weeks. It's his first game back, and he's on fire."

"I know," he says knowingly, shooting me a wink.

I don't think he does it to concur with my assessment of the QB's playing tonight. He never tells me names or any personal details about his patients, but I think that wink was just an exception to share some insider information with his boyfriend. At least, I've been living off the high of believing we are ever since he held my hand on our walk last week and didn't correct my word vomit.

If he's not my boyfriend, there will be some awkward questions the next time I talk to my sister. I may have gushed to Alice about not being single for the first time in my adult life. Hearing how happy she was for me made me feel foolish for ever wondering how she'd accept my sexuality. For years, I was happy to live with the suspicion that she always knew, but never pressed me like I owed the world a confession.

The Cougars make a brutal tackle of the Panthers' wide receiver, bringing a collective reaction of horror from the home team section. Rubbing Remy's knee idly, I feel him lean in close to my ear to speak over the noise in the stadium.

"We're going to have to go to a gladiator competition on our next date to compete with this."

I think my heart just stopped. When I look over, he's seemingly oblivious to the palpitations his wonderful words caused, stuffing one end of his hot dog into his mouth. Have I been overthinking things? I guess this is pretty much a date. Two guys who kiss each other, enjoying a public outing.

"You just want to see a bunch of men parade around in pteruges. Admit it," I tease him, barreling my ass onto the dating train.

"Oh, my gosh!" He barks out a laugh. "No, but I can't even describe how sexy it is that you know whatever that word was that their outfits were called."

When the game ends and we make it back to my truck, I open his door for him. I need to do whatever I can to make it a notable date since I only realized halfway through that it was one.

"Are you still hungry? I'll take you anywhere you want to go for dinner."

Leaning over, he grips the back of my neck and gives me a slow kiss that makes me forget where I am. "Thank you, but I think I ate enough hot dogs to last me until lunch tomorrow, unless you're hungry…"

I am hungry, hungry for him. And finally, freaking finally, it's not just a broiling sensation in my chest and groin with no evidence of proof. We need to fucking get home ASAP.

"No, I'm good."

I somehow make it back to my house without getting a speeding ticket or blowing any traffic lights. Fortunately, Remy looked like he thought

I was just joyriding, as though I was high off the Panthers crushing the Cougars.

When we've parked, in my haste, I round the front of my truck before he does, so I miss the chance to see if he was going to head for my front door or his car. "Do you want to come in and pick out some bad TV?"

Fancy, Chris. Real smooth.

"Only because that *is* the only kind of TV I watch."

He reaches for my hand, and we walk up my pathway. I'm going to count that as walking him to the door, even though it's not his.

Remy gives Gale welcome scratches and the sweet talk she's a glutton for whenever he's around. I head to the sunporch and let her out to do her business, hoping she makes it quick while my blood still feels like it's flowing where it needs to go.

As I lean on the doorjamb and wait for her, Remy sidles up to me and rests his hand on the small of my back. Leaning up, he gives me a kiss.

"Thanks for taking me to a game with you. I hope I didn't interfere with your getting all the notes you need."

Notes? Who cares about notes?

Circling my arms around him, I brush his top lip and then the bottom one with my own. He does that thing where it feels like he's melting into me, which drives me mad, parting his lips in invitation. This time, it sends even more blood to my half-hard cock. When my tongue slides against his, the static it sends through me is like seeing an old black-and-white film remastered into color. I grunt and hold him tighter. Just the simple graze of his hand up my side over my sweatshirt has amplified results. It's like making out with Remy two-point-oh.

I don't know if this was technically a first date, and I know going all the way isn't first-date protocol, but we put the cart before the horse years ago. Shifting my hips forward, I press my erection into his thigh, sliding my hands down to his ass to hold him closer. He gasps and glances down between us.

"So...*this* has been happening all night, if you want to take advantage of it."

"Was it from watching me shove hot dogs in my face?"

"It's from you being *you.*"

I kiss him again, deeper this time, hoping he'll take me up on making use of my development. He makes a satisfied noise, leaning harder against me. Maybe it sounds sophomoric, but it's incredibly validating to have a hard-on and be able to show your boyfriend. I can't count how many times I got one just from thinking about him years ago and had to try to hide it. I never had a good reason to hide, even if it took me years to realize that. I sure as hell don't want to hide now.

"Come home with me," I whisper.

"I think I already did," he chuckles.

"I mean for Christmas…if you didn't make other plans already. I'd love to bring you home with me to meet my family." I rub my thumbs anxiously against the small of his back, praying I don't scare him. This is definitely not a *first-date* conversation. When the flicker of surprise in his eyes passes, he smiles.

"Okay."

"Okay?" He didn't even hesitate, so I want to make sure I heard him correctly.

"Yeah."

Pushing off me, he takes a step back, peeling his sweatshirt and undershirt over his head in one go. His bare chest is a more radiant sight than the warm glow from the light in my living room. He keeps stepping back, the corner of his mouth curved upward, as he reaches for the button of his jeans. It's a slow, traveling striptease, and I can tell its end destination is my bedroom. It's the same stupid way I used to try to lure him into getting into bed more quickly; however, his doing it has to be a hell of a lot sexier than when I did. I don't even look at his hands when I hear his zipper lower. The heat in his eyes and the hopefulness are barer sights than any naked flesh.

Fuck me. How did I get this lucky?

I take a step toward him, but then remember I was standing by the sunporch door for a reason. "Shit," I mutter, spinning around and opening the patio door. "Gale! Get your ass in here!"

As soon as her tail clears the door, I shut and lock it. When I turn around, Remy is gone, but I hear the *thud* of shoes hitting the floor in my bedroom.

Giving myself a stroke over my jeans, I stalk to my room and start lifting my sweatshirt up with my other hand. I feel like a damn hunter who came home empty-handed but is about to be rewarded for putting in a good effort all season. Flinging my shirt to the floor in the hallway, I stop to admire the view when I reach my doorway.

Remy slips his boxer briefs down over his hips, his perfect cock springing free. Shorts now pooled on the floor, he kicks them out of the way and licks his lips. In two steps, I'm kissing him, slipping my fingers into his hair, and running my hand down his back to the smooth skin of his ass. His hands wrench open my fly like he just ate a gummy and has the munchies again. I can't get enough of his mouth. Each kiss rockets another stream of blissful static through my veins. It pools in my groin, building momentum and feeding my cock for an overdue step in our long-awaited reunion.

Drawing back, he shoves my pants over my hips as I hastily kick my shoes off. "Is it weird that I feel like Jamie might burst in?"

"Yes," I deadpan, leaning into him until he falls back on the bed with a laugh.

I crawl onto the mattress and sigh at the feel of his warm body when I settle against his side. Skin to skin, my hard cock pressed against his thigh, arousal pumping through me unfettered, I feel free and capable of taking care of my man. Leaning in, I seal his smile with my own. Our cocks brush together, and we exchange sounds of relief as I wrap my hand around both of us, giving us a stroke. His fingers dig into my hips, hungry for me. I want to pound on my chest for being able to give him that sensation.

"Do you want to?" I rasp, tearing my mouth away and skirting my hand to give his ass cheek a squeeze.

He groans and settles onto his back, spreading his legs and bringing his feet to the base of his ass. '*Yes*' has never looked or sounded so sexy. With his cock ready and leaking, his sac plump and drawn up high, I'm in danger of coming just from the sight of him. Knowing I'll be able to look into his eyes like this only makes it all the more intimate.

Shuffling to the side of the bed, I fetch the new bottle of lube I bought. It was a manifestation of sorts—if you purchase the necessary items, it might happen. His crease is like an inferno when I settle between his legs and circle his hole with my slickened fingers. The way his eyes slip closed and his facial muscles go slack is a picture I'm going to live off in my mind.

"Fuck Chris," he slurs, running a hand down his stomach when I press my index finger inside his heat.

How this man wants me is beyond me. Planting my hand next to him, I feed on his panting open mouth, working him open. He moans my name against my lips, a dream I never thought I'd have again.

"*Now*, please," he begs, his hands cupping my face.

"Do you want a condom?"

"No. Just you, if that's okay."

I'm grateful he doesn't mind. I don't want to chance losing any of the sensation in my dick right now since it's finally working when I want it to. Sitting back on my feet, I scooch forward, slicking myself up while I watch Remy draw his knees up to his chest. I was so ignorant when I was younger that I didn't even know men could have sex like this. The internet and television have made leaps and bounds since those days when society was too shocked to become educated.

As I drag more lube over his twitching hole, teasing it, a feeling too big fills my chest. It's possessive, proud, humbled, and grateful all at the same time. Remy is my boyfriend, and he's coming home with me at Christmas to meet my family. We're in my bed, free of expectations, about to claim each other with our bodies in a way we never have before—with deep emotions. If it wasn't love that brought us to this moment, I'll never understand what love is. Because I swear I see it in his eyes, and it's all I can do not to cry.

"I dreamt about this," I whisper, my voice sounding thick.

"What?"

"Deserving you. You looking at me like I earned you."

A wash of tenderness spills over his features, and he pushes up on an elbow. His fingers slide to the back of my neck and tug me down for another kiss. Just as my lips meet his, a sharp blade of pain slices up my spine, locking my body up and stealing my breath.

The strangled sound that tears past my choked airway isn't even a word. The pain is so debilitating, I can't even breathe and have to grip onto Remy's shoulder for support.

No… not now. Not fucking now!

"Chris! What's wrong?"

I can't even tell him, but I'm too pissed and ashamed to even if I could, slowly slumping to the side to get my palm on the mattress for balance. I let out another pitiful sound, but leaning to my right and forward as I brace myself finally helps stop whatever my back didn't like about my quick movement.

"Oh, God. I'm sorry. Here, can you lie down?"

His gentle hand glides soothingly across my shoulders, and his other hooks underneath my armpit to help me lower myself. I crash onto my side and flop over onto my back. The sensation of a spike being driven up my spine stops, finally allowing me to take a gulp of air.

"I am so sorry. Are you okay? Do you need an ice pack?"

"I'm fine," I pant. I'm not fine. My fucking cock is a hundred percent deflated, and my boyfriend is lubed up and unfulfilled right next to me. Giving myself a few strokes, I take him in, visual therapy from the upset, and rub his thigh reassuringly. "Just…give me a minute."

"Chris," he scoffs, eyes wild, "I'm not worried about that. I'm worried about *you*."

Fucking hell. Compassion is the last thing I want right now. "No. I want to," I reassure him, hoping there are no lingering signs of agony in my expression.

Shaking his head, he leans down and strokes my jaw with his thumb. "I want you to get off, too, but more importantly, I want you not to be in pain."

Only Remy would care more about someone else than having a passionate moment ruined. This is why he deserves to have his mind blown. I keep stroking myself idly, willing the blood to return now that whatever got pinched before seems to be at ease.

"I've got some pills the doctor gave me." I nod toward my bathroom, rubbing my palm up and down the curve of his hip. "They're in my medicine cabinet. Let me go get one, and I'll make you forget everyone's name but mine again."

The incredulous look on his face isn't the response I was hoping for to my backup plan. Apparently, there's no sexy way to say, *'Hey, wait, I'll go grab my Sildenafil so I can fuck you.'* If I could just get my cock to stand up, though, I'm hoping it will wipe that worry out of his eyes. I push on the mattress, intent on sliding my legs gingerly over the side of the bed, but he puts a hand on my chest to stop me.

"Wait. I have a better idea."

I stay put, wondering what on earth could make the dead rise. My cock is shriveled and stuck to my thigh like it's still winded from whatever nerve just pinched its life supply. Remy shifts and settles on his knees between my thighs, a tender smile on his face. His palms glide up my thighs, and he bends, pressing a kiss to the juncture at my hip.

Great. Now I get to disappoint him twice.

"Remy," I warn gently, "I don't think that's going to work."

He makes a shushing noise and places another kiss at the top of my right thigh, his hands lightly caressing my legs. "It's not for your dick. It's for your back."

Now, I'm fucking lost. He must see so on my face when he glances up at me.

"It's a relaxation technique I've never tried on a patient before. Just humor me," he adds playfully. "Besides, if it's me you're worried about, I'm pretty sure I could come just from touching you."

If he was trying to boost my confidence, that certainly did it. Sighing in defeat, I close my eyes and imagine I'm sitting on my couch. He walks in and stops in his tracks. His jaw falls open, and a sharp gasp leaves his lips as he grips the wall for support and comes in his pants. I could definitely live with possessing that talent if it were possible.

I feel warm breath against my sac and then the wet tip of his tongue. My eyes flutter open as he kisses one of my testes. He takes it into his mouth, engulfing it, and swirls his tongue around its circumference.

Shit. Just the thought of it is hot.

"I think I'm going to have to report you to your boss if you ever…try this technique at work," I caution, my voice coming out like gravel.

His nose nudges lower, right to the place where my cheeks begin behind my taint. The slippery wet tip of his tongue traces the seam there, making me gasp. On an instinct I didn't know I possessed, I slide my feet up to the base of my ass to open myself as a swirl of arousal starts brewing in the pit of my groin.

"It would need *lots* of workshop trials at home before I'd even consider mentioning it at the center," he purrs, drawing his tongue over my hole.

"Fuck," I slur, my lungs burning in a good way now, and little tingles trickling down my cock and balls.

He was right. The muscles that tensed up when that javelin of pain fired earlier are now sedated from Remy's every touch. I reach for my cock to stoke the static there and find it thickening again. I already knew he had magic hands. I'm adding a magic mouth to that list now, too.

Dragging his nails lightly through the hairs on my thighs, he unfurls a mastery of seduction. Kisses to my inner thighs, flicks and swirls of his tongue to my crease, the base of my cock, and even my knuckles when my hand gets in the way. He buries his face in the juncture of my hip, his cheek nestled against my cock and balls, and sucks on the skin there. Tickling sparks zip down to my toes and up my spine, making it increasingly difficult to remain still. A bead of precum glistens on my tip. I haven't seen that in months, and even longer with another person involved.

Remy surfaces, moving toward my cock. And hell, he's the eighth wonder of the world, his eyes hazy with desire, all from just touching me.

"Remy…"

I only get his name out before his lips wrap around the head of my cock, and his tongue claims that drop of precum he worked so hard to create. My nuts want to follow the suction all the way up through my shaft. I need to finish my sentence before I come in his mouth.

"Remy, lie down. I'll get you now."

He draws off but shakes his head. Why is he shaking his head?

Holding my gaze, he places a hand on my knee and shuffles around my legs. I just went from being out of commission to being in dire need. Please don't tell me he's changed his mind. His cock looks just as engorged as mine does right now.

He swings a leg over me and plants his knee on the other side of my hips, straddling me. Biting his lip, he reaches back and presses my cock between his cheeks. Fuck. He's so warm there. His hips arch, dragging my length through his seam.

"This okay?" he whispers.

Is he kidding me? I run my hands up his thighs and squeeze his hips.

"Very okay."

How stupid was I, thinking I had to be this big, tough guy who takes charge all the time? I thought that's what he saw me as in college, so that's what I tried to give him. I was so ignorant about so many things, sex being one of them.

Remy straddling me? Looking like he's drunk on the idea of riding me and taking what he wants? Yeah. I am definitely okay with that.

Bending down, he leans in to kiss me as he angles my cock against his entrance. "If something hurts again and you don't tell me, I swear to God, I'll twist one of your nipples off. Okay?" he warns, circling his index finger around one of mine.

"Okay," I laugh, holding up a hand in surrender.

"Good."

His smile presses against mine, the tip of his tongue licking the seam of my mouth. I feel him pulse against the tip of my cock, the tight pucker kissing me at the same time he does. And then, he presses back.

His body squeezes my tip, drawing me into a tight sleeve of slickened heat. Remy blinks, his mouth parted enough that I can see his teeth pressed together. Spots of pink pop up on his neck and cheeks as I knead his hip and thigh, feeling utterly useless and yet spoiled as all hell. He feels so damn incredible. Each centimeter he takes me shoves the pressure to my balls, which are crying to force it in the opposite direction.

"Chris," he gasps.

His chest heaves. A flood of breath rains down on me. With a determined look in his gaze, he rocks, capturing more of me. Oh, God. I try to breathe through the pressure of his channel's hug. My fingertips are probably leaving bruises on his thighs. Hand pressed against my chest, he rocks again, and I feel the soft shell of his ass brush against my thighs.

Eyes slipping closed, he moans long and guttural. Fucking hell.

"Remy…you're not real. How are you real?" I choke, a well of emotions threatening tears.

His eyes flutter open, mouth panting. He smooths his hand over my heart with something a lot like gratitude in his eyes, and then he moves. Slow undulations of his hips, his body pumping me, his movements pull incoherent sounds from my throat.

He's so handsome and sweet, perfect in every way. And he wants me. *Me!* The rhythm is like making love in slow motion compared to how we used to mess around. It's as though time has stopped and I'm in a dreamlike state, one where the focal point is every micro-expression on Remy's face and the heady sounds he's making as he stares into my eyes. This is really our do-over, this time we've spent together. It's really happening. He's really mine. I'm so damn gone for him; he can do whatever he wants with me. I just hope it's for a very long time.

"Shit. Oh, shit," I grit, the ache to release becoming the equivalent of a migraine in my balls. "Slow down. I'm—"

"Let go," he cuts me off, bending down and cradling the back of my head. His lips drag over mine, and he whispers again, "Just let go. I want to feel you."

My hips jerk without permission, my body obeying his sweet request. My cock makes up for the lack of use, pulsing so hard it makes me dizzy as I release into him. I have to blink through the spots in my vision, so I don't miss his reaction. What I see only makes the weight of bliss more overpowering.

Mouth parted, his gaze looks drunk, as though I'm giving him an indescribable gift. My sweaty palm fumbles between us, taking him in my grasp. He groans, his eyes slipping closed. His cock is slick with dribbles of precum. I stroke through it, spreading it as I go until he jerks in my hand and his ring clenches around me.

"Yes. Yesss," I pant, watching his head fall, a broken cry spilling out of him along with his release.

He moans my name and then whimpers it. Every nerve ending in my body sings at the sound. I use the last strength in my sapped appendages to pull him to me. We're a pile of hot skin sticking to hot skin and winded, satisfied noises.

"It's probably good we…haven't been doing that…for fifteen years," he pants against my chest, slipping onto his side next to me. "One of us would have had a heart attack."

My tired laugh pulls me out of the darkness behind my heavy eyelids. "Just one of us, huh?" I tease, giving him a kiss.

"*Me.* One of us is me." His hips shift away from my thigh, the air cooling the damp skin where his cock was sticking to it. "Shit. Sorry. I'll go grab something."

I roll with a grunt, putting him half under me to get him on his back and give him another kiss. "No. Stay. I'll go."

I get my feet on the floor and rise. My muscles feel as pliable as chewed bubble gum as I tromp to the bathroom. Hell, I think I might sleep like a brick tonight. Glancing back, I find Remy propped against a pillow, exhausted and smiling. He looks so happy and satisfied. I feel like a man, a whole man, for the first time in my life. Ironically, I don't think it has anything to do with sex. I think it's because he's looking at me like I'm his.

REMY

chapter 21

Cameron University's auditorium is surprisingly full. I wonder if that means some professors still offer extra credit for attending these things. I'd like to believe it's because the students know my man is about to speak, but that might just be me. It's surreal to stand here at the back of the room where I spot a few professors doing the same near other doorways. On my way in, a gaggle of kids who looked like lost fresh-men called me '*sir*' and asked me if this was where the winter break safety briefing was. That expounds on just how long it's been since any of them could have been me or Chris. God, we were just kids when we met.

People act like once you turn eighteen, you're an adult. I used to think that too. It takes a hell of a lot longer than that to figure yourself, the world, and life out, though.

The emcee concludes her opening address and announces Chris. My stomach flips with nerves. He's being so freaking brave doing this. I know he tried to act like he wasn't freaking out the last few days, but I think I'm freaking out. He's so hard on himself. I'm terrified he'll either not get through it or critique himself too harshly afterward. He was up late last night, poring over his notes on his computer, Gale asleep by his feet, until I dragged him back to bed, insisting he try to turn his mind off.

The introductory applause sounds obligatory until Chris walks out on the stage. Immediately, a few catcall whistles echo through the auditorium, making me chuckle. Chris' stoic face looks like he's ready to go into battle, but his gaze darts to the crowd in confusion for a second. He really has no idea how handsome he still is. This man.

He reaches the podium, and the dean shakes his hand, turning over the mic to him. To my surprise, he doesn't stand behind it. He takes a few idle steps, explaining his affiliation with the university—his college football career, getting drafted and playing for the NFL, and how he's a sportswriter covering their games for the paper now.

"So, why am I here to give you your winter break safety meeting?" he asks rhetorically. "I'll let you in on a little secret. I didn't want to be here about as much as you probably don't want to be right now either." That gets him a laugh, but my stomach muscles tighten, and I press the skin at the tip of my thumb between my teeth.

"That's what bad decisions do to you," he explains. "They make you want to hide, not show up, or walk around with your head hung in shame, because they never go away. You can learn from them, sure, but you spend a lot of time wondering what life would have been like if you'd never made them in the first place."

He then explains some details about the night of his accident; some I knew, some I didn't. It only gets worse when he talks about waking up in the hospital, his surgeries, and his recovery.

"But it wasn't exactly a recovery," he adds. "Because guess what I did? I made yet another bad decision."

He elaborates on the temptation of the opioids he was taking for pain management. How they numbed his emotional pain. How it got easier and easier to rely on them. How it seemed easier to numb the physical pain than to do the actual work of physical therapy. He tells them that by the time you realize your decision was bad, you might already be trapped. I swipe a tear off my cheek, grateful he hasn't looked up here, even though I told him right where I would be if he needed to see me to ground himself. All the while, he paces slowly back and forth across the stage, one hand tucked in his pocket, in front of a sea of silence as though he's a natural. Should I have expected anything less from Chris when he puts his mind to something?

"When you head out for the holidays, and even when you come back, I hope you can take something from this throughout the rest of your time here because you've got your whole lives ahead of you. There will be days, weeks, or months, even, when you might feel like no one understands you or what you're going through. There will be times you won't think you're enough for yourself, your family, or maybe a special someone."

My breath catches when he pauses and searches the back of the room until his eyes land on me. He flashes me a sympathetic smile that heals an old wound I didn't know was still there.

"Or your introduction to a bad decision might just look like celebrating when you feel so good you think you're invincible. But we aren't," he affirms with finality.

"I could have made this university very proud once, but a bad decision found me, and I took it. I was on top of the world, living a life some people only dream of living for a twenty-three-year-old. That party I told you about? The one where I was at a mansion, surrounded by celebrities and women throwing themselves at me before I got in my car—a car that would take me twenty years to afford now. I wasn't happy. I was miserable, in fact. I'd never felt so alone or trapped in my life. And the pressure I thought I'd overcome by finally making it seemed like it had just been reset, knowing I'd have to keep being the best every single day on the field after that. All I wanted was someone to talk to and maybe a hand to hold, not champagne, money, fancy cars, or a Super Bowl ring. The hand I wanted to hold belonged to another student here at Cameron U." He pauses, and I don't know how I'm still standing. "Because there are a lot of happy times you're going to have here, too. Some of the best times of your life. But back then, I was so conflicted, thinking there was no way I'd be able to hold his hand and be allowed to play on national television. Walking away from him was actually my first bad decision and cost me more than I can ever explain."

A few whispers float over the audience. Chris runs his hand over the top of his head and clears his throat. God, I just want to run to him and tell him he's done enough.

"I didn't know if the team would drop me, if my family would look at me the same way. If anyone would. I was scared and overwhelmed by expectations I didn't think I had control over. So, I got in my car and drove as fast as I could, chasing that feeling of invincibility, to let life know that it couldn't break me. Just so I could feel like I was in control of something for a few minutes."

He finally comes to a stop, squaring off with the audience. He shakes his head.

"Life doesn't break you. But your bad decisions can feel like they do for a long time. So, when you're out there, think about what it is that you really want. Think about what you want your life to look like when you're faced with drugs, alcohol, or feeling like you don't belong here. They're not decisions; they're just temptations. Saying *yes* to them is the bad decision. Don't let them win, or you might never know how great you really could have had it after you overcame your struggles on your own. Because they're sure as shit not going to help you."

I hiccup out a laugh that they got a glimpse of the full Chris. Only one expletive is impressive. He thanks them and waits for the dean to walk over to retrieve the mic. She doesn't let him sneak away, though. The attendees are all on their feet, applauding, a thunderous sound.

Trembling with anticipation, I push out the door, the noise erupting with me out into the hallway. My pulse is pumping with every step down the side corridor that leads to the back of the auditorium, where I told him I'd meet him.

It's my turn to pace now, anxiously walking in circles as I wait for him to appear. Each time the door swings open and a staff member comes out, my heart jumps into my throat.

Finally, the hinges creak again, and out walks Chris. His complexion is pale, his eyes searching until they land on me. He looks like he just came from a bomb blast.

I smile encouragingly and open my arms as he lumbers over. He buries his face against my neck and grabs onto me like he's about to collapse. His chest pushes against mine, a heavy exhale ghosting against my skin.

"Hey," I coo, rubbing his back.

"How awful was it?" he mumbles against my shoulder.

"Awful? Chris, I'm not letting you go because every man and woman in there probably wants your phone number right now."

My flattery earns me a scoff against the seam of my sweatshirt. I practically have to pry him off me just to get enough space so I can cradle his face and force him to look at me. I've never seen a more pitiful and yet endearing sight.

"I'm serious. You were fantastic. You were…*you.*" I wish there were better words to reassure him, but that seems appropriate. I suck in a breath, trying to hold my tears at bay. "I'm so fucking proud of you."

He searches my watery eyes, shaking his head. "How?"

"Because I could never do what you've done."

I want to rattle that skeptical look off his face. Brushing my thumb against his cheek, I shake my head, insisting, "I *couldn't.*"

He sighs, giving up arguing with me, and chews on his lip. I wish he'd been in that audience so he could have seen and heard himself. My big man with his big feelings.

Running my hands down his arms, the smooth fabric of his dress shirt feels damp in places. Someone was clearly sweating himself into a tizzy. I lace my fingers through his, realizing I have one other idea on how to boost his spirits.

"Listen, I need to ask you something…"

That gets him to lift his head. The wariness in his features tugs at my heart. I remember how vulnerable he looked last week when he told me he wished for me to look at him like he deserves me. Each time I look at him, I ask myself what I did to deserve him, and I think now is a good time to reassure him.

"I was wondering if it's okay that I'm in love with you?"

His mouth falls open, and he blinks several times, looking at me like I'm not real again. God, could I have ever asked for more love than that?

His features crumple suddenly, scaring me into thinking I said something wrong. Then, he yanks me against him, crushing me in his arms, and sputters.

"Thank you," he heaves against my neck like the words freed him from a prison. I'm jostled, and he pulls back, cupping my face with tears in his eyes. "Thank you," he whispers again, kissing me. His mouth moves to my cheek, but doesn't stop there, peppering little kisses all over my face. "I'm going to make sure I deserve it every single day."

Love is now not a big enough word. I squeeze his arms, pressing my lips to his cheek near his ear. "You *will* deserve it. It doesn't cost anything."

"I am *so* in love with you." The words flow out of him like he's been holding them in.

I feel them pour through me, over me. They're as strong as his arms that wrap around me. The door hinges creak behind us, and a janitor rolls a cleaning cart inside. Chris smiles down at me, looking more composed. I reach for his hand and tug.

"Come on. Let's go home."

Home. I want to laugh at how different that word sounds than it used to. It doesn't matter whether it's my house or Chris', whether it's a co-lease or not. Home is wherever he and I are. Together.

CHRIS

chapter 22

Sitting on my parents' couch, arm proudly and protectively draped over the back of Remy's shoulders, I smile at his amusement over my nephews teaching Mom how to use her new smartphone. She looks up over her bifocals at my nephews, who are groaning over her last question about the confounding technology in her hands, and then flashes Remy a look of exasperation like a cry for help. He chuckles and reassures her it will be second nature to her in no time.

Last week, when I told her I was bringing someone home with me for Christmas and that someone happened to be a guy I was dating whom I'd known in college, there was the expected pause. I had kind of hoped

Alice would have dropped a few hints, so I wouldn't even have to have the conversation, but I'm glad she didn't. I'm too old to have my older sister fight my battles. Plus, Remy deserves a relationship with a man who will go to bat for him if necessary.

'Well…what's his name?'

Her excited reply when I told her the news will live in my memory forever. I think I was expecting the worst because I've been primed to expect the worst for so long. Her barely checked glee of a mother hoping her child would finally settle down with someone was a nice outcome instead. She's as wonderful as she's always been, even if the first person I ever brought home ended up being a nice *man* rather than the nice *woman* she used to wish for me.

He baked a tray of seven-layer brownies and brought them with us, which pretty much won her approval the second we walked in the door. I can't say I blame her, but my nephews better not have eaten all of them. I have plans for the leftovers coming home with us. My boyfriend is a damn good cook. Seeing her and Remy in a moment of solidarity now warms my heart. This feels like it could be the start of many more happy years of him at my side for family gatherings. Almost.

My father's easy chair sits empty to my right, the Hawai'i Bowl playing on the living room television. I saw him slip into his den earlier, which isn't uncommon for him on game days, but we always watch whatever bowl is on in the living room on holidays. I know I'm being avoided, and it's pissing me off more and more with each minute that ticks by without him resurfacing.

He barely said a word at dinner, and certainly none to Remy. A hand squeezes my kneecap. I find Remy's concerned face looking at me.

"You all right?"

"Yeah." I give him a reassuring smile and a peck on the cheek, even though I'm pretty sure he knows I'm lying. Motioning to the door of my father's den, I let out a sigh. "I'd better go get this over with. I'll meet you upstairs after?"

"All right."

He nods, trying to look encouraging. The fact that he looks worried I might be faced with something unpleasant compounds my aggravation with my father. How can anyone not see that this man deserves kindness or, at the very least, acknowledgement?

Hoisting myself off the couch, I pass by Alice, who's sitting on her husband Dean's lap with her head on his shoulder while he's fast asleep in the recliner. She yawns, and I ruffle her hair. I get a half-hearted swat from her, but she smirks.

"Lightweights," I tease.

"Food coma," she mumbles, closing her eyes.

The door to Dad's den looks equivalent to a gallows as I stare at the handle. On the other side, adversity. Always. Except, I can't be the pacifist son this time. Pulling the lever, the door swings open, and the sound of the Hawai'i Bowl immediately touches my ears, dubbing over the echo of it out in the living room behind me.

His gray eyes flick to mine momentarily from where he's sitting in his leather chair, legs crossed, and he nods, raising his bottle of beer before fixing his gaze back on his TV screen. The sleeves of his red sweater are rolled up his forearms, exposing the memories of strength there on his weathered skin.

I used to be in awe of this room when I was younger. I viewed it as a trophy room of my father's life. Staring at a poster on his wall of me in my NFL uniform, I remember how proud I was when my achievements made it into his beloved space. Below the poster, framed pictures of me playing in college and high school sit in a row on a shelf. I look determined and in the zone in them. All I see in the NFL poster, however, is turmoil in my eyes. For years after my accident, I thought maybe I hadn't been grateful enough for my successes. It was easier to appreciate them once I had regrets than to live them before I did, I suppose.

"It's a miracle Conrad made it to the bowl," Dad comments as a play recap is broadcast over the TV. "You would have had twice as many yards as him."

Would have…

I know he's just posturing, reliving the good old days by comparing my former abilities to the college player in the game who's playing, but it hits the wrong way today. I'm tired of being a '*was*' instead of an '*is*.' Sometimes it feels like I stopped being his son the second I crashed into that guardrail.

"What did you think of Remy?" I ask, still staring at that conflicted face in the poster.

"That's a good program they started with that center at the college."

I guess his ears were working at dinner when Mom, Dean, and Alice were asking Remy about his job. Ironically, though, the family member at the table with the most knowledge of sports injuries didn't contribute an ounce of conversation. His response about Remy is no response.

I turn around, possibly hoping for another comment, but he's still watching the game. No father-son chitchat on his lips, just dull interest in his television that looks a lot like avoidance. I take a few steps until I block his line of vision. I'd given him the benefit of the doubt at dinner and while we opened gifts, thinking maybe he was just in a mood. That's what being around Remy does; it makes you optimistic. I'm about out of optimism for the day now, though.

"Did you know he called to check on me after the accident? He was worried about me."

"We all were," he says matter-of-factly, adjusting the sleeve of his sweater.

My stomach twists into knots, seeing the ugly truth of being ignored.

"That wasn't rhetorical. Did you know?"

His gaze flicks to mine, but no sooner it shifts to the line of windows overlooking the backyard. He gets up out of his chair, which only infuriates me more. Clearly, the game that was holding his attention isn't all that interesting after all.

"That was a long time ago."

Another non-answer. Unbelievable. I've never disrespected my father in my life, never even stood up to him at times when I thought he was being too critical and pushing me during my training. I can't let this go, though.

"Because I think you did."

I stare at his stiff back. His unflinching silence. The image of the once proud, indestructible, and all-knowing man I thought him to be—my hero—crumbles. All I see is a gatekeeper, a tired old puppet master who held my strings. And I fucking let him.

"Did you see our messages and put it together?" I laugh for some reason, but it's not amused laughter.

I can hear him sigh a defeated sound from where I'm standing. That tells me everything I needed to know but didn't want to believe. I'm shaking, my heartbeat pounding in my ears. Remy and I can go to a hotel or drive back to San Antonio after this. I'll just apologize to Mom, and Remy, bless him, will understand. I need to get this out. The gloves are off.

"Is *that* why you didn't tell me? Was it not in line with Vince Mightener's dream for his football protégé? Because it really would have helped if I'd known he'd called, if I'd known *someone* out there who didn't care about me because of a fucking game was happy because they knew I'd lived. I might have—"

My voice cracks over the possibilities and how the last decade and a half could have gone so differently. Swiping my hand over my face, I can feel it trembling. I take a breath to calm my nerves and get control of my voice. I just spewed all my dirty deeds to an entire auditorium the other day. Dad is just one man. I can do this.

"I'll never forget what you and Mom have done for me, but you've been pulling my strings and making deals for me since I was a kid. And I *trusted you*. I thought *you* knew best. That if I did *everything* you said I should, life was going to be great."

I throw my hands up, unable to contain my sarcasm, but my audience is still a statue. In the grand scheme of things, I know that I might have been too immature to make a go of anything with Remy back then. I might have screwed it all up, even if I'd felt I had the chance. But damn it, it sure would have been nice to know I'd had one.

"I know I messed up, and I've paid for that, but…you didn't have the right to do *that*. I'm not always confident because being too confident leads to bad decisions. I'm not going to be a coach or in some hall of fame, and I'm gay." I have to pause to take a breath, the vibrations coursing through me threatening to make my knees buckle. "But you know what? Life is pretty great, even when your own father can't look at you at the dinner table."

Dad's head lowers, and I hate myself for sounding so treacherous, but I don't regret the context. I wait, my heartbeat still thumping in my ears. If I stand here any longer, though, the tears in my eyes might end up spilling over, and I'm not about to ruin Remy's Christmas by making him see me like that.

"You've got nothing to say? For once, the great Vince Mightener has nothing to say?"

Scoffing, I shake my head after yet another beat of silence. Spinning on my heel, I march to the door of a room I'd now like to take a wrecking ball to.

"Chris..."

It comes out calm, not with commanding retribution for my tirade, but it hits like a punch to my back after he stayed quiet for so long. I stop, telling myself I do only because he didn't say *'Champ.'*

"I thought I knew what was best for you." His gravely voice is sub-dued, but I roll my eyes at the pathetic excuse he's offering, grateful he can't see my face. "I have this son who shines brighter than I ever did in every single way, and I...wanted to show him off to the whole world however I could. I still do. It doesn't mean I was right."

I find myself turning around without even thinking about it. I'm too confused over what sounded like a vote of confidence that, for once, wasn't laced with a dozen reasons for how I'm failing to live up to his expectations. It's also the closest thing Vince Mightener has ever come to saying he was wrong about anything.

His chest inflates on a ragged breath. Pursing his lips, he looks like words are barbed wire, and if he spits them out, he'll bleed. There's nothing proud about him at the moment, such a stark contrast from the image I've had of him my entire life.

"I've been trying to think of how to say that for weeks. Years, maybe." His free hand fidgets with the label on his beer bottle, and he sighs. Angling his chin, he motions in the general direction of the living room. "And then you bring home someone who makes it look so simple; it was like a splash of cold water to the face. *That's* why it was too hard to look at you. Somebody'd already given you what I should have a long time ago."

He finally looks right at me, his gray eyes holding a well of remorse. And I swear he just tried to smile because it felt like the equivalent of a hug.

Something hot and wet hits my cheek. Swiping at it, I'm still shaking but for different reasons now. Maybe it's merely seconds, but it seems like an eternity that we stand, facing each other, neither of us saying a word. He shifts in place, but keeps holding my gaze. The expression on his face is clearer than any words could ever be—he's wondering if he can be forgiven for a lifetime of pushing me.

"Merry Christmas." I nod. It's the only thing I can think to say that sounds like, *'All right then.'*

"Merry Christmas."

I leave, so neither of us has to endure any more emotional turmoil for the evening. I'm grateful that Remy's not in the living room when I come out. Neither is Mom. The boys are playing a *Nintendo* game while Alice and Dean are now snoring in the recliner. No one needs to be any wiser about my heart-to-heart with Dad. I assume he'll appreciate that as much as I do.

I head upstairs to my old room, swiping at my face in the hopes that any sign of tears will be gone before I have to face Remy. Except, he's not in the room where we dropped our bags earlier. One guess says he's with Mom somewhere, so at least I know he's in good hands.

Slipping into the attached bathroom, I close the door behind me and turn on the shower. I strip out of my clothes and step under the hot spray, letting it rain down on my face. In less than a minute, my skin is pleasantly numb from the scalding water. It melts away the tension and the last of the adrenaline rush I had from confronting Dad. I watch the suds swirl down the drain, imagining they're taking with them the years of animosity I've carried. My limbs are heavy, but I feel clean and rejuvenated, body and soul.

REMY

chapter 23

If I sit here any longer, waiting for Chris to come out of his father's den, I might have a nervous breakdown. Alice and Dean are fast asleep in the recliner like two overworked, overtired parents who deserve a nap. Gale is passed out on her back, sporting her brand-new Christmas bandana from '*Grandma*' and possibly chasing a squirrel in her dreams. Rose disappeared into the kitchen a little while ago, and the boys are transfixed by a new game one of them got for Christmas—a football game, imagine that. That leaves just me and my thoughts.

Ugh, I can't do this.

Shoving off the couch, I amble back through the dining room. Maybe burning off my restlessness will keep me from worrying that any semblance of peace Chris has found over the past two months won't be shattered by whatever is happening behind that closed door. I already called my parents earlier and sent a message to Jamie. I could go up to Chris' room to wait for him there, but that won't keep me from wondering how his chat with *'daddy'* is going either. Or keep me close enough by to hear if it comes to blows.

It wouldn't go that far, would it?

Not the image I needed right now.

The sound of dishes clanking on the other side of the kitchen door catches my attention. I think I just found a distraction that will keep me near the potential war zone in the other room. Swiping two dirty mugs off the dining table, I take them with me. Rose is elbow deep in soapy water at the sink, doing a mother's labor of love.

"Oh, did you find more for me?" she asks, gracing me with an appreciative smile.

How the woman can manage to sound cheery about that further solidifies the picture of patience and exuberance I saw from her over the evening. Smiling, I set them down on the counter and then move to the other side of the sink and grab a hand towel.

"Oh, you don't have to do that. You're our guest," she scolds.

"You made dinner. It's the least I can do. Besides, Chris and I do dishes together all the time. It wouldn't be fair if I dry for him and not his mother."

"You're so sweet," she says softly, affectionately, not just a throw-away comment.

But is your husband? I want to ask.

Chris hasn't mentioned much about him other than Vince may not approve of his current career choice. If he could have seen his son the other day at the college, he'd have known he was meant to use his voice.

It takes me a second, but I locate the cabinet where Rose keeps the dinner plates. I set the ones I dried inside and turn back to my duty station. Her forearms are resting on the edge of the sink, head hung, eyes closed. Did she…fall asleep standing up? Is she sick?

"Rose…are you all right?"

I hear her before I put two and two together—a sniffle. Her lower lip quivers. The sponge in her hand splashes into the water. Just as I lay my hand on her shoulder, she practically throws herself at me. Arms going tight around my waist, she hugs me and sobs against my chest.

I am officially terrified, a thousand-pound weight dropping into my stomach. Did something happen to Chris? What is going on?

"Rose?"

"Sorry. I'm sorry," she sniffles, straightening up. Swiping her eyes, she takes a second to compose herself. "Do you know *how long* it's been since I've seen my son smile?"

The question stuns me. It sounds rhetorical, emphasized by the watery appreciative look on her face. She reaches out and gives my hand a squeeze, whispering, "Thank you."

I thought I knew how much Chris loved me, but the weight of it settles on me more now, hearing her words. And now *I* might be on the verge of crying. Clearing my throat, I squeeze her hand in return.

"No thanks needed. I like making him smile, and I should be thanking your good parenting; he makes me smile, too."

The loving look she gives me is as powerful as if she were my own mother, and I'm grateful to know Chris has her in his corner. We finish up the dishes, and she hugs me again, wishing me a good night.

I find the same scene in the living room when I return. The door to the den is still closed, so I give up and head upstairs. Inside Chris' bedroom, damp heat and the scent of shower gel hit me. Light from the bathroom spills out, but it's interrupted when Chris steps out, a towel wrapped around his waist. His gaze seems far off as he rubs the muscle in his shoulder before spotting me.

There are tired lines around his eyes, but he's still as handsome as ever, flashing me an exhausted smile. He put on a good face at dinner, laughing with me and the rest of his family, but I didn't miss the way his expression shuttered when it became apparent that Vince had little to contribute to the conversations.

"Feel better?" An hour and a half drive in a truck for Chris feels a lot different than it does for me.

"Yeah. A little bit."

Moving to the side of the bed, I pat the top of the mattress. "Come here." The look he gives me doesn't change my mind. "No arguments."

His shoulders sag with a defeated sound, and he crawls onto the mattress, settling on his side so his back is facing me. I'm curious to see his reaction tomorrow when we go home and he opens the Christmas stocking I made up for him. Santa had time to track down some flavored massage oil this year.

I set to work on his shoulders. Little bells of victory ding inside me when he sighs. I'm afraid to ask him about his talk with his father, but I don't have to remain in suspense too long.

"It went all right," he murmurs against his forearm.

That information does as much to relax me as any massage. Bending down, I press a kiss to the back of his neck.

"I'm glad."

I had asked him if he'd ever brought a man home before, to which he replied that he'd never brought anyone. He said he suspected his father may have known about his sexuality all along, but that it had been one of those unspoken things that became more difficult to broach the more the years went by. And then, of all things, he apologized to me, as though he'd been hiding me from Vince for fifteen years, and asked if I was sure I still wanted to come to his family's Christmas. I told him I'd ride into any battle with him, and I don't think I let go of his hand for the entire drive.

"He just stood there…not saying anything," he adds, the words cracking something in my chest, hearing what he just went through. "I got more and more pissed off, even though I didn't want to be. And then…" My hands still in the middle of his back as he makes a disbelieving sound. "I found out he's just as fragile as me, just as fragile as anyone else." His ribcage heaves, and he reaches back, squeezing my hip. "I love you, Remy."

I think I understand now why people adore fairy tales. You can't help but want a happily ever after for the hero when they have to fight so much. I rest my hand in front of him on the mattress, leaning down to kiss his shoulder.

"I love you too."

Chris doesn't let me get away, though. I don't mind at all when he turns his head, cups my face, and tastes me like I'm the last drop of water in the desert. His skin is still warm against my palm from his shower as I make soothing passes across his chest and down his stomach. His hand covers mine, redirecting it to a bulge at the front of his towel. He tightens his grip, making me hug what's underneath the terry cloth fabric. A grunt spills over his lips and into my mouth. That is certainly one way to ask for what you want.

"Does your door lock?"

"Oh, yeah, but they won't come up here."

I'd feel better if it were locked, but I take his word for it, slipping loose the knot in his towel. It falls away, leaving him looking like a Greek god who was meant for loving. This was supposed to be a massage. I make up for the deviation by trailing a path of kisses down his spine, cascading my palm across the velvety skin of his ass. I know he scoffed at me for saying that taking care of him is like an addiction, but making him feel good does as much for me as it does for him. It's why I don't stop when I reach the seam between his globes, too tempted by the work of art he is that he'll never see.

The first kiss I land on that tight dark crevice is followed by Chris' deep exhale. He reaches up for one of his pillows, brings it to his stomach, and rolls onto his stomach. Clearly, he was full of shit when he once insinuated he'd like his belly scratched. Smoothing my hands down the uncharted territory, I wet my lips and drag them in a slow kiss between his cheeks.

"I think I like this massage," he whispers, shifting his legs apart.

Tomorrow cannot come soon enough. I might have to unpack his stocking for him as soon as we walk in the door. I've decided there are some things I don't want to chance my new friend Rose seeing, so I rush to lock his door. She doesn't need to discover all the ways I make her son smile. Planting my hands back on the mattress on either side of him, I let my breath ghost his seam to tease his senses. How many times did I dream of doing this to him? Merry Christmas to me.

He's hot and soft, the hair in his crease tickling the tip of my tongue when I drag it up and over his pucker. The moan he lets out vibrates all the way to my cock, firming my nuts behind my jeans.

"*Fuuuck.* Remy…"

The amount of contentment his reaction brings me is obscene. I don't hold back, making love to his entrance with my mouth, intending to make him forget any troubling thought he's ever had in his life. Groaning, gasping, whimpering; he's writhing so much he's twisted the comforter into a snarled mess by his head. He drops one foot to the floor off the side of the bed, hiking his hips up to chase my mouth, riding my tongue as I tease his channel.

"Remy…*you*," he pants. "Give me your cock."

Wiping my wet, swollen lips, I blink, assuming he must mean he wants to taste me or stroke me. I've practically driven him mad and know how much emphasis he's always putting on getting me off before himself, but he doesn't move. It's nothing I ever expected he was up for, and it makes me wonder just how emotional today made him. Is this more of the guilt he felt for bringing me here? Because if it takes all night to reassure him that I want to be wherever he is, I'll gladly do that.

"We don't have to do that," I assure him, running my palm in a circle over one of his globes.

"I want to."

Head canted to the side, I can tell he's serious and curious about my answer. I'm still hesitant, though. I've never gotten the impression that he's bottomed.

"How long has it been?"

"Today years long…"

The confession comes quietly. I might have swallowed my tongue processing the weight of knowing that means I'll be the first.

"Please," he adds.

Chris begging me to fuck him is not something I ever imagined I'd hear. Falling forward, I brace myself on my forearm, hugging him against me with my other. I hope the way I sweep my lips over his tells him my answer and how careful I'll be. Running my hand down his hip, I detour to retrieve my wallet from my back pocket. When I get the packet of lube out of it, I watch him put the cart before the horse. Still craning his neck to kiss me, he reaches back, unfastening the button on my jeans and lowering my zipper. When he reaches inside, his kisses grow hungrier, his breathing more rapid. And me? Well, my head is spinning already.

Rising, I have to extricate myself from his hand. "Gonna need that back," I tease, shoving my jeans and underwear down my hips to coat myself in the liquid.

I save an ample amount to dribble in his crease, swiping my trembling fingers through it. With each circle I trace around his circumference, he spreads his legs, arches his hips, and groans. Carefully, I press the center and slip inside. My ears are attuned to his every sound.

The way he relaxes so quickly and accepts me humbles my heart. Trust from Chris isn't easily given. I know how precious this gift is.

Working the lube inside his heat, my fingertip brushes against his bundle of nerves. His head arches back. The moan he lets out had to have been heard by Gale and every dog on the street. Holy hell, he is beautiful.

"My prostate works," he gasps. "Thank fuck something works. Aw, thank fuck."

I choke on a bubble of laughter, smoothing my hand tenderly over the uneven line on his spine. "It works just fine," I assure him. "But your parents might not invite me back if you get any louder."

Grunting, he shifts his hips back, taking me deeper. "They sleep… downstairs. It's fine."

He went from being a Nervous Nelly about essentially coming out to his parents at Christmas to riding my finger on the same night under the same roof. In the years after college, I sometimes told myself that he used to only think with his dick. Tonight, I can safely say his prostate is running the show with that kind of unabashed talk.

Leaning over him, I sweep into his mouth while I continue to work him. It's the only way I can think of helping to keep him quiet so he regrets nothing during breakfast tomorrow with Vince and Rose.

When my second finger makes a sweep of his gland for the third time, he reaches back and pulls my hips closer. Tearing away from my mouth, he gasps, "You. Now you."

As I tear my shirt over my head and take in the sight that his bare skin and glistening crease make, I want more than I ever have. I want to go home. I want to crawl into one of our beds. Want to curl up on the couch. Watch Gale run around his backyard. See how the afternoon sun kisses his frame, and how sexy he looks in sweatpants. I want to watch the way his face looks when he falls asleep with a book open in his lap. I want to go anywhere, holding his hand. I want to feel it age in mine. I want to live…just live with Chris at my side for however long life will let us.

Bracing a hand on the bed, I line myself up and hold a kiss to the side of his neck. When I tell him to push, he does, and then his body grabs me, pulling me in the way his presence has ever since the first time I laid eyes on him. Urgent and all-consuming.

Sounds of shock fall from both of our lips. We hang in the silence and the pressure until his body calls for more, easing the way. I brace my other hand on the bed, brushing his pinky incessantly with my thumb through each nudge of my hips. Head hung, mouth gaping, the soft whines that fall from his lips dance charges of static through my groin as I pepper his shoulder with kisses.

"*This…*" he pants a moment after my hips touch his ass. "This is what I needed—*the man I love inside me.*" A shaky exhale racks his body beneath me. "The only man I've ever loved, Remy."

My heart overflows, my arms quivering. I have to bite the inside of my lip and think of awful things to resists the temptation of coming and weeping. Blowing out a breath, I rest my forehead against his shoulder, pinch my eyes closed, and move.

"You have me...for as long as you want me."

Going slow, so I don't hurt his spine, is a torture of its own. I find the right angle and the perfect rhythm soon enough. His sounds of pleasure rise, filling me with gratitude.

He cries out my name, and his body demonstrates how strong it still is, clamping around me in pulses that make me go lightheaded. I give him what he wanted, what I can no longer hold back, getting drunk off the change in his sounds when he feels me release. He reaches back, fingers digging into my hip to hold me there like he doesn't want it to end. We may go slower than we used to, but we're still two forces of nature that boggle my mind.

Heaving, I slip out and raise an arm while he turns over, then collapse on the bed next to him. I wrap him in my arms as we come down.

"You okay?"

He nods, looking too sated still to speak. His hand grips my forearm and squeezes. Turning his head, he presses his forehead to mine and whispers, "Thank you."

"For what?" I chuckle. "Sex?"

His droopy eyelids rise, and he shakes his head against mine. "For giving me a chance again. For loving me."

This from the man who once referred to himself as a grumpy asshole. "You were always my only chance, Chris. I love you."

The bed dips when he rolls to his side, his big arms swallowing me in a hug. The kiss he gives me is an extension of an orgasm, slow and lazy, deep and soulful.

"Thank you," he whispers again, smiling and looking into my eyes. "But you can still show me with your dick now and then."

I bark out a laugh. I don't mind anymore that a part of us will always be twenty-two, but the way twenty-two-year-olds shouldn't take everything as seriously as we did back then. We get up eventually and wobble to the bathroom, exchanging more touches and kisses. I pause when he steps inside the stall for his second shower of the night and glances back to see if I'm coming. I think whoever dubbed him Mighty was correct. As for the fallen part, well, that's accurate too. He reaches out for my hand, and there's no denying the love in his eyes or how deep it runs.

REMY
epilogue

7 Years Later

Wiping down the kitchen table, I glance through the doorway to the living room and smile at the sight that greets me. Gale flashes me a pleading look, so I hurry back to the stove to avoid the guilt that comes with direct eye contact. Dogs, I've learned, excel at manipulating emotions.

No matter, though. She'll be freed from her obligations as soon as the big man I spot out the kitchen window, lumbering up the walkway, comes through the door. The hinges creak, and the familiar sound of weighty footsteps against the hardwood floor makes my heart do a little somersault. It's the most comforting white noise in the world.

"Daddy!" a delighted squeal in the living room shouts with the same exuberance I feel in my chest. Our daughter's greeting is followed by the frenetic excitement that is the language of all toddlers. "*Look-she'ssopretty!* She's a princess!"

I chuckle softly, wondering if Chris thinks the word *'pretty'* was delivered as demonic-sounding as I do. Scrubbing the frying pan, I keep my ear trained to the exchange.

"Delia…what did Daddy tell you? Gale's too old to play dress up, honey. You can't be hanging on her like that."

Like clockwork, our little impressionist switches to her sugary sweet logical tone. "But I made her *beudfal.*"

Ah, the price we pay for vanity.

"I know she's beautiful, but she doesn't need a crown or a cape to be beautiful. Wait…are those my sunglasses?"

The sound of Gale's nails clipping down the hallway tells me she's found her chance for escape. Poor old girl. A conspiratorial murmur of conversation closes in, laced with undertones of doting and affection. Oh, how the Mighty fell again three years ago when she came along, as well as the grandparents. At least Delia's arrival stopped Grandma Rose from tormenting Gale with bandanas. She instead showered her generosity on her granddaughter in the form of all things frilly. That child has enough tutus to clothe a ballet troupe.

"Sorry," I call, knowing I can't hide from my crimes now that he's found me. "I tried to stop her but gave up after the fourteenth warning."

"Softie," he teases, giving me a peck on the cheek. Delia smacks her palm against her lips and blows a kiss to me from her perch on one of his forearms.

"I don't have the magic touch that you do. You know this."

I lean in, however, and fake gobble the poofy sleeve of Delia's nightgown, unable to resist hearing one more of her giggles. Chris flashes me a suspicious look and then directs his gaze to Delia.

"Mhm. Well, how about the baby whisperer puts little miss here to bed?" The way he puts jubilant emphasis on the word *bed* as though it's the equivalent of *Disney World* works for him in ways it never works for me.

Delia throws her arms up and cheers, "Yay! The Hoppy Song!"

The '*baby whisperer*' loses all signs of smugness. I choke to keep my snort from coming out in full force. Too little, too late.

Wow…what a salty baby whisperer.

"Hey, remember what I said?" he warns Delia. "You're never supposed to tell anyone Daddy sings you that." To me, he mutters, "Don't judge my methods. It works. She'll be out in ten minutes."

"Hey, no judgment here." I extend my arm to the doorway regally. "By all means, Hoppy King."

He leans in to let me give Delia her goodnight hugs before carting her off to tuck her in. I finish stowing the leftovers in the refrigerator and cover the plate I left for Chris on the table before heading into the living room. Delia's accessories litter the place on the floor in front of Chris' recliner. I set to picking up her plastic dress-up heels, a sparkly wand, and a tea set, tossing them all inside her toy box by the bookshelf. Seeing the children's books that have been added to the shelves makes me smile. It reminds me of a conversation four years ago when Chris asked if I thought we were too old to have children. I think the man reverted to being ten years younger when we adopted her a year later.

The floor creaks behind me, and I feel the life force that is my person soothe my soul. He wraps his arms around me, and I lean into his chest, turning my head for a kiss.

"Nine minutes," he declares proudly.

"You haven't lost your touch. How was practice?"

"Sam and Marcus head-butted each other with their helmets for a solid five minutes. Rudy chased a rabbit while he was holding the ball, so the entire team ended up joining in," he informs me with mirth in his voice, turning me around to face him. "It was great."

I kiss the smirk on his face, wondering what Vince thinks of the irony that his son did get involved in coaching after all. Junior Peewee football, but coaching, nonetheless.

Chris' hands slide down to my hips. The grimace he makes gives me a feeling of dread. I know that look.

"So…I have to fly to Denver next Friday."

"Nooo," I groan, dropping my forehead onto his shoulder.

I knew he said he might have a speaking engagement coming up there, but I was hoping it wouldn't be so soon. He just went to one in Tennessee last week.

He gives my hips a squeeze and tries to root my face out of the crook of his neck with his own. "Hey, you, me, Delia, and the great outdoors this weekend. Remember?"

We've been looking forward to this family trip to Montana to see Jamie and his husband, but it would be better if mine didn't have to fly off somewhere else the day after we return. My rendition of The Hoppy Song doesn't go over like his does, and, well, I'm greedy and like having him here.

"Yeah."

I manage a smile. I'm too proud of the work he does and the sense of worth it's given him to make him suffer a guilt trip just because I miss him when he has to do one of these engagements. His safety briefing at Cameron U years ago led to more at other local colleges, where several people asked if he had a book. It took me giving him a few boosts of confidence that what he had to say was important, but the end result was one of the most touching, inspiring stories I'd ever read, even if I knew most of it already. Who knew a self-proclaimed 'grumpy asshole' would be invited to give motivational talks around the country several times a year?

Patting his chest, I step away to stow the last of Delia's chaos. "I saved you a plate. It's on the table. You might have to pop it in the microwave, though."

Something tugs at the belt loops on the back of my jeans. "Come to bed, Papa," he rumbles at the back of my ear. "I'll eat later."

That sounds like a much more enticing idea than cleaning up princess time. Arching a brow, I reach back and run my hand down his side. "Oh? And do what?"

"That thing we used to do a lot that we're still really good at when we find the time."

I toss the plastic crown in my hand into the air, not caring where it lands, and start toward the bedroom. "Okay."

His chuckle follows close behind me. When we pass by his desk, Snowflake hops into his hamster wheel in his cage on the stand next to it and starts running. Three-year-old girls name everything snowflake.

"Ugh," Chris grunts. "That thing stinks."

"*You* tell her you want to get rid of it then."

His hand swats my ass. "Why are you so mean, Tanner?"

"Because my husband is an antagonizer, *Mr. Tanner.*"

My comeback loses all its clout when something sharp stabs the sole of my stocking clad foot and I stumble.

"Ah, shit! What was that?"

Hopping, I catch sight of one of Delia's wooden blocks skating across the floor before it comes to a stop. Chris bends to retrieve it and presents one of its sides to me. "The letter *R,*" he grimaces sheepishly, stepping close to wrap an arm around my waist. "I'll have it stricken from the alphabet." Rubbing my back, he urges me forward. "Come on, I'll kiss it better."

"Oh yeah? Maybe I should smack myself with it in a few other places then."

His stubble brushes against my neck where his lips press a kiss. "Not necessary."

The feeling of completion that surrounds me brings me back fully to the baffling joy that is my life. Sometimes we bicker. Sometimes we fall asleep without even saying goodnight, but then I remember that neither of us is perfect. And neither is life. Perfect doesn't exist. Happiness, on the other hand… It might look a little messy at times, but you can't beat the sight of it with the right person in your life, no matter how long or how many chances it took you to get there.

One of my exes once told me I could be too much in social settings, the way I ramble when I'm excited or nervous. Chris used to think he wasn't enough, and sometimes still does. Maybe that's what makes us work. Together, we're enough to overcome the lack of faith we have in ourselves.

DEAR READER

Thank you for reading *Mighty The Fallen*. I hope you enjoyed Chris and Remy's journey.

If you struggle with chronic pain and/or illnesses, and all that comes with them, please give yourself some grace for the days you can't be the version of you that you'd like to be. You are a warrior going up the same hill as everyone else but with a hundred pounds more on your back—I call that pretty damn amazing. The world needs tough people like you around, so hang in there and keep inspiring us even if what you think you see in the mirror doesn't always look inspiring to you.

BOOKS BY DIANNA

M/M ROMANCE

THE SHUTOUT
THE HOLIDATE RESCUE
SILENT IS THE HEART
CONTINGENTLY YOURS

BROKEN HEARTS
UNTIL I SAW YOU
IN THE EYE OF THE BEHOLDER

MEN OF OLYMPUS
YOU AGAIN
TOUGH LOVE

CARVER BROTHERS
THE GENTLEMAN
THE IDIOT

BARNES BROTHERS
THE FATING

BAD DECISIONS
CAGED BY THE STRANGER

SHATTERED
MIGHTY THE FALLEN

M/F ROMANCE

A FAIR WARNING

for signed copies visit:
www.diannaroman.com

www.ingramcontent.com/pod-product-compliance
Lightning Source LLC
Chambersburg PA
CBHW020038310726
48970CB00007B/2311